Julie,

One who reads lives a thousand lives and one who doesn't read lives only one.

Happy reading!

Y0-DOL-730

D!SSENSION

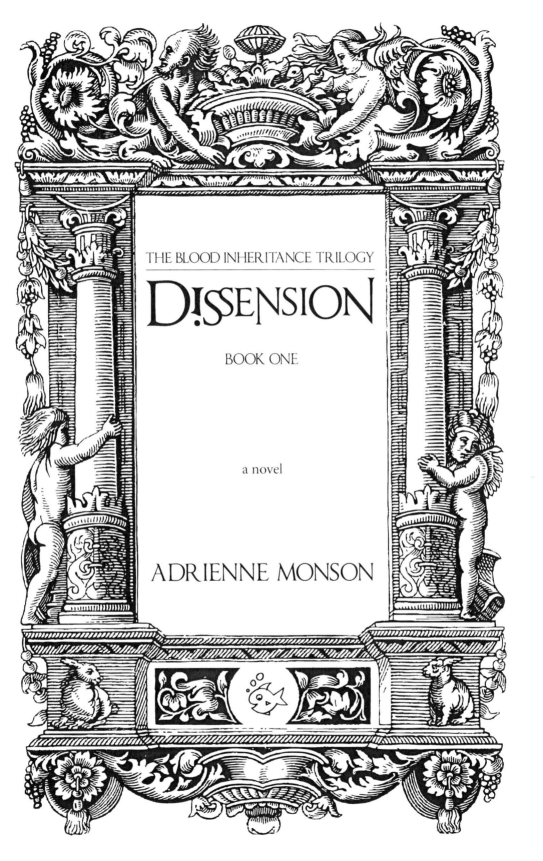

THE BLOOD INHERITANCE TRILOGY

DISSENSION

BOOK ONE

a novel

ADRIENNE MONSON

D!SSENSION

This book is a work of fiction. Names, characters, places, and incidents either are products of the author's imagination or are used fictitiously. Any resemblance to actual events or locales or persons, living or dead, is entirely coincidental and not intended by the author.

Copyright © 2013 by Adrienne Monson

All rights reserved. Except as permitted under the U.S. Copyright Act of 1976, no part of this publication may be reproduced, distributed, or transmitted in any form or by any means, or stored in a database or retrieval system, without the prior return permission of the publisher.
The scanning, uploading, and distribution of this book via the Internet or via any other means without the permission of the publisher is illegal and punishable by law. Please purchase only authorized electronic editions and do not participate in or encourage electronic piracy or copyrighted materials. Your support of the author's rights is appreciated.

First Hardcover Edition: February 2013
First Paperback Edition: February 2013

For information on subsidiary rights, please contact the publisher at rights@jollyfishpress.com. For a complete list of our wholesalers and distributors, please visit our website at www.jollyfishpress.com.
For information, address Jolly Fish Press, PO Box 1773, Provo, UT 84603-1773.
Printed in the United States of America

THIS TITLE IS ALSO AVAILABLE AS AN EBOOK.

Library of Congress Control Number: 2013930182
ISBN 0984880194
ISBN 978-0-9848801-9-5

10 9 8 7 6 5 4 3 2 1

To Dennis, my father, who introduced me to
my first love—books.

DISSENSION

JOLLY**FISH**PRESS
PROVO, UTAH

CHAPTER 1

The floor was filled to capacity. Hundreds of sweaty, young bodies pumped and gyrated rhythmically to the beat of the music blaring from oversized speakers placed throughout the room. There was no talking; no one could be heard even if she were to scream at the top of her lungs. Of course, none of them had come to talk; they were here to get drunk and rub up against each other. They came to get laid.

The bar overflowed with women wearing tops that left little to the imagination, and men openly ogled those assets to the point of drooling onto these women's cleavage—it was impossible not to bump into each other as they danced, and no one seemed to mind the invasion of personal space.

Kyle used that excuse to get as close as possible to the beautiful woman he was dancing with. They had only been dancing for fifteen minutes, and it was all he could do to resist from twisting his hands into her long, blond hair, and wrapping it around him. He couldn't wait to caress her plump lips with his own and make her scream like she'd never screamed before.

He wanted to see terror in her eyes—those emerald green eyes.

He had to have her. Tonight. Right this minute. Kyle took a deep breath to fortify himself, but it was ruined by the scent of roses emanating from her delicate skin.

The tension in what little air that separated them was palpable. That meant she must want him just as badly as he wanted her. The knowledge gave him reason to smile. He knew women couldn't resist his smile. He always got the girls he wanted.

His eyes nearly rolled back in his head when she returned his smile with an equally seductive one of her own. She was far too pretty—exotically so—and he had to do something about it very soon.

Kyle pressed his body even closer and stroked his hands down her back. She had a small waist that spanned into the most perfectly curved hips he had ever felt. She reciprocated by snuggling her face into the crook of his neck and creeping toward his jaw with provocative little kisses. He groaned and moved his hands lower, stroking every curve on his way to her thighs. She stayed relaxed in his arms, moving against him.

That was it. He couldn't last any longer.

Kyle pulled back and gestured to the backdoor with his head. She arched her brow in interest and nodded. He grabbed her hand and led her outside.

They both took deep breaths of fresh air as soon as they walked out and smiled to the bouncer as they passed him. The large bouncer kept his beefy arms folded, barely glancing at them as he watched a couple just a few feet in front of him. The woman, wearing a skirt short enough to see that she'd foregone underwear, was frantically kissing her date, pinning him to a sticky wall that smelled of urine and alcohol.

Kyle felt himself losing control as they walked down the alley. He had planned to take this lush piece back to his apartment for a long night of forbidden pleasures, but he wasn't sure if he could last that long.

The knife was with him, strapped inside his pants at his hip. He never went anywhere without his trusty bit of silver. It was named Sylvia, after the first girl he'd had.

With his weapon handy he could have her right now in the alley. His heart sped up at the thought of taking her on the filthy ground, making her dirty, making her his with so many people nearby. No one would hear her screams, and even if they did, nobody would come to investigate in this part of the city.

With his decision made, he paused to look around. They were in the darker part of the alley where the wall curved and no one was in sight. It was perfect.

Kyle turned to his date and pulled her in by the hair for a

hard, urgent kiss. She tasted so sweet—he couldn't wait to taste more of her. And to see her blood strewn all over the ground—to look into her eyes and see her fear—he would be her master.

Becoming unhinged, he broke the kiss, pulling back just a little, giving her an intent look. He pushed her back into the cement wall behind her, making her glorious hair stick to its dirt. She'd make a lovely picture by the time he was finished with her. He licked his lips as he eased his hand up to his hip. Slowly, he unsheathed Sylvia as his eyes perused her body. He usually liked to start at the stomach and move out from there, but maybe tonight he would start with her flawless face. Yes, he wanted to see this angel's skin pouring red.

He raised his hand high for the first slice, the gleaming silver of the knife barely reflecting in the dim streetlight. He brought the blade down slowly, watching her eyes intently, anticipating the fright he would see there. But to his surprise, she smiled at him.

Before he could register her rapacious look, her hand struck out in a blur, squeezing his wrist and forcing him to drop the knife as his bones made a distinct grinding noise. He screamed. Her arm moved at that same unimaginable speed and impacted with his neck, crushing his windpipe.

Kyle struggled as she pulled his head down toward her. His feeble attempts to strike out at her were no match for the steel grip she had on him. When she could reach his neck with her mouth, she bit down and sucked.

There wasn't much pain from her bite; he tried to scream past his broken throat, but nothing came out. He was helpless. There was nothing he could do while this woman, half his size, sucked the life right out of him.

He felt himself grow weaker and tried once again to struggle, but it was no use.

Memories of his life flooded his vision, and suddenly, he was a little boy, leaving gutted rats under his sister's pillow. He grew older and saw his first kill with that whore, Sylvia. It had been unplanned. She had led him on and teased him, but wouldn't put out. It had enraged him so much that he had forced himself on her and then sliced her pretty face and delicate neck until she was unrecognizable. Then, he was a man of twenty-eight, experienced in his kills, thinking of himself as a master hunter. His last kill had been so beautifully brutal. He had managed to drag it out for the entire day, just slicing her up here and there to make her wondrous screams last as long as possible. It was one of the most fulfilling days of his life . . .

HOLDING HIS NECK TO HER mouth, Leisha was in her own mind again, the screams of his latest victim echoing in her head. The poor man was nearing his death and she was able to control the visions emanating from him and focus on the ambrosia of liquid pouring down her throat. She couldn't think beyond the rapture as his blood slid into her stomach, settling it. She gulped without spilling a drop.

Within just a few seconds, her body was already feeling energized. The aching in her head subsided and she felt elated. She closed her eyes in relief as The Hunger retreated from her mind, leaving her to herself again. She adjusted her hold on her victim and continued feeding on him—there was still a little more blood left in his body.

Feeling more than satisfied, Leisha opened her eyes and looked directly into a pair of silvery-blue eyes framed by an ebony face. She knew those eyes well; she had stared into their depths in endless fascination in a time long past.

The rapture of her feast vanished quickly as she stood frozen by his penetrating gaze—her temporary paralysis vanished with the thought of why Tafari was here. She let go of her victim, allowing the still-warm body to slide down her legs onto the filthy ground.

Leisha crouched in a defensive position, wishing she had worn pants instead of her sleazy skirt. Her black heels would make fighting a little more difficult, but she had done it before. She stayed where she was, allowing Tafari to make the first move.

She'd wanted to avoid this moment, and had successfully done so for well over a thousand years. But now it seemed Tafari had finally sought her out. They would be evenly matched in combat, and Leisha truly had no desire to kill him. Of course, she did not want to be killed *by* him either; she would do what she must to survive.

"Hello, Leisha," he said, his voice hollow. That was his whole demeanor; his expression was flat, withdrawn. His

arms were folded over his expansive chest with a leg cocked to give a pretense of being casual. But being of large stature and still able to carry himself with lethal grace, he was never simply casual.

He glanced down at the body lying on the ground by her feet. "I see you have not changed much." Then he smiled, cold.

Showing no reaction to the insult, she kept herself steeled both physically and mentally for the altercation she knew would ensue. "Tafari," she said, surprised at the sound of her affection. She quickly cleared her throat and attempted to sound more nonchalant. "So what do we do now? Fight each other to the death? Seems so cliché, don't you think?"

"I did not come here to fight you."

That was not what Leisha was expecting to hear. She studied him for a moment, trying to decide whether or not he was toying with her.

His firm, square jaw was freshly shaved, and a sudden memory of brushing her cheek against his smooth skin intruded her mind. She shook her head to keep those thoughts at bay, but Tafari had always had that effect on her. She could never think straight around him, and after two thousand years of being separated, she would have expected her emotions to have dried up.

She straightened and schooled her expression into one of indifference. It was offset by the fact that she was having a hard time looking directly at him. She didn't want to

be distracted by those captivating eyes; she focused on his chest instead. "So, why are you here?"

He took several steps forward and cupped her face, his fingers digging into her cheeks, forcing her to meet his gaze.

"I will tell you that I certainly did not come here so you could avoid looking at me as if I were beneath you," he said firmly, a British accent lightly threading his tone. His voice was flat, but it seemed to have a little quiver to it.

Her breath caught at his touch. It felt electric and made her feel alive in a way she hadn't felt since she was human. She had not even bothered to defend herself from his out-stretched hand, a realization that jolted her.

At five-foot-six, her neck was at an awkward angle compared to his six-foot stature. He let his hand drop but didn't take any steps back, apparently oblivious to the corpse at their feet.

They were close enough to kiss, the energy that flowed between their bodies was of a charged violence with an undertone of undeniable chemistry. They stared into each other's eyes.

"That is better," Tafari said after a few minutes.

Leisha blinked, then scoffed, and would have taken a step back if the wall had not been directly behind her. "Oh, please, Tafari. You say I'm acting like you're beneath me? I think that's the pot calling the kettle black."

Tafari crossed his arms and smirked. "Seeing as how I *am* black, would you call me the pot or the kettle?"

She rolled her eyes, but she could feel herself relaxing a little.

"I think I should be allowed one paltry pun considering that is the second cliché you have used thus far," he said.

Leisha's lips twitched.

Tafari cleared his throat. "I have not seen you make any reports to Ptah for some time. Is it possible that he has allowed you to go out on your own?"

Whatever warmth she had felt quickly shriveled within her. "How would you know that? You've been following me? Watching me?" She was agitated with herself as much as with him—not having had the slightest inkling that someone had been following her. She didn't like the thought of Tafari being near without her knowing.

"I needed to talk to you," he said, "but I did not want to walk into an ambush of twenty bloody vampires just to do that. I did what I had to do to protect myself." He stared hard. "It is likely you have forgotten I serve a higher purpose than most people could fathom."

Leisha felt like sputtering. "Right. A higher purpose? So, murdering me is a higher purpose." He opened his mouth, but Leisha kept on. "I didn't realize your duty was so glorified. Should I bow down to you now, or after you've elevated yourself in my presence? It would certainly make it easier for you to cut my head off!"

"There will be no need for that. I am sure there will be plenty of time to kill you later. I did come to speak with you. So, either you can be civil with me as I am attempting

to be with you, or we can just end the conversation now."

She studied him. "Tell me what it is you came to say so we can both be on our way. That is, if you really meant it when you said you weren't here to kill me."

With an edge to his voice he explained, "I came here to warn you."

"You came here to *warn* me? About your superiority or your higher purpose in life?"

Tafari's eyes flashed violence, then he took a deep, calming breath. "The planets are beginning to align as it has been foretold." Leisha felt a chill run down her spine. "The prophecy child is coming."

"Thanks for the information," she said. "But that still doesn't answer the question of why you're telling me."

For a second, Tafari looked as confused as she felt, but then his face went back to its passive state so quickly that Leisha thought she must have imagined it. "I have come to inform you so that I might make a request of you in return."

"What could you possibly want from me?"

"I know Ptah is going to seek you out to rejoin him for the war that may be approaching. I ask that you stay away from the other vampires until this is all over."

Leisha's brain was trying to process several things, especially why Tafari would want her to stay away from the vampires, but she focused on the important one. "Who says there's going to be a war? There's nothing in the prophecies about any war."

"You know the prophecies as well as anyone else. Both

immortals and vampires have prophesied of his coming. Most believe that he will have the ability to control both of our kinds; he is connected to us all in some way, yet none of us know exactly what he is supposed to do."

Comprehension trickled in. "If he can control us, then both the immortals and vampires would want to find him and exploit his powers to gain the upper hand. They will go to war with each other over the child."

Tafari nodded.

Leisha folded her arms beneath her breasts. "Doesn't anyone remember that we tried that five hundred years ago? It didn't work. Both of our people had almost the same losses. This is a foolish idea, especially since neither side has found this prophecy child yet. The prophecies about him are too vague to make any kind of plans. What makes you think we can control him?"

Tafari actually grinned, and it looked genuine. "If only you were an immortal." His smile faded into sadness as he spoke.

Leisha mirrored his sorrow and bowed her head. "I can't tell you how many times I have wished that."

Tafari didn't bother to hide his confusion, and maybe there was some curiosity in his face as well. "Are you still the same Leisha that I married? Why else would you wish to be an immortal instead of the monster that you are?"

Leisha took a deep breath. This was not going to be a pleasant conversation, but if she could only get him to understand what had happened to her. She lifted her face.

"I'm the same. My soul hasn't left me; it is only my body that is different."

Tafari shook his head and took a step back. "No, it cannot be. The Leisha I married would never have become a vampire. I know that a person has to agree to become a vampire or the metamorphosis will not work. And I saw"—his voice broke—"I saw what you did."

How could Leisha explain the truth? How could she make him understand? The memory of her first kill flooded her mind. She had fought off The Hunger long enough to run away from her daughter and father so they would not fall victim to her. But she'd had nowhere to run—

LEISHA FELL TO HER KNEES, *panting more from mental strain than physical exertion. She didn't know what to do or where to go. The thought of going back to Ptah made her stomach reel even more.*

She began to sway. The Hunger was crippling.

She couldn't begin to describe or understand the pain it caused. Her head was splitting to the point that she could hardly think. She was shaking and weak. Too weak.

Her stomach rumbled, but she couldn't hear it. She only felt the pain; her core was acid, and a demon was clawing at her brain.

Then she heard a heartbeat. There were footsteps approaching and her nostrils filled with the scent of sweet, young flesh. Musky with male spice and a hint of saltiness. She salivated uncontrollably.

"Are you all right?"

She couldn't answer, couldn't think past that appetizing blood

flowing through his veins. She wanted so much to fight, but there was no more energy. She had no strength to run away and could not escape from this temptation that was leaning over her.

He gently touched her arm, and that was all it took. She didn't remember much of what happened next; just that primal creature taking over. It was as if she had blacked out and some vile instinct had taken control over her body.

When Leisha became aware of herself, she was sitting in the middle of the scattered remains of bones and viscera. It was such a gruesome sight, one could hardly tell if they were of a human.

Leisha didn't feel sick at all anymore. In fact, she felt great. All the pain that she had experienced only moments before was a distant memory.

Yet, even the euphoria of how she felt could not shield her mind from the crushing guilt of what she had just done. Not only had Leisha killed a man, she had torn him to shreds and devoured him. She hadn't even seen what he looked like, didn't know his name. It seemed so . . . cold.

Then another thought dawned. Ptah had known The Hunger would take over. That was why he let her bid one last goodbye to her daughter and her father. He was setting her up to kill her family.

She said a small prayer of thanks to the gods—she'd managed to control herself long enough to spare them.

But what should she do now? She stood and looked around. Leisha froze when she saw the last person in the world she'd wanted to see at that moment.

Tafari wasn't moving; he just stood down the path and stared at the sight before him. His face was a mixture of grief and revulsion.

Yet, his eyes were glazed as if he couldn't quite understand the scene before him.

"Tafari." Voice shaking, she reached a bloody hand toward him.

"You are one of them," he whispered through tears that were threatening to come.

Her tears flowed down her face, leaving red streaks on her cheeks. "Yes," she whispered back. "I am sorry, my love. I truly did not want this."

He doubled over as if in great pain. "I have to kill you, then." It was barely a whisper—she wouldn't have heard it if it hadn't been for her heightened senses.

She stepped forward with her hand still reaching for him. "Please, you do not understa—"

"You are one of them*!" he screamed. The sorrow had left his face, but the rage remained.*

The torment in his expression seared into her brain. "I am sorry," Leisha said again.

Taking one step toward her, Tafari pulled a machete from its sheath on his back. Leisha didn't wait to see what he would do. Instead, she ran away as fast as she could to the only place she would be accepted. To the one being she loathed more than anything else. She had made her choice, and now she would have to find some way to live with it . . . even if it meant becoming the monster that she feared.

THE MEMORY HAD RESURFACED, AND talking about it was almost too painful. But she had to try. "Tafari, it's still me." She paused to search for the right words. "You don't

understand what it is like when The Hunger takes over. I have no control. What you saw . . ." She stopped when she saw his jaw clench. "I'm different now." Leisha wanted to shoot herself for her lack of eloquence. She'd had this conversation in her head dozens of times, but she couldn't seem to grasp any of what she'd wanted to say.

Tafari scoffed. "Different?" He gestured to the dead man lying at her feet. "Just because you are not tearing up the bodies when you eat them does not make it any better."

"This man," she said heatedly, "was planning to rape and murder me. He's a serial killer! I did humanity a favor by killing him, and you have no right to judge!"

Tafari narrowed his eyes. "How could you know that about him? From what I saw, you just met him inside the club thirty minutes ago."

"I have the ability to read minds."

A black eyebrow arched. "That ability is a myth. None of the immortals can do it, and both sides have developed the same psychic abilities over the years."

Leisha kept her gaze level. "It's not a myth. I can do it."

"Really?" he mocked. "What am I thinking right now?"

Leisha shook her head. "It wouldn't work on you. It's a limited power and doesn't work on the strong-willed unless they're drunk or somehow impaired."

As if he had been expecting that explanation, he nodded smugly.

"Look," Leisha's tolerance was thinning considerably, "you came and sought me out. So don't try to criticize me for how I live my life."

"Life? You call this a life? Look at yourself, Leisha. You justify killing because they are murderers themselves? Who are you to play God, deciding who lives and dies?"

Leisha leaned forward slightly. "Are you really so much better? I once saw an immortal shoot a human so that a vampire would not be able to drink their blood and restore the vampire's energy."

Tafari nodded wearily. "Sometimes we have to sacrifice for the greater good." It sounded forced though, detracting a bit from her anger. "Besides, *I* have never taken a human life."

Her spine straightened. "And that would somehow make it all right for you to judge me for it? You don't know anything about me, Tafari."

It would be pointless to tell him about how she was barely surviving by merely snacking, about how she would go to the clubs and dance with men, and when they thought she was kissing them roughly, she was really sneaking a couple swallows of blood. But it wasn't enough to sustain her, and every so often she had to make a kill. She decided if she tried to explain, she would only sound more pathetic.

"That is for the better, Leisha. The more I know of you, the more repulsed I become." Leisha ground her teeth. "Thank you for the warning, Tafari. As for your request, I see no reason to grant it to you. I suggest you rejoin your own kind before you say something that will really piss me off."

Leisha didn't wait for a response. She turned and leaped onto the rooftop of the dance club, running and bounding from one building to another until she was on the same block as her car, all the while denying her pain, trying not to feel the hurt from Tafari's words.

CHAPTER 2

Leisha pulled into the garage, her movements mechanical as she pushed the remote to close the garage door behind her. She sat in the car for a while, staring at nothing.

She didn't blame Tafari for hating her; she wished she could have told him long ago why things turned out the way they did. The few times she had seen Tafari over the last two thousand years had never been private. This was the first opportunity she managed to talk to him alone, and she had permitted herself to take offense at his insults.

Leisha pushed her shoulders back, got out of her Dodge Viper and walked to the door that led into her kitchen. This place had been her home for almost a year, which was a long time for her.

Her kitchen was of simple décor, her cupboards stocked with barely enough food just in case she had company, or if she was in the mood to eat something herself.

The living room was connected to the kitchen and din-ing room with wide open doorways. Leisha could see the flat screen television from the kitchen if she wanted to, though she usually enjoyed watching TV relaxing on her plush sofa.

As Leisha entered the dining room, the hair on the back of her neck prickled. She was not alone in the house. There was a presence here, and she could not identify exactly what it was.

Fully alert, she crept cautiously into the unlit living room, her hands poised at her sides, ready for attack. As she walked through the doorway, she sensed more than saw a shadow move toward her from the left. Before she could turn and confront her intruder, he grabbed the nape of her neck in a steel grip and pushed her down. She lost her balance and felt her forehead slam into the hardwood floor.

Before her attacker could move, she swept out her leg and knocked his feet out from under him. He landed with his face less than five inches from hers.

She was about to strike out when recognition bloomed; she made a sound of annoyance in the back of her throat as she took her time to stand and walk over to the light switch. When the corner lamp came on, Ptah was still in the shadows.

Standing, he took his time studying her. His long, silky black hair was tied back at the nape of his neck, as usu-al. Even though his eyes were black, they stood out even among the darkness, absorbing what little light was left in the shadows around them.

Ptah smiled. "I enjoy so much to look at you, Leisha." His voice was just as she remembered it; silky smooth with a razor sharp hardness lying in wait under the surface. He could convince anyone that the sky was really green with that voice, and with the steel that waited beneath it, he could make the toughest man lose control of his bladder. "It truly has been too long."

He was wearing a black button-up shirt and khaki slacks over his lean, toned frame. The last time she had seen him was a hundred years ago, wearing more sophisticated, high class attire. Yet he still had a presence that filled the room, even with his modern, ordinary clothes. He could wear fig leaves and still dominate the room with his powerful aura.

"I thought we had an agreement, Ptah." Leisha continued to look into his eyes. It was like looking into a bottomless pit, causing her to feel queasy. But she was used to it.

"Yes, we did. In which you agreed to come back should my need for your aid arise."

"The vampires," she clarified. "I would come back if the vampires needed me. If this is a personal favor to you, then you can forget it."

Ptah smiled ruefully. He stepped closer until they were half a step apart and lightly traced his fingers along her clavicle and up her neck. "Do not worry, beautiful Leisha, I know what the arrangement is. However, I would not object if you wanted to give me some personal . . . attention while you are back home."

Shivering, as lewd images from the past assaulted her vision, Leisha took a step back. "This is my home. Any place you live in will never be my home again."

Ptah chuckled at her reaction. "I shall not argue with you on that matter," he said pleasantly. "With the condition that you remember to treat me with the proper respect, most particularly when you are among us." His voice hardened. "I will not have any of the other vampires following after your pathetic example of striving to hold on to your *humanity*."

Leisha leaned a shoulder against the wall. "What's the matter, Ptah? Are you worried that I might sway some of those village idiots to my way of life?"

Ptah was unaffected by her mockery. "At least those village idiots, as you refer to them, know how to live in the present. They actually enjoy what they are. Something you have yet to learn for yourself."

Leisha shrugged. "That means nothing to me. I've enjoyed my life for the past century without you." She sighed. "Regardless, I promise to treat you properly . . . in public," she added in a too-sweet voice.

The master vampire ignored yet another jab. "You will return with me tonight. I have a private jet that will fly us directly there."

"No, that won't work for me." She hurried on before Ptah could reply to her protest. "I have to do a lot of paperwork and tie up loose ends before I can leave. I need to get this house sold and make sure no one who knows me wonders what happened to me. You wouldn't want the police to have my picture as a missing person, would you?"

Ptah's soulless eyes roamed over her intently. The memories they brought back she would rather keep suppressed. Instead, she focused on his smooth olive complexion, his straight nose on his soft, boyishly charming face.

"Agreed. I must return tonight to meet with Victor and the captains on our strategies against the immortals."

Too fast for her to react, he grabbed her by the shoulders and leaned down until their noses were touching. "You will come as soon as you can. It should not take you more than a day or two." His grip on her shoulders became painful. "Do not even think of running, because I will find you. And when I do, I will make sure you live a most derisory and contemptible existence. I will punish you worse than ever before."

She knew by his tone he was referring to the time she had rescued one of his victims. Ptah had managed to find the victim again and tortured her to death in front of Leisha. Then he caged Leisha in the sewers below his lair, where all the vampires were directed to dump their victims' corpses in the cage with her. She had been stuck in the darkness, sitting in refuse and rotting bodies for an entire month, gnawing on her own arms to keep herself from attempting to eat the poisonous, decaying flesh around her. And that was only the beginning of that particular punishment.

"I understand," Leisha said, refusing to be affected by the intimidation.

Ptah hesitated a moment before releasing her. He walked back to the couch and sat down, making himself comfortable. "Besides," he said softly, "I think coming home and living amongst your own kind again will be rewarding. The last time I saw you, you were conflicted inside. I could almost feel the hate that you had for yourself." He looked her up and down appreciatively. "You are so lovely, my sweet, yet I can feel that same self-loathing in you now. I had hoped that being independent would have helped you to move beyond that."

His voice carried a trace of sympathy and concern. It wasn't truly genuine, though she knew Ptah had always wanted her. He'd treated her specially after Tafari shunned her—she remembered it as well as she remembered Ptah was also the one who'd forced her to betray her family in the first place.

Leisha crossed her arms. "You didn't allow me to leave because you wanted to help me, and we both know that."

He shrugged. "It does not change the fact that you need to move past this selfishness."

Leisha blinked, taken aback by the bald comment.

Ptah sighed as if he was irritated, and without warning, shot off the couch at incredible speed and grabbed Leisha by the wrist, forcing her to turn her back toward him, pulling both her arms behind her at a painful angle, before walking her to a mirror on the wall next to her front door.

"What are you doing?" she asked, but didn't bother to fight him off.

He put her wrists in one hand and pulled her hair with the other, impelling her to look in the mirror. "You are a lovely creature, and you know it as well as I," he said. "But you are so focused on yourself and your petty little depression that you are wasting all of your potential." He tugged on her hair. "You are not the pathetic creature you pretend yourself to be. Once you can get past this juvenile concept of good and evil you're stubbornly holding on to, you and I will do wonders together."

She struggled against his grip and Ptah pulled her wrists higher. A cracking sound came from her right shoulder as it dislocated, an excruciating pain shot up her neck. Leisha grunted and kicked her leg back hard enough to make his knee snap in the wrong direction.

Ptah did not react, but leaned on his good leg and released his hold on her.

Leisha spun around and worked her arm back into the socket, gritting her teeth against the burning, throbbing sensation. "You are still not concerned for me or upset over my 'waste of potential.' You're just angry because you never got what you expected when you forced me to join you." She flipped him off.

Ptah growled and lunged at her, knocking her to the floor. Locking his feet over her legs, he held her arms above her head with one hand while squeezing her neck with the other. Leaning close to her ear, he whispered, "You know nothing. You have been with me from the beginning and you still have no comprehension." He leaned back and

looked into her eyes. "It amazes me when I contemplate how talented you are—you learning new skills and adapting to new eras—yet your mind is so obtuse when looking at yourself."

Again, Leisha was speechless. Ptah had never spoken to her like this. It took her completely off guard and made her feel strangely vulnerable to him in a way she'd never experienced before.

Ptah had abused her in every way imaginable, had forced her to warm his bed and cater to his sadistic sexual appetites. He had manipulated her and beaten her more times than she could remember, and yet she had never felt as exposed to him as she did in that moment. And she had no idea why.

As if sensing her confusion and her newfound sense of vulnerability, Ptah gently rolled off of her, picked her up and carried her to the couch, his knee having healed by that time. After settling himself, he turned to her and lightly stroked her hair, the way he'd done in the past when he wanted something from her. She knew it was just another ploy, yet it soothed nonetheless. She didn't want to think about Ptah and his effect on her; it was unnerving.

"Tell me, Leisha," Ptah said gently. "Why do you hate yourself so much?"

"Because I'm a monster," she whispered. She didn't mean to answer; it came out of its own volition.

"That is part of it," he agreed. "But there is more essence to it at your core. While you think what we are is wrong and unnatural, there is something else I know you're feeling. Do you want to tell me what that is?"

She shook her head, her gaze on the floor.

Ptah put two fingers under her chin and pulled her eyes to him. "The real reason you hate yourself so much," he explained, "is because there is a part of you that enjoys being a vampire. There is a part of you that revels in drinking blood and being immortal. And you hate yourself for this." He paused with deliberation. "You hate me because I made you the way you are."

She nodded, the emotions and confusion within her swelling at each word he spoke.

He leaned close. "Well, my sweet, let me confide a little secret with you." His hand moved to her mouth, his thumb caressing her dark pink lips. "While I have no doubt that you harbor some token of hatred toward me, you are also grateful to me for giving you endless life. That is why you will always come back to me, and that is why it took you so long to leave me in the first place."

He leaned over and kissed her.

Leisha closed her eyes and felt a pain deep within her emerge. She did not want to fall into the trap Ptah was luring her into, yet she felt some truth in his words. She pulled back from his kiss and his hands, but made no move to escape as she'd initially intended.

Ptah held up his hands. "I understand you may not be ready to face the truth as of yet, but one day you will"—kissing her hair—"and once you do, you will thank me."

Leisha swallowed and felt herself trembling. It would be so much easier to give in to him. She could go back, and he would take care of her, in his own twisted way. She would once again be revered as a powerful vampire and would no longer worry about feeling so alone in the world. She was tired of trying to control her hunger, at making an effort to do good in order to make up for all of her sins.

It was such a tempting thought that she was on the brink of folding. Maybe it wouldn't be so bad to be in that life again. She had friends who'd enjoyed her company. They'd include her in their hunts and orgies . . . in the bloodshed and torture of innocent people who had never done any-one harm. She would go out in the daylight and bring back "young pretties" for their enjoyment. She would once again be enabling their twisted habits.

"No!" she screamed as she slapped him on the cheek. She stood and looked down at him. "I'm free of you now. I don't want to come back to you and play your sick games." She pressed her lips together and forced herself to calm. "I don't want to go back, Ptah, but I will because I gave you a blood oath that I would come if you needed me. But know that I will leave you again as soon as this nonsense is over. And *I* will be the one who decides when you no lon-ger need me."

Ptah stood and smiled as if he knew something she did not. "We shall see." He walked over to the television. "I think once you are among us again, you will be enlight-ened." He turned back to her. "You need to understand that you never were, nor will, ever be free of me." He began sauntering around the room, studying her decorations. "You may even begin to understand that it is useless for you to continue pining after that sorry warrior of an immortal. After all, he never truly loved you, did he?"

Intense pain rippled through her chest.

Ptah waved away any possible denials. "Do not bother to lie to me or yourself. We both know you still think of him as some paragon. But think on this for a moment. What happened when Tafari's love and loyalty were put to the test?"

Leisha felt the old hurt of Tafari's rejection as if it was just yesterday that it happened. She stumbled to the couch and sat, overwhelmed with the mix of feelings and memories that protruded.

"You have never been accepted by those you loved, Leisha. Even when you were human, you were not accepted."

"That's not true."

He smiled. "The witch doctor took you in, yes. Then there is Tafari, of course. But what happened after that?"

She could not speak, could not move. His words were like acid running through her body. The pain of becoming a vampire would have been more preferable than this.

"You did something so noble." Ptah's voice was patronizing. "An act of true love. Something humans are supposed to admire, yes?" He was beginning to look smug. "But what happened when you did this? You were rejected by the

only people you loved. The only people who had supposedly accepted you. Their love was supposed to be unconditional, was it not?"

Every word that came out of his mouth killed her just a little more, and she knew it would not hurt this much if it was not true. He was obviously trying to manipulate her, but she could not argue with what he was saying.

"Would you like me to continue?" he asked.

She shook her head.

He walked over and knelt in front of her, taking her hands in his. "My feelings for you are unconditional. I will always welcome you. Even after you left me over a hundred years ago, I am here now to take you back. Come with me Leisha. I will always want you. Always."

These were the words of the devil. But she could not argue against the truth, the logic in them. She could feel herself being seduced by what Ptah was offering. Leisha had no other choice—Ptah had deflated every sense of hope she'd ever felt.

The master vampire was correct; she was going to return to him. There was no use in fighting what she was anymore. As much as she tried to hold on to her altruism, it did not prove redeeming. *After all,* she thought to herself, *Tafari still doesn't want me and never bothered to find out why I became a vampire. Maybe he never cared enough to know in the first place.*

Ptah's arms embraced her, and she burrowed into his body. She gave in and willingly allowed it. Just for this night, she told herself, the way she'd been telling herself

every time Ptah sought for her. In such moments, she took the comfort he was offering her. *Just one last time.*

CHAPTER 3

Despite her current grief, Samantha couldn't help but be curious about this place. The decent size house was in a quiet neighborhood. Her father had told her that most of the people in this area frequently traveled on business. Apparently, it wasn't much of a family community and she wouldn't meet anyone her age around here.

That was fine with her, though. She'd always gotten along with adults better than people her age. She was used to hanging out with her mom and her mom's friends. Mary had been as wonderful a friend as she'd been a mother.

The vision of her mom bloody and dying appeared suddenly in Samantha's mind, and she shut her eyes against it.

"Headache?" her father asked.

She shook her head.

He hesitated for a moment, then walked past her and carried her suitcases up the stairs. "Your room is up here," he said over his shoulder.

She followed without comment. It had been years since she last talked to her father, and it showed. They hardly spoke more than a few words to each other since he picked her up from the airport.

When they got to her room, she saw that he'd made a feeble effort to make it look feminine. The bedspread was a pink floral design; it was definitely new. She didn't tell him how she hated floral designs. Instead, she continued to survey what was now her quarters.

Apart from the bed, a brown Formica desk sat in the corner next to a window with no shades. The closet was directly across from the bed; its doors wide open, exposing a row of empty metal hangers. Beside the closet stood a small white dresser.

It was nothing like her room back home—that room was bright with cheerful colors everywhere. It was also spacious. She wondered if she should bother putting up all the pictures that used to adorn the walls of her old room. Maybe they would help liven up the place.

Samantha suppressed a sigh. "It's nice. Thanks."

Her father put her suitcases in front of the closet and stood to look at her. His dark brown hair was combed neatly in his usual "professional" look. His shoulders were broad and his build could easily be intimidating, but the nervousness Samantha felt had nothing to do with her

father's athletic physique. It was the look in his piercing blue eyes—the same color as hers—that held some emotions of uncertainty, perhaps even a little fear. But what she mostly saw was a scrutinizing look. He probably didn't even realize he was doing it, but he was studying her as if she were a bug under a microscope.

She pushed away the urge to ask about his work. He'd never told her mother when they were married, so she knew it would have been a futile effort to try to assuage that part of her curiosity.

"I'm glad you like it, Samantha," her father replied.

They stood there for a few awkward seconds.

He glanced at his watch.

"Don't let me keep you from anything." She hoped she came off as casual.

He smiled. "I do have some errands to run before it gets too late. Are you all right being here by yourself?"

She forced a small chuckle. "Of course, Dad. I'm sixteen, not six."

He twitched slightly when she called him Dad. It was the first time she had addressed him, and it did feel disagreeable leaving her mouth. He stayed composed, leaving her to unpack as he exited the room.

Samantha slumped to the bed as soon as her door closed. Traveling was supposed to make anyone feel tired, but she was sure her exhaustion had a lot to do with the last hour of arriving in Nevada and dealing with her father.

She wondered if maybe he wouldn't mind her calling

him Mason instead of Dad. She was sure he didn't really think of himself that way. Why would he? The last time she saw him was over ten years ago when her mother left him. Her parents' separation hadn't been that difficult for her, since her father wasn't around much anyway.

She pushed her thoughts away as she got up to unpack. The Spartan room could be worse. Maybe she could ask her dad if she could paint it. Possibly buy a colorful chair to brighten it up. *Oh, well.* It wasn't really important in the grand scheme of things, although it would certainly help her feel better.

She hadn't known what to expect from her dad when she arrived. On the plane over she had thought that maybe they could at least share a connection of grief for her mom, but he had simply asked her if she'd checked in any luggage. He was all business when it came to locating her bags and getting everything loaded up in his car.

The drive to her new home was silent. No music. No conversation. She simply reciprocated his stoicism, and wondered if it would be like this until she graduated. If so, she would seriously think about early graduation, then off to college immediately after that. A college that was at least a few states away.

Samantha sighed. It was possible she might be too hard on her dad. After all, her mother had once been in love with him enough to marry him. Samantha suspected that her mom had never stopped loving him. So that meant he couldn't be all that bad. Hopefully.

Samantha pulled out a few pairs of jeans, and was starting to lay them in the middle drawer of the dresser when—

SUDDENLY, SHE WAS NO LONGER in the house. Instead, she was in what looked like a warehouse. It was practically bare except for a bunch of boxes lined up against the wall to her left. To her right, a room separated her from the rest of the place with a simple white curtain. There was screaming coming from behind it.

Samantha walked over to the curtain and pushed it aside. It looked like a medical laboratory. Tubes filled with various liquids lay systematically on one table. On another table were other kinds of instruments that sent an ice-cold chill down her spine—knives, saws, and blades shimmered in the fluorescent light.

Between the two tables a group of men wearing what reminded her of SWAT uniforms—though they did not look like they belonged to any police force—stood guard around a dentist chair.

Except this chair had metal bars that held down the arms and legs of a woman with long, blonde hair and large almond-shaped eyes, the most striking green irises Samantha had ever seen. The woman's high cheekbones and angular jaw line defined her beauty—that even under such unflattering circumstance she still appeared beguiling.

One of the men probed a metal object against the woman's neck. It seemed to be giving her a sort of electrical shock. The woman screamed every time he touched it to her neck.

"Interesting," said an all-too-familiar voice behind her.

Samantha turned to see her dad in his usual suit and tie under a white lab coat looking at the woman as if she were a lab rat. "Let's

try it at a higher velocity and see if she can take some more." He
pulled out a clip board from behind him and began making notes ...

SAMANTHA GASPED AND PANTED AS she came back to herself. She was again in the gloomy house and her father was still gone. She realized the jeans were still in her arms, and that she was clutching them tightly to her chest. Letting them drop to the floor, she went back to lower herself on the bed.

She always had to lie down after a vision. The lightheadedness that came afterward did not last long, and in fifteen minutes she would be able to stand again. Her mother had always warned her that no one should ever know about her psychic premonition ability. "Especially not your father," her mother had emphasized.

What was he doing to that poor woman? *Or rather, what is he going to do?* Experience had taught her to rely on the visions she received; they always came true. The problem was she never knew when it would actually happen.

She knew that she couldn't ignore this vision. There must be a reason why it appeared in her mind. Now she just had to figure what action she needed to take.

She wished her mother were here. Mary would know Samantha's options whenever she had a vision.

When Samantha was twelve she had a vision about an old woman's death. "The woman was ready to die," Samantha had told her mother. "It was as if I could hear her thoughts while she was getting ready to move on to the next life. She

felt content with everything except for a misunderstanding between her and her granddaughter. She left a bunch of messages for her granddaughter, but the girl wouldn't even talk to her. The woman died regretting not having the chance to explain the situation and apologize to her granddaughter."

"Well," her mother mused while she sipped her morning coffee. "Do you know who that young girl is?"

Samantha nodded and explained that through the woman's thoughts, she was able to capture the girl's contact information. The girl's name was Mallory. Then her mother told her to locate Mallory and explain to her what the old woman had wanted to say. It was the first time Samantha had even considered doing something about her visions.

Going to the house of a complete stranger so that she could help the dead fulfill some unfinished business was awkward—she had to tell Mallory that her grandmother sent her—but it turned out well. After Samantha relayed the grandmother's message, Mallory cried on Samantha's shoulder, then sat up and gave her a brilliant smile. She thanked Samantha and attended the funeral service the following afternoon to pay her final respects.

It was then that Samantha realized all the good she could do with her visions. Since that time, she always found a way to help those in her visions any way she could. Now, she would have to figure out a way to help the woman cuffed in the dentist chair. The thought of what this woman was going through made Samantha shudder.

Maybe she could just follow her dad to work and see if there was a way to help the woman escape.

Again, the curiosity about her father dove into her thoughts. What would happen if he did find out about her psychic ability? Was the woman in her vision psychic as well? Her father did work for the government, and there were plenty of conspiracy theories in the world about the government. Samantha usually paid no mind to them . . . but what if? What if her father was involved in some kind of experiment with people? She could still see her father's scrutinizing gaze in her mind. Was she living with a monster?

Her body started to tremble as the possibilities came to mind. It took her most of the night to think things over. She contemplated confronting her dad as she put her clothes away and wondered how she could save the woman from her fate. She still wasn't sure what her course of action would be when she climbed onto the soft mattress and pulled the covers to her chest. But she did know one thing—she would do whatever it took to get the woman out of that nightmare.

CHAPTER 4

L eisha had finally finished preparing to leave. She had packed up all of her belongings and sent them ahead to India. Ptah would send someone to pick them up. That way, her room would be ready for her when she got there. It had been Ptah's suggestion, and Leisha very well knew that it had more to do with him making sure she got to India as soon as she could.

Leisha made a stop to the grocery store to purchase some iron pills. She had a long flight ahead of her and would not be able to feed on the flight. Iron and the plane food would have to suffice for the duration.

Walking out of the store toward her car, she felt a sudden and intense sensation of danger. She wasn't sure what was going to happen, but whenever she got that feeling, she knew some kind of threat was just around the corner.

She stopped and looked around. The parking lot was

mostly empty, with a few cars parked here and there. No one was in sight, and no customers were heading to or from the store. The street beyond the parking lot was pretty busy with the evening traffic full of commuters getting home.

She strained her ears to see if she could hear anyone approaching, but heard no footsteps or even a heartbeat. There was a faint sound from a distance. It sounded like a high-pitched whistle, and it was getting louder.

Realizing what it was, Leisha abruptly hurled herself to the ground.

As she did, something grazed past her right shoulder.

They were far away. From what she could deduce, she decided that it had to be a sniper on the roof of a building somewhere, not the roof of the grocery store—she would have noticed. That meant it had to be a pro. Someone who could shoot at long ranges with deadly accuracy.

She heard the whistle sound again as she rolled through debris and gravel until she was beneath an old pickup truck. The bullet smashed into the front tire of the truck, and she realized too late, that there was a third whistle sound coming right on top of the second one that met its mark this time. She felt the pain explode through her hamstring and bit her lip. The pain was fiery and intense, already coursing through her whole body. She looked at her leg and saw that what she thought had been a bullet was more like a long silver rod poking out of her leg. It had to be a tranquilizer.

Swearing under her breath, she hurried to pull it out.

She cursed again as it tore through muscle and skin on its way out. The rod had a dozen small spikes sticking out of the head that must have popped out once in contact with its target.

Leisha was already starting to feel the effects of whatever drug had been in the bullet. Instead of the burning, her body now felt numb. She had to get away before whoever was out there came to get her.

She forced herself to roll over and get onto her hands and knees. As soon as her head was up, her vision swam. She took a deep breath and continued to force herself up on her feet. Once she was finally standing, someone grabbed her arm.

She jerked away and heard a baritone voice in her ear. "Oh, honey, I didn't mean to startle you."

Her brain was slowing to a crawl and she couldn't figure out what was going on. Who was the man holding her arm? Was she pretending to date him to drink his blood? No, that wasn't right.

She was only vaguely aware of herself moving, propelled by the man behind her. She blinked and squinted through her blurred, murky vision. How did she get into a car? Who was driving and why was she in the backseat? What was that man in the backseat with her doing? Why couldn't she move her arms? Suddenly, the fuzziness and the confusion were gone and a vast darkness loomed before her to swallow her whole . . .

SAMANTHA'S HEART WAS POUNDING SO hard, she thought she might go into convulsions.

She was in her father's trunk for over an hour while he drove around. She had been monitoring his daily routine for the past few days, and decided that tonight was the night for action. The image of that tortured woman had been haunting her to the point where she could no longer sleep.

Mason had followed his usual routine of coming home to have dinner with his daughter before driving back to work for a few more hours. Since the air between them was still intensely awkward, it was easy for Samantha to quickly retreat into her bedroom after dinner. Once there, she'd rapidly changed into darker clothing and snuck her way into her father's trunk in the garage before he left for work again. She couldn't figure out what direction the car was heading, but somehow, she felt deep within herself that she'd reached the right destination.

Her father got out of the car and was walking away. It didn't sound like he had parked in a garage—she heard no echoes. That meant she would be more in the open than she'd hoped.

She wished her vision had at least shown her the layout of this place, but she would just have to follow her instincts. She pushed the trunk release button from the inside; it opened with a pop. She cringed at the sound.

She eased open the lid just barely enough for her to peek out. The sun was at the horizon in its setting, leaving long

shadows to cover a regular looking parking lot. There was a lot of gravel on the pavement; she would have to be careful when she climbed out. It would be such a waste to go through all this trouble just to slip and announce her unauthorized presence to everyone.

The parking lot was lined with cars. Trees grew sporadically on islands separating the parking spaces. Samantha strained her ears for suspicious sound, but heard nothing. She took a deep, calming breath that did nothing for her racing heart, and opened the lid all the way so she could jump out quickly. She landed lightly on her feet and squatted as she eased the trunk shut.

Crawling to the side of the car for better cover, Samantha planned her next move. She could see the building now. It looked like a regular, plain warehouse, a rectangular building with double steel doors at the front entrance. On the side was a large set of vertical sliding doors—the loading dock. She didn't want to imagine the kinds of things trucks brought to this place.

There weren't any surveillance cameras she could see. She wasn't sure if she was going to come out of this alive; but she figured it would still be best to remain inconspicuous. While her actions tonight might save some woman's life, it would kill any chances of a relationship between her and her father.

Samantha pushed the thought away. It wasn't like she was going to have much of a relationship with her father anyway, knowing that he was torturing people as part of his work. She looked around again before running in a crouch to the next row of cars, bringing her a little closer to the building. As she studied the building, she noticed a keypad next to the double steel doors in the front. She would have to sneak through their security system. Although she was far from qualified to accomplish the task, Samantha wouldn't allow herself to feel discouraged.

Approaching the large sliding doors on the side, she studied them for several minutes, trying to see if there was any way to break the code. With the doors shut and padlocked on the bottom, Samantha couldn't think of a way to get in at all.

She shouldn't have come. She didn't know what she was doing anyway; she wasn't some 007 agent or anything. Who was she kidding? Samantha turned to go, her grief for the woman in her vision overwhelming. She ached with regret.

As she was turning, she noticed a group of people approaching. There were five men and three women, all dressed in business suits, talking. From what Samantha could hear of their conversation, they were returning from dinner, and had a long night ahead of them. They didn't pay attention to their surroundings much, and a few of them even appeared a little tipsy.

Samantha was wearing black slacks and a dark blue shirt. Her shirt—scoop neck and cap sleeves—wasn't exactly professional. Her shoes were black sneakers and definitely didn't look anything near the business attire the

other women were wearing. Still, she had already thought of what she would tell them. If it didn't work, she could try and play it off as some juvenile prank.

They were getting closer and would be passing her in a matter of seconds. She didn't have time to think anymore. Samantha drew a deep breath, squared her shoulders, and stood up to her full height of five-foot-nine, trying to give the impression that she knew exactly where she was going. She approached the man who was leading the group.

He was quite handsome, with a thick head of brown hair and a lovely tan that complemented his blue eyes. "So then, she said she was just dating me for my money!" He paused from punching in the code to laugh heartily. The rest of the group laughed with him.

The woman next to him clutched her stomach from laughing too hard, then straightened and pulled her auburn hair from her eyes. "I guess she found out that a government salary is not what it looks like."

The man telling the story grunted in agreement as he placed his face in a small alcove where his retinas were scanned. "It was my car that made her think I was rich. When I told her I bought it with my parents' inheritance, she asked if there was anything left from that."

Everyone chuckled and Samantha finally reached them.

"Oh, thank God!" She managed to make her voice a bit older by deepening it. The brunette man looked over at Samantha and squinted at her as if his vision was blurry. "I went to dinner and left all my stuff inside." The group was already starting to appear skeptical, but no one looked intimidating. "Mr. Campbell told me I had to finish this mundane project by midnight and I still have so much to work on before it's anywhere close to completion." She shook her head and gave a tentative smile. "Not good for my second day on the job, is it?"

A woman with black curls gave her a sympathetic smile. "No harm done." She checked her watch. "You can get in now and have a few hours to work on that project." She met Samantha's eyes. "Mason Campbell was my first boss when I started and I had daily fantasies of tearing his arrogant head off to keep me sane."

Samantha smiled gratefully to the woman and again the brunette who held the door open for her.

The first thing she noticed was the strong stench of ammonia. The second was the bland and empty hallway gaping before her. A moment of paralyzing foreboding crept up her throat, but she swallowed it down and walked forward.

She barely contained a scream when one of the men, wearing a bright pink tie, grabbed her arm to stop her. "I thought you were on Campbell's team." His tone was irritated.

"I am," she said hoarsely.

"Then why are you headed there?" He pointed down a corridor to their left. "His work station is down there."

"Right," she quickly agreed. "I just needed to ask, uh, Karen a question first."

"Oh." He seemed to accept that and let go of her arm before walking straight ahead with the rest of the group, leaving her alone in the echoing hall.

Samantha exhaled slowly. She hadn't realized that she'd been holding her breath that whole time, and was feeling lightheaded. After taking a couple of deep breaths, she felt better. Having a better idea of the general direction she needed to go, she went to the left.

The place was lit by cheap fluorescents, the floor a generic tile, the taupe walls completely bare. The air conditioner was on full blast, and her arms were covered in goose bumps. She could see security cameras on the ceiling and averted her face every time she passed one, but knew she probably wasn't going to get far in this labyrinth.

LEISHA WOKE FEELING GROGGY. SHE couldn't remember ever feeling so tired. Moaning, she tried to put her hand to her head, but her hand wouldn't move. She opened her eyes to see that she was lying in a chair with her arms and legs clamped on it. They weren't just any clamps; these were steel clamps about four-inches thick. Even so, if she applied enough pressure at the right angle, she could get free.

She looked around to see what her full situation was but couldn't see anything. There was a lamp just above her head that was blindingly bright, making it impossible to see anything outside of the light. She tried to break through the clamps, pulling with all of her strength. But they wouldn't budge.

"You won't get them off," said an ominous voice to her right. "They're being held by an electromagnetic charge that will hold even the strongest of your kind." The voice was smug. Probably from having captured her so easily.

Leisha laid her head back and closed her eyes, trying not to give away any feelings of panic or anger. She had to think. There had to be some way to manipulate her way out of this, but first she needed to know who these people were and what exactly it was that they wanted from her. He had said "you people," assuming that he meant vampires. So, he knew about her physical abilities, but maybe if she concentrated hard enough, she could read his mind.

It was hard to read the minds of people with strong wills, but maybe there was someone in the room with them who wasn't strong-willed. It would be difficult to probe the minds of people she couldn't see, although not completely impossible. Leisha concentrated on her breathing, taking deep and even breaths, in through her nose and out through her mouth. Once she was in a calm and relaxed state of mind, she began reaching out mentally to scan her vicinity.

There were a total of eight men around her. No women. She could tell these men had had some military training by the way their minds held. They were strong and determined, their minds somewhat blank. Military people knew how to keep their thoughts impassive; they were trained to do so.

That wasn't good, of course, because Leisha had no way of knowing what was going on if they weren't thinking about it. Knowing that they were some kind of military did nothing to help her feel better. These men were trained for all kinds of situations and would be ready to spring at any sign of struggle. Plus, they simply would not listen to anything she told them, killing any chances of her trying to talk her way out of this—whatever "this" was.

Her thoughts were interrupted by the same man who had spoken before. "Now that you are fully conscious, we can finally begin." His voice sounded somewhat eager.

"Begin what, exactly?" Leisha asked, consciously maintaining a cool composure.

The man chuckled. "We want to know more about your kind," he said conversationally. "We have already established how strong you are and what most of your capabilities are. Now we want to see exactly how much of a pain threshold you have."

With no other warning, a hand holding a Taser device came into view and pressed it to her neck. Leisha felt an electric jolt throughout her entire body. It filled her from her fingertips to her head to her toes. The first time was too much of a shock for her to react in any way. When the Taser was pulled away, she was left gasping. Then it came again, even stronger, and this time it went for so long that she couldn't hold back the blood-curdling scream.

Her vision was starting to go, the bright light looking dimmer. "Interesting," she heard the man say through a

haze of dizziness and nausea. "Let's try it at a higher velocity and see if she can take some more."

Leisha's scream now penetrated every room and hallway in the building.

SAMANTHA SAW A WOMEN'S RESTROOM and ducked inside so she could hide away to think for a minute. It was a small bathroom, with just one sink and three stalls. She turned on the tap and splashed cold water on her face.

As she patted her skin dry with a paper towel, she noticed another door marked "Lounge" on the other end of the room. Uncertain of what to expect, she cracked it open and peeked through. There was a rocking chair and a couch with a long counter on the other side. She immediately recognized it as a mother's lounge, where women could go pump milk while they were at work. The only reason she knew that was because she used to take naps in the mother's lounge at her mom's office.

She wasn't sure if that should be a comfort to her—to know that mothers work at this creepy facility. Of course, her father *was* a father. Before today, she simply couldn't imagine him running a place like this.

There was a coat rack in the mother's lounge as well, and Samantha couldn't believe her good fortune when she saw a white lab coat visible from under a windbreaker. This would help her to be less conspicuous.

After donning the somewhat large lab jacket, she felt more confident and forced herself to leave the false safety

of the bathroom to look for the woman. She was certain that the rooms around her were a lot smaller than what she had seen, so she decided to keep walking.

At one point, she thought she heard the high whine of an electric saw of some kind from behind the door to her right. She froze when the man's screaming reached her ears. It was a scream of painful agony. She tried to swallow, but her mouth was too dry. *What is this place?* She felt like she was in some kind of haunted horror house. Even though the fluorescent lights kept the place well illuminated—and there were no frightful images on the walls— there was a sense of evil lurking throughout the building. Everything seemed completely surreal.

She must be naïve to think she could storm in here and save some poor woman from being tortured. The same people who were holding her captive would find Samantha and do the same to her. She needed to get out of there as fast as possible.

Samantha was just starting to turn around and run when the door on the right a few feet ahead of her opened. She froze momentarily, a deer caught in the headlights. There was a woman who looked to be in her mid-thirties wearing a business skirt to her knees, a button-up white blouse that was mostly covered by a white lab coat. She was holding a clipboard, looking very distinguished.

The woman did not see Samantha when she opened the door; she was busy giving instructions to someone inside. Samantha would not be able to get around the corner before the doctor woman saw her, so she acted by instinct. She stood as tall as she could, trying to embody the essence of confidence, and ready to walk right past the door as if she had every right to be there.

Just as Samantha took that first step forward, she heard a growl coming from the room. The woman in the doorway had gone pale, but was trying to control the situation.

"Just stay calm, Beth. He won't hurt you. Isn't that right, Thomas? You remember Beth, don't you?"

There was another ferocious growl, and then an ear-shattering scream that made Samantha want to shriek in fear herself. The woman in the doorway gasped in horror and moved to close the door. She almost had it latched when something began to pull it back open.

Samantha ran to the door and held its handle next to the woman's desperate grip. Together, they used all their strength to pull the door closed. When the latch snapped shut, the woman pressed her badge into a scanner on the wall, and Samantha heard more than one dead bolt screech into place. The woman slid to the floor. She was pale and shaking while something pounded the door with tremendous force from the other side.

Samantha wasn't sure what to do. She certainly didn't want this woman to be asking her any questions about why she was there, but on the other hand, she felt for her. The woman looked like she might be in shock.

"Are . . . you all right?" Samantha asked.

The woman looked at Samantha with slightly dilated

pupils and cleared her throat three times before she was able to respond. "I'm fine." Her voice was a little shaky, but she managed to sound composed. She struggled to stand, and when she did, she looked as though she had gotten herself completely under control.

"We all go into this job with the knowledge that we make many personal sacrifices, don't we?" She gave Samantha a rueful smile, which Samantha hesitantly returned.

The woman squared her shoulders, but was too embarrassed of her momentary breakdown to look directly at Samantha. "Thank you for your help, but if you'll excuse me, I'll need to report this incident." She walked away without waiting for Samantha's response.

Samantha wondered exactly what had happened in that room and was sick with the thought that there might be a girl named Beth dying just a few feet away from her. What was foremost on her mind, however, was the comment the woman had made about personal sacrifices. Is that what her father had done for the sake of his career? Sacrificed his wife and daughter? She wondered if that was why he had never been good about keeping in contact with her. Maybe he didn't want anyone getting too close to him because of the "strange duties" the government required of him.

Samantha must have been walking blindly, for she couldn't tell how long she'd been wandering. She was now in a completely different corridor. What if she were caught while questioning things to which she would probably never get an answer anyway?

She pushed away the sound of an electric saw followed by a horrid cry. She needed to stay alert and find the woman from her vision as quickly as possible. She was too deep into the building to leave empty handed.

She was coming to the end of the corridor. There were double doors directly ahead of her, with small windows in each door. There were more corridors to each side of her, forming a T-junction. Samantha wondered what hid behind the doors directly ahead of her—they looked like they opened into a large and spacious room, exactly what she was searching for. Before she actually reached the end of the corridor, she heard footsteps coming down the hall to the right.

Immediately, she fled to a doorway on her right just before the corner of the junction. There was about two feet of wall protruding from the doorway, giving her barely enough hiding space. She flattened herself as best she could, hoping to be invisible.

Samantha kept her breathing under control, rubbing her sweaty palms absently over her pants. Suddenly, the door next to her swung open toward her, barely skimming her toes. She froze. A man had exited that room, and was now well down the hallway toward the opposite direction.

Samantha released the breath she'd been holding and glanced around the corner from her hiding spot to check on the previous person coming down the corridor. Bile

froze in her throat as she saw her father, a white lab coat over his suit. He was standing in front of the double doors, entering a security code.

There was no question now; she had found the place she was looking for. The doors opened and her father entered. There wasn't much time left for her to think things through—the doors were slowly closing again. Samantha took a deep breath and ran to the door in time for her to wedge herself through before they sealed shut.

Her father turned around the corner to her left. There was a wall directly in front of her, leaving her the option of going left or right. She knew her father would lead her to the woman, but wasn't sure if directly following him in such small corridors was such a good idea. She crept to the corner where he had disappeared and peeked to see if it was safe to follow.

There was a doorway about twenty feet ahead she could try and run to, but it was too risky. Mason Campbell had walked to the end of the hall, and was accessing a room straight ahead. The room had windows instead of walls; she could see five computers with people slouching over them.

Samantha turned around and decided to go toward the opposite direction. At the end of this corridor, she saw the large doors of the loading docks. At least now she had a clearer idea as to where she was in the building. She looked around before taking her first fateful step down the corridor.

At the end of the hall, she saw an assorted collection of storage boxes. Perhaps these boxes were used as part of a cover at the loading docks. In a corner next to the boxes was what looked like a power panel. It was at least ten-feet long and five-feet wide. *Could that control the power to the whole building?*

Samantha walked as soundlessly as possible, hoping no one would be in the room she was about to pass. The door stood wide open; it appeared to be a lab. There were only two women in it, both enthralled by a test tube holding a red liquid. Samantha scurried past, running as fast as she could to the boxes.

As soon as she reached them, she squeezed into the tiny space between the boxes and the power panel. She scanned the labels on the switches to locate the main power switch, but before she attempted to cut the power, she must first find the woman. From where she was, Samantha could see the rest of the corridor. The room with the two women met up with the glass room her father had entered.

Mason Campbell came out holding a metal cup, walking toward an all too familiar alcove in the hallway covered with a white curtain. As he pulled it back, Samantha gasped at the sight.

The woman was lying unconscious, strapped into the same chair Samantha had witnessed in her vision. There were several spots of blackened skin on the woman's body. Samantha knew if she were close enough, she would smell burnt flesh; the woman's arms were completely swollen.

"This'll wake her up." Her father gave the cup to one of the men guarding the woman.

This was her chance—Samantha knew—but it was an incredibly sloppy plan. There were six guards with guns— who knew what else they concealed in their uniforms. Cutting the power would give her an advantage, but she didn't know if she could actually sneak past any of them to get to the woman.

The woman was sputtering blood, trying not to choke. She was waking up, and Samantha knew more horrendous torture would ensue. She could not stomach anymore of it. Impulsively, she strode to the power panel, threw the main switch, and immediately found herself shrouded in impenetrable darkness.

CHAPTER 5

At first, there was nothing but pain. Leisha hurt everywhere. The electric shocks were at such a high voltage that if it weren't for the pain, she would have thought herself paralyzed at this point. The men had also broken both of her arms, and not just once. They pounded her bones into powder with sledgehammers, starting with her wrists and slowly working their way up to her shoulders. The vampire did not even know when she lost consciousness.

When Leisha came to, she became aware of a warm, sweet liquid pouring into her mouth. She choked at first, but then was able to swallow the blessed ambrosia of blood. Her mind became more alert. The blood stopped abruptly, and she realized they were only giving her enough to keep her awake, not enough to heal. The frustration was too potent. She wanted to scream, but was too weak to do anything at all.

She could hear the voice of the man who was in charge of her torture. He called it an experiment, but it was torture. She knew this degradation would not stop until they learned everything they could about vampires. Then, they would kill her.

The sudden dark seemed to freeze everyone. For a split second, Leisha thought that she had lost her vision, but when she heard the man say, "What's going on?" she tried to unscramble her thoughts and focus. Her eyes quickly adjusted to the abysmal black, the current in her restraints gone.

She mustered all the strength she could, and pulled the bands on her arms. The broken bones and shattered ligaments protested in unimaginable agony, but Leisha did her best not to faint from the pain and continued to pull. Finally, her right arm came free with a loud *clink*. Before anyone around her was able to comprehend what the sound was, she forced herself to reach out through the throbbing agony to the first person on her right and yanked him down to her mouth. He hadn't even had time to grunt before she was desperately gulping his blood.

Within a matter of seconds, she was beginning to heal, tearing through the metal restraints on her arm and legs. By this time, the men realized exactly what was happening and were beginning to take action. A flashlight shone on the now vacant chair; the military men spun, trying frantically to locate their captive.

Leisha didn't waste any time killing them. She came up

behind the men on one side and used both arms to simultaneously twist their necks so fast that they didn't feel a thing. She leaped, just barely avoiding the bullets aimed at her. She flipped over backwards in the air and landed on slightly bent knees behind the rest of the men on the other side of the chair.

Twisting the necks of the two men directly in front of her, she brought her leg up and kicked the other man in the face. His nose and jawbones shattered; he wouldn't be a threat to her anymore.

The three remaining men, not wanting to take their chances, ran away as fast as they could.

Hearing heartbeats pounding ahead, Leisha deduced that a bunch of people were hiding in a room in that direction. She felt a sense of empowerment, knowing she was the one causing their fear. They deserved worse than to be temporarily terrified.

She wanted to go into that room and kill every one of them. She wanted to twist their demented heads off their shoulders, but she restrained the rage. They had weapons and bullets that could incapacitate her, and she needed to get out of there before they could organize an attack that would put her back in that ghastly chair.

Instead, she turned around and ran through the pitch-black darkness. She could see a little, but not much more than shadows. She gasped when she ran into a bunch of boxes. Empty plastic bottles bounced all around. She was just about to spring away when she heard groaning.

She had hit someone who had evidently been hiding behind the boxes. Leisha had wanted to move on to locate an exit, but keen inclination tugged at her to check on the person. She could not say why exactly, and didn't have the time to examine her motives at the moment. Whatever the reason, she bent toward the person and reached out.

By the feel of the face, it was a young girl, definitely in her teens. Leisha hoisted the girl to her feet by the shoulder and whispered in her ear.

"Do you work here?" Leisha asked gruffly.

The girl stiffened in her grip, but tried to reply calmly. "Yes, of course, I do." Her voice had a slight tremor to it, but was perfectly calm. By sensing the pulse of the girl's heart, Leisha knew she was lying.

"My name is Leisha, and I've been taken against my will. Are you a captive as well?"

"No, I'm not," the girl said, skipping a heartbeat. "I mean, I'm trying to get out of here, and I was trying to help . . . you're the woman who was strapped to that chair over there? With blonde hair?"

"Keep your voice down!" Leisha hissed. What on earth was this girl talking about? Leisha decided to worry about that later and accept whatever help this girl could offer. "Yes, I'm that woman they were torturing. What's your name?"

"Samantha," the girl replied in hushed tones.

"Samantha, do you know a way out of here?"

Leisha could feel Samantha shrug. "There are big

sliding doors just over there for the loading docks, but they're locked at the bottom. I think I could find the front entrance—"

"Don't worry about it," Leisha interrupted. "I can get this sliding door open. Stay next to the boxes so you don't get hurt."

Samantha obliged and Leisha felt her way over to where Samantha had pointed. The sliding door was made from thin metal; Leisha had no problem kicking through. She pried open the flimsy door, wide enough to walk through. The small opening let in a mixture of moonlight and fluorescent lighting, providing Samantha with plenty of illumination to maneuver around.

Red backup lights came on just as Leisha was pushing Samantha through the opening. Guards were rushing toward her from two directions, but Leisha didn't stay to fight. She went through the hole and saw the girl looking about them nervously.

"Do you have a car?" Leisha asked.

Samantha shook her head, jumping at the sound of gunshots. The girl looked through the hole to where the shots originated. Instead of jumping out of the way, she froze. A bullet whizzed past them and Leisha pushed the girl on the ground, using her own body as a shield. The vampire looked up to see her torturer staring at Samantha, his face pale. The man's icy blue eyes seemed to panic.

Bright spotlights came on, their beams moving around the parking lot. Leisha heard what she could only have

guessed were armored vehicles grinding their way toward her location along with men on foot.

She looked down to see Samantha unconscious, probably from the impact. She picked up the girl and carried her around the side of a large container unhooked from its diesel engine. Once unburdened with the human, Leisha rushed to the closest car and pushed it to the gaping hole in the sliding door. A couple of guards had already made it out by then, but the majority of them were either still in the compound or crushed by the car.

She took no time to sprint at the two men aiming their weapons at her, and was fast enough to hit them both in their stomachs, giving them enough internal damage to kill them, albeit slowly.

Before the rest of the men approached, Leisha hurried back over to Samantha, picked her up, and ran like she'd never run before. Within minutes, she was already fifty miles away. The only thing surrounding them now was desert. She laid Samantha down and patted her cheeks lightly. The girl's eyelashes fluttered, then slowly opened. When her eyes finally focused on Leisha's face through the moonlight, they widened in recognition.

SAMANTHA'S HEAD WAS POUNDING AND she felt exhausted. It took her a few moments before the events of the evening came flooding back into her brain, and she instantly recognized the woman hovering over her. The woman was covered in blood from her hair to her clothes, but her emerald green eyes radiated beauty.

Samantha sat up and swayed a little—her injury must not have been too bad. "What happened? Where are we? What did you say your name was?"

"My name is Leisha. You were knocked out," the blonde responded. "I pulled you to a car and we drove for some time. But the car broke down, so I carried you out here in the desert." She paused. "I believe we are safe. For now."

"How were you able to escape?" Samantha asked, her voice shaky.

Leisha smiled at the girl. "You helped me escape."

Samantha shifted nervously under the gratitude. "I mean, I just turned off the power. I was going to try and get you out, too." She glanced at Leisha, still calm and serene, and not a mark on her. "But you were at my side before I knew it. How did you get out of those binds and away from those men? And how did you know where I was? What happened to all those bruises I saw on your body? I thought you were close to death!"

"The metal stirrups that held me down were powered by electricity. Once you shut off the power, I was able to sneak away from the men in the dark. It was pure chance that I ran into you."

Samantha studied her rescuer before responding. Everything she could see about Leisha seemed to say she spoke the truth, but for some reason it just felt wrong. She knew it wasn't the whole truth; Leisha hadn't said anything

about being miraculously healed. Samantha would pursue that question later. "You must have great instincts."

Leisha shrugged. "What about you?" she asked. "How did you know where to find me, and why rescue me at all? I don't believe we've ever met."

It was now Samantha's turn to hedge the truth. She looked down at her lap. "I . . . I know one of the men that captured you." At the thought of her father, his image came to mind—they had made eye contact just as the shooting had started. The look on his ashen face was seared into her mind. Obviously, after today, there would be no doubt about her involvement in helping Leisha. "I decided to follow him to see what he was up to, and when I peeked in and saw what they were doing to you, I couldn't help but to stop it." Changing the subject quickly, Samantha continued, "Are you all right? I mean, how *did* you heal so rapidly?"

"Maybe you should ask the man whom you know captured me. They gave me something to drink that would heal me."

"Why would they want to heal you after torturing you just a few moments before?"

Leisha gave Samantha a level stare. "So they could torture me some more without killing me." She said it simply, with no emotion, but there was something about Leisha that Samantha could read. She knew Leisha had been more than unnerved by the experience, though she played the cool and unaffected persona beautifully.

Samantha was shaken up herself. To imagine being

tortured to death was horrible enough, but to not even have that final escape was beyond what she wanted to comprehend.

Again the image of her father's cool and calculating eyes filled her vision and she shivered. How could she go back home and face him after all of this?

As if reading her thoughts, Leisha said, "Do you have a way to get home?"

"I haven't gotten my driver's license yet. So, no, I don't have a car." She felt so much like a child admitting it, but brushed off the feeling. "I did bring my cell, though."

She pulled it out and handed it to the woman. Leisha stood and checked the bars to make sure it would work before dialing. She didn't have to wait long before someone answered.

"I know!" Leisha snapped at the person who answered. "You wouldn't believe what just happened to me." By the look on Leisha's face, the person on the other end must have said something rude. Samantha felt steady enough to stand by herself while listening to one side of the conversation. "Look, Ptah," Leisha continued, "someone had the *gall* to actually kidnap and attempt to torture me, so I'm in absolutely no mood to deal with you right now. What I would love from you is if you would send out your private jet to come and get me," Looking around, she voiced, "I'm not exactly sure where I am. It's somewhere outside of Vegas; I think maybe to the south." She listened some more and looked momentary impressed.

"That works for me." Leisha hung up and handed the phone back to Samantha.

"You should call a friend to come pick you up as well."

"You know someone who has a private jet?" Samantha asked. "Who exactly are you? That guy's name is really *Ta?*" It had never occurred to Samantha that this woman may have been kidnapped because of some political battle, but if Leisha had those kinds of connections, then maybe there was more to her situation than Samantha had originally speculated.

"I'm no one of consequence, really. I just happen to know someone who has become very wealthy over the years. You really should make a call to have someone get you before my friend shows up. I don't think you would enjoy meeting him."

Suddenly, Samantha felt all alone in the world. Who could she call? The only person she knew in Nevada was her father, and there was no way she would call him. Tears welled up. She missed her mother terribly.

Turning to hide the few silent tears from Leisha, she said, trying to steady her trembling voice, "I don't have anyone to call. I can just go back to the road and hitch a ride. It's no big deal."

Leisha seemed torn—her eyes downcast in thought. It was obvious she did not want Samantha to be there when that Ptah guy arrived. Hitching her way back home where she knew her father would be waiting wasn't Samantha's first choice either, but there wasn't any other way around it.

"You have lost a loved one recently, haven't you?" Leisha asked, to Samantha's surprise.

Samantha didn't bother to hide her tears this time. "My mother," she whispered, staring at her feet. She hated having to admit her mother's death out loud—every time she did that, it seemed realer. So much had happened in such a short amount of time—her best friend was dead, she couldn't trust her father, she had just snuck into some government compound and witnessed unspeakable atrocities, and now she was all alone with nowhere to go and no one to turn to for help. It was just too much for her to handle.

Leisha was suddenly beside her and holding her gently. Samantha hadn't expected it; she'd stiffened at the sudden embrace. She hadn't cried about her mother in front of anyone and didn't think it was right to burden the woman she hardly knew with her emotional baggage.

Leisha murmured something in her ear she did not understand. She thought they might have been French—whatever it meant, the tenderness in Leisha's voice pulled at her heart. Before she knew it, Samantha was hugging Leisha back and sobbing into her shoulder. At that moment Samantha was a lost little girl clinging tightly to a stranger as if she were her lifeline.

Samantha didn't know how much time had passed, but she felt utterly drained. Every emotion she'd suppressed

had come racing back to the surface, and it had exhausted her completely.

Leisha had not said a recognizable word the whole time. She just stroked Samantha's soft, fine hazelnut hair and let her cry everything out. It was good for Samantha to finally have some kind of emotional release no matter how awkward it felt.

Samantha felt the need to say something, but nothing came to mind.

It was at this moment that she noticed a man coming from over the crest of a hill. He was tall, with light brown hair. His hazel eyes focused intently on her, and when she met his gaze, the rest of the world ceased to exist. His thin, lithe frame filled her entire vision. This mystery man had just become her whole world. She knew she needed to be closer to him as she was aching to touch him, smell him. And before she knew it, she found herself walking toward him, a lustful smile on her face.

CHAPTER 6

Leisha did not hear any footfalls, but when she saw the dreamy look on Samantha's face, she knew a vampire was behind her. Turning, she saw Nikita staring Samantha down. Nikita had a skill the vampires referred to as luring, and he was currently using it on the girl.

Leisha bolted to her feet. "Stop it, Nikita."

Nikita broke his gaze on Samantha, and turned to face Leisha. "She is fair game," he said, his Russian accent barely noticeable. "You have not marked her."

"I haven't, but you may not touch her. She is under my protection." As soon as the words came out, Leisha wished she hadn't said them. The only reason vampires kept humans under their protection was because they intended to make them human servants. Nikita would now expect Samantha to come with them; the binding process would have to commence soon.

Nikita shrugged. "If you really like her that much, then by all means." And with that, he broke the trance, and Samantha came to herself again, blinking several times and looking around as if she were just waking and couldn't remember where she was.

Leisha stepped forward, her arm around the girl's shoulder. "Don't worry, Samantha. You're safe with me. I promise." She didn't like manipulating Samantha and exposing her to vampires, but she had no other choice now. It still amazed her how quickly a situation like this could go downhill so rapidly—no matter how many times Leisha had experienced the same thing, it still astounded her.

"I'm afraid you will need to come with us, Samantha." The girl was still recovering from Nikita's spell, no sign of comprehension on her face. "It's for your own protection. I promise that you'll be able to contact your family and let them know you're all right." Leisha couldn't say anything more with Nikita standing there. She knew she would have to explain everything to Samantha in another time; she would have to reveal the monster that she was. For reasons she couldn't explain, she wanted Samantha to like her, not to fear her.

An image of her daughter's wide, frightened eyes filled her vision.

Samantha looked like her lucidity was coming back, though she remained subdued. She was dependent on Leisha to take care of things. Seeing the innocent look of trust in Samantha's face pained Leisha even more. But she

ignored the feelings and turned back to Nikita with a cool gaze.

"You got here rather quickly," she said. "Did Ptah even leave the States?"

Nikita gave his usual soft smile. "Of course, he left. There was plenty for him to do at the base," His gaze roamed over Samantha's figure in a casual manner. "He didn't trust you completely. He wanted me to stick around to make sure you followed through on your word."

The insult thickened Leisha's blood. "I still hold my word as my bond, and Ptah should know that will never change."

Nikita shrugged nonchalantly. As usual, nothing ruffled him. Not even when Ptah approached him four hundred years ago and asked him if he wanted to join the undead. Leisha remembered her shock when Nikita studied Ptah's obsidian eyes passively. He'd shrugged then, too, and said, "I have nothing better to do."

She decided to return to the original subject. "You saw me being taken and did nothing to stop them?" The austere edge in her voice had no effect on him.

Nikita walked over and sat down on the boulder next to Leisha. She decided to mirror him and repositioned herself on another boulder nearby. Samantha, now beside her, was fully alert, but stayed quiet, observing everything with intent curiosity.

"I was going to get you out," Nikita said. "I was studying the compound, and trying to figure out how to get past their security so I could find you before I had to fight them.

I heard you screaming, but they weren't killing you, and I certainly didn't want to be the next subject for their little science project. I was rewiring the security cameras in the parking lot when you two came bursting out." He appeared undaunted, but Leisha had the feeling that he was somewhat jealous that a mere human girl had beaten him to the rescue. Maybe he had a soft spot after all.

Samantha piped up with wide eyes. "There were security cameras in the parking lot? I didn't see any . . ."

Nikita nodded.

"So," Leisha said, somewhat impatient, but mainly irritated that Nikita had heard her screams. "If you were right there, why did you wait so long to show up?"

"I was waiting for Ptah's orders. Not sure what he would want." Meaning, he wasn't sure whether to approach with Samantha being around.

"I see," Leisha said. "Well, did you bring transportation? Or do we still have to wait for Ptah to send his plane?"

"I got a car from the parking lot. Ptah is sending the jet to the airport."

"Is the car going to be reported any time soon?"

Nikita gave his infamous shrug and stood, brushing dirt off his black slacks. It was time to go.

Leisha rose and turned to Samantha.

Samantha seemed a little hesitant to come with them. She obviously knew there was something unusual about them, but Leisha knew she would never guess just how unusual.

Leisha hesitated at the thought of exposing this beautiful young woman to her sordid world, but she knew there was really no choice since she didn't want Nikita to suck this girl dry.

They got to the car in no time and were on their way, with Nikita driving and Leisha in the passenger seat. Samantha was in the back.

"How long until we get to the airport, Nikita?" Samantha asked.

Nikita glanced in the rear view mirror at her. "About an hour. Please, call me Nik. It hurts to hear you mar my name like that."

Samantha actually smiled quite warmly. "Sure, Nik. Thanks for coming to get us."

Leisha wasn't sure what to think of her response. What was the girl thinking? She shouldn't make friends with a vampire. Especially Nikita, who cared so little for human life, or anything at all. Leisha was definitely going to have a long talk with Samantha on the plane. Nikita would probably be piloting the plane himself with the pilot door sealed shut; he wouldn't be able to hear her. That was lucky, since it was going to be a tedious conversation.

She couldn't do anything about it now, so she sat back and closed her eyes to rest.

Leisha woke when Nikita made a thoughtful humming noise at the back of his throat.

"What is it?" she asked, instantly alert.

"I believe we have a tail," he said, in his usual calm

voice. "No doubt, it's the people from whom you have just escaped."

Leisha's blood went into a boil, her body pulling itself into fighting mode. She looked back at Samantha, who appeared pale and more than a little frightened, and changed her mind. "Can you lose them?"

Nikita shook his head. "It's quite obvious we're headed to the municipal. Even if I lose these ones, more will follow."

He was right. Leisha cursed her frustration. "We have to get to the jet. Once we're in the air, they won't be able to touch us."

Nikita nodded. "I have a few weapons under the seats and in the glove box."

Leisha stared at him in surprise. Most vampires considered themselves more dangerous than any weapon a human could manufacture.

Nikita was unperturbed by her shock. "I was going to go into that compound by myself. I figured a little backup would come in handy."

Leisha nodded and checked under her seat. "Nice."

She reached for the pieces of the Parker Hale sniper rifle and assembled it within seconds, hesitating for a second before aiming it out the window at the Humvee that was quickly gaining on them. She generally didn't like killing, but figured these guys were just as bad as the murderers she put to rest.

As she started to point the rifle out the window,

Samantha grabbed her arm. "You can't! You don't know who's in that car."

Leisha studied her briefly. Samantha had mentioned she knew someone who worked in the compound.

Struggling momentarily, Leisha tried to decide what was best. She definitely was not going to be taken again, no matter what. But she also didn't have to be so aggressive so soon. She must first know their next move.

"You're right," she said to Samantha. "But I will act to defend myself, you, and Nikita."

Samantha withdrew her hand and sat back. She didn't look happy about Leisha keeping the weapon in her lap, but did not protest. She was completely on edge, drawn with dilated eyes. Leisha couldn't blame her.

The car was right behind them now, trying to blind them with their bright lights.

"These guys think they can intimidate me with lights?" Nikita chuckled.

Samantha focused her eyes intently on the car, Leisha assumed, to see if she could find a familiar face. Of course, the build of the Humvee and the bright headlights made that impossible, but Samantha looked anyway.

The back windshield shattered as the first bullet fired. Samantha screamed and ducked low. Nikita swerved to throw off their aim. Leisha concentrated her senses on the vehicle and was able to detect five passengers. She didn't need to read their minds to know they were all military

trained. Leaning out the window, Leisha took two seconds to aim before blowing out the two front tires.

The Humvee swerved both ways before spinning out on the highway.

"I'm pretty sure I hear a helicopter approaching." Nikita was so casual in his comment that it took a second for Leisha to fully comprehend him.

Leisha put her head out the window and searched the sky. Sure enough, a black helicopter was quickly making its way toward them. When it was a hundred feet above and directly behind them, bullets flew. They first struck the pavement just behind the car, quickly making their way to the car and up the trunk.

Leisha and Nikita exchanged glances when they heard another vehicle heading toward them from the opposite direction. It was a classic ambush.

"We have more advantage fighting on ground than in the air," he commented. Leisha reluctantly nodded in agreement.

Nikita slammed on the breaks and manipulated the steering wheel as the car swerved dangerously in every which way. It finally came to a halt, but they didn't have much time. The helicopter had turned around and would be on them in fewer than twenty seconds.

Leisha jumped into the backseat and pulled Samantha out the door. Nikita was already beside her by the time she got Samantha out.

"It looks like she hit her head or something," Nikita

observed. "She's barely conscious." It was true. Leisha was holding the girl upright, but Samantha's head was lolling to the side.

Leisha turned to Nikita. "I'll find some place safe to put her, and then come back to help you fight."

"There is no time."

She followed his gaze to the second Humvee that was almost to the car. The vampires could hear the men from the first Humvee trying to sneak over to them on foot. Leisha cursed under her breath.

Nikita would have been a blur to any human eye, but Leisha could see him clearly as he ran back to the car and pulled out another rifle and a couple of handguns stashed under the seats.

There was no more time. Leisha sped forty feet away to let Samantha rest on the ground and hurried back to Nikita.

He was already aiming his rifle at the helicopter. He fired and hit one of the shooters right between the eyes.

Leisha directed her attention at the Humvee parked next to Nikita's stolen car. There were four men inside, one of them being a four star general. She could see the man behind the passenger seat clearly enough to catch the freckles lining his face. The one behind the driver had a distinct square jaw, and was loading a shotgun with more of those specialized tranquilizer bullets.

In her peripheral vision, she could see Nikita running,

and then leaping high into the air, landing with perfect grace in the cabin of the helicopter.

Leisha nearly flew as she raced toward Square Jaw. Apparently, no one was expecting her to take the offensive, and they were momentarily paralyzed when she punched through the window, stabbing her fingers through Square Jaw's eyes with one hand while pulling his shotgun out the window with the other.

The men got over their shock and scrambled out of the vehicle with their weapons ready. It was a cinch for Leisha to take out the driver. She pulled out his throat before he got his second foot out the door.

Four Stars fired his handgun and hit Leisha in the shoulder. She hissed at the pain and was immediately up in the air, flipping over the Humvee, landing behind the general before he could blink. Pulling him toward her with her right arm, she grabbed his handgun with her left and proceeded to bite into his neck, at the same time, clipping Freckles in his heart, giving him no time to react. She didn't like the taste of her victim's blood—he ate way too much salt and had marijuana in his system. But he was a well of information. It was difficult to sift through all of his memories as they poured into her brain faster than his blood poured into her mouth. She figured out that he had been on this latest assignment for three years and was beginning to lose his sanity with everything he'd seen, though he agreed with the results the scientists were trying to achieve.

These people were part of a secret sect of the FBI. The Attorney General was the top guy in charge, but he only saw reports of their progress from afar. About thirty years ago, they discovered vampires were no mere legend; they studied everything they could find about vampires, and developed weapons to be used against her kind.

Then they decided if they could combine the blood of a vampire with a human, they could create a new breed of super soldiers that would be faster, stronger, and could heal quickly in combat. For the last six years, they had managed to capture four vampires, testing their strengths and weaknesses before draining them and experimenting with their blood. So far, this FBI division hadn't been able to create a formula that the soldiers could use. Most of the men who volunteered for the experiments had to be killed after trying to go on a murderous rampage.

Leisha pulled away from the general, panting with his memories overflowing in her mind; he'd given her more than enough information to digest. Leisha would never want to be in that compound again. Ever.

A bullet penetrating her side snapped her back to the situation at hand. She spun and crouched while aiming her gun at the direction of where the shot came. When she saw the spark of a second shot, she fired and hit her target while her opponent's bullet whizzed past her head.

Something exploded in the sky. Leisha looked up to see Nikita hurtling into the night air, his arms spread wide, showing a slight smile on his face. The other men,

distracted by the fireball, plunged toward the ground. Leisha seized that moment and ran in their direction.

But no one was there. The assault team was not in the small sand dunes where she'd suspected. In the darkness in the field, a movement caught Leisha's attention. It was a hundred feet away from Nikita and close to the spot where Leisha had left Samantha.

No! Leisha leapt to her feet and ran to the movement she had seen without any thought of the other men around.

She felt sudden pains in her calf but didn't break stride. Another pain shot through her left side into her liver—that one really hurt. She ground her teeth against the pain. How was it possible for her to be hit when she was moving faster than her assailants' human eyes could follow? She tossed the thought aside and continued to her destination. There was no place for her to hide for cover; she just had to keep going and get to Samantha.

When she finally reached the spot where she had left the girl, Leisha found nothing. She scanned the surrounding area. Before she had time to look around, she heard a footfall directly behind her.

Leisha turned to see a man holding a specialized gun, aimed at her head.

"You may be fast, but the tranquilizer bullet will go directly into your brain before you'll be able to kill me." She stared into his hard brown eyes, unmoving. He might have been military, but the longer she stood there, the more his hand began to shake.

When his arm slipped about an inch, she lunged for the gun and was able to barely tip it before he got off a shot. The tranquilizer hit her in the neck, just below her jugular. Leisha gripped his wrist in her viselike grasp. He groaned and the gun fell from his hand as she heard his bones snapping.

The drugs were starting to affect her already. She moved her hand up to his neck to crush it.

"Don't do it!" came a frantic plea to her right.

Leisha looked over at Samantha. She knew Samantha had some reason about not killing these men, but couldn't remember what. Leisha shook her head.

Samantha put her hand on Leisha's arm to move it, but Leisha didn't budge. She was supposed to kill this man . . . wasn't she?

"Leisha," Samantha begged. "You don't have to kill him."

Leisha was on the brink of consciousness when she saw Nikita's blurry figure appear and twist the man's head, killing him instantly.

Samantha's horrified screams were the last thing she heard as darkness engulfed her.

CHAPTER 7

Samantha leaned her head back in her seat. She had spent the first two hours in the plane sobbing and it gave her a headache. Her eyes were now puffy, and she wasn't feeling any better. She had cried herself completely dry and felt too drained and exhausted to shed more tears. Her emotions were starting to numb, and she was beginning to welcome it.

That soldier's death kept playing in her head.

Nikita had patiently tried to explain to her that killing the man was the most logical and practical thing to do. No matter how she had tried to protest, he wouldn't be moved on the matter. When he finally convinced her she was safe with him, that nothing more could be done after the matter, she grudgingly allowed him to walk her to the car, Leisha's unconscious body carried over his shoulder like a sack of grain.

Amazingly, she did feel safe with Nikita, even after witnessing what he was capable of.

Samantha cradled her head in the backseat of the barely functioning, bullet-ridden car the whole way to the small airport. She didn't know how Nikita was able to get direct access to the plane hangar—they hadn't seen a soul on the tarmac; there were no security checks.

Once they had gotten on the plane, Nikita left her to look after Leisha while he went in the cockpit and flew them out of there. Samantha had no idea where they were going or who this Ptah was, but she knew by going with Leisha, she had just changed her life dramatically.

There was something otherworldly about Leisha and Nikita. She had seen them in action on the highway. They were downright superhuman. Their strength and speed was astounding. While she watched them kill all those men, she wondered if she might have made a mistake in freeing Leisha. Could they be the "bad guys," while her father and his men were the "good guys"?

The thought of her dad brought back a memory of him at the compound, in which he was staring directly at her through the torn door. He knew she had helped Leisha escape. If she was in the wrong, would he ever forgive her? But she knew in her heart she had had that vision for a reason. She was supposed to rescue Leisha. Not knowing how her gift worked, it wouldn't make sense for her instincts to inspire her to save someone evil.

All those people killed . . . Samantha felt a wave of

compassion for all the men who'd lost their lives tonight. Before her mother, she had never experienced death, personally, though her visions had introduced her to the concept at an early age. Somewhere in the world in this very moment, loved ones left behind by the dead grieved.

Samantha got out of her seat and went to the back of the plane where Leisha was lying across the seats. The plane was decent sized. She had never been in a private jet, so she didn't know what to compare it to, but it seemed pretty nice. The seats were large and plush, complete with foot rests that folded out like recliners. There were ten seats all evenly spaced, except for the four along the back—those were right next to each other, which was good for Leisha, who remained unconscious the entire time.

Nikita had assured her Leisha would be all right, but Samantha could not help but worry. Leisha was shot in the leg and in her side. She'd also been hit in the neck with some kind of tranquilizer. That would take a while to recover. To add to the damage, Nikita refused to take her to the hospital, giving off an air of impatience. Samantha had to press him until he finally agreed to dress the wounds with strips from an extra shirt he'd found in the trunk of the car. The whole time, he acted like he was indulging a little child.

Samantha laid her hand over Leisha's forehead. Leisha felt slightly cool—Samantha didn't know what to make of it. Leisha stirred under her touch and Samantha jumped back, startled.

Leisha, groggy, opened her eyes, taking a few minutes to focus on Samantha.

"How do you feel?" Samantha asked. She knelt by Leisha's side and took her hand.

"I'll be fine in a few minutes. I just need this stupid drug to wear off." Leisha pulled her hand out of Samantha's and very carefully sat up. She closed her eyes briefly against a dizzy spell. "Nikita didn't hurt you at all, did he?"

Samantha suppressed the memory of Nik twisting the soldier's neck. "No, he's been pretty accommodating, actually."

Leisha's eyes widened at that, but didn't press the matter. She looked at Samantha with a kind of gentleness. "Are you ready to tell me who you are and why you tried to rescue me from that compound?"

The pregnant silence filled the air. Samantha pursed her lips and looked to her right, her eyes burning with unshed tears.

"I'm giving you my protection, Samantha," Leisha squeezed her arm, "which is a big deal, and I think I deserve to know what your situation is."

Unable to protest, Samantha sighed. She sat next to Leisha and explained, "My father works there. I don't know details about what he does. Anyway, I already told you that I followed him to the compound tonight." She wrinkled her nose. "Actually, I hid in my dad's trunk and snuck in that way." She omitted her unique ability. Though Samantha knew she'd end up confiding in Leisha about it in the near

future, for the time being, she'd keep the knowledge of her gift to herself—she'd promised her mother this much.

Leisha accepted the information as if it were no big deal. The woman's facial expression suggested she could see holes in her story, though wise enough not to push.

Staring at Leisha's bandaged leg, Samantha couldn't bring herself to meet Leisha's gaze.

"Does it hurt a lot?" she was surprised that the make-shift bandage wasn't already soaked in blood. The bandage on Leisha's side hadn't bled very much, either.

"No, it doesn't hurt anymore." Leisha bent down and slowly unwrapped the bandage. She lifted her pant leg to show Samantha smooth, unscarred skin. Samantha gasped at the sight.

Samantha reached out for Leisha's torso, fingers shaking, and removed the dressing. The woman's tan skin showed no signs of scars, either. So, this woman had super strength and speed, and could heal rapidly, too. What in the world was she?

As if she could read Samantha's mind, Leisha spoke quietly, "I am a vampire."

The simple statement was enough to floor Samantha completely. "T-th-that . . . No." She swallowed. "They don't exist." She had been helping the wrong side after all. She had betrayed her own father for a vampire! It couldn't be true. Samantha's heart leapt.

Leisha made a soothing gesture with her hand, but did not touch her.

"The story I have to tell is very long. It happened about two thousand years ago." The vampire paused. "Are you ready to hear it? I can give you time to get used to the idea of our existence, if you need it. But I must explain everything to you before we arrive in India. You have to be prepared before you go to the vampire's lair."

India? Vampire's lair? Leisha couldn't be serious, could she? Samantha groaned.

She had been a complete fool! She was going to be surrounded by vampires. They were going to ravish her flesh and drink her blood, and kill her. Everything around her suddenly started to shift, her head spinning. The day had already been a lot to take in, but this was just too much!

"I promise you will be safe," Leisha reassured. She deliberately put her hand on Samantha's shoulder and rubbed her back in soothing circles.

The motion eased Samantha's tense muscles and she felt herself relaxing. Her breathing became even and she no longer felt lightheaded. Samantha lifted her head and met Leisha's gaze. The woman's green eyes were full of concern and something else. Shame, maybe? "You don't like what you are, do you?" Samantha whispered.

Leisha looked to the floor. "I have to accept what I am. There is no other choice."

"How old are you?" Samantha asked, her inquisitiveness piquing.

Leisha seemed amused. "I'm not exactly sure. You lose track after a time. But I was turned into a vampire with the

first of us. That was approximately two thousand years ago."

This beautiful young woman sitting next to her was two thousand years old? It seemed too impossible to fathom.

"This will be a lot to take in, and I'm sorry that I have to give you so much information. But there is little time. It began in my village in Africa, near Egypt."

"You're from Africa?" Samantha interrupted. "But . . . you don't look . . . you know . . . African," she said lamely.

"I don't know who my biological parents were." She said it matter-of-factly. "I was found on the north shore of Africa. I believe my parents died at sea, but I have no memory of it myself. I was only a baby at the time."

"But you didn't stay in the village close to the shore where you were found?"

"There was a terrible storm that killed half the village the day after they found me. I was considered a bad omen." Leisha continued conversationally. "I was passed around to a few different villages until the shaman of one village agreed to take me in. The village witch doctors were highly esteemed, so when he decided to raise me, the rest of the village grudgingly accepted me." Her face softened as she reminisced her past. "The shaman raised me as if I were his own daughter. I loved him deeply." Leisha swallowed. "Anyway, when I was probably around the age of eighteen or so, there was an awful drought in that area. The drought was large enough that simply moving to a more fruitful area wasn't an option. It got so desperate that many people

in the village wanted to offer me up as a blood sacrifice to appease the gods, but my father wouldn't allow it. He tried every calling spell he knew to bring the rains, but nothing seemed to work.

"That's when Ptah first arrived into the village. He wanted to harvest our land for gold to pay homage to Ptolemy XV Caesarean, the last Pharaoh of Egypt." Leisha paused and looked at Samantha. "You see, we had already traded all of the gold from the surfaces near our village for what food we could get. What Ptah wanted to do was dig deeper for more gold. There was a belief that digging too deep in the earth could unleash things from other worlds, and our people would never have agreed under normal circumstances. But we were desperate, and in exchange, Ptah promised us food and water. It was an offer we simply couldn't refuse."

"So . . . vampires are from another world that you unleashed when you dug too deep? But we mine in Africa all the time now. It's a huge source for diamonds. Are you saying that every time someone is mining over there, they unleash more vampires?"

"No, that's not it." Leisha took a breath. "As far as mining today, I have a theory: Because so many people have become more practical and less superstitious, it has simply taken away the powers from other worlds."

"So, if you have faith in it, then it will happen, but if you don't believe, then the powers can't touch you?" It seemed a weak explanation to Samantha, but if Leisha's

story was really true, then what other explanation could there be?

"It's just a theory. May I finish?" At Samantha's nod, Leisha continued, "Nothing happened at first. Ptah had workers from all over mining just outside of our village, and they were bringing up an abundance of gold. Our village was being fed as if we were all royalty. Everyone was happy." Leisha smiled, a mixture of nostalgia and sadness. "I'd never been happier."

There was a story in itself from just that comment. Samantha could sense it. "What made you so happy?" she asked.

Leisha stared out the window to the night sky. "I was in love," she said simply. "His name was Tafari. He was one of the workers in the mine. It had been my job to bring the miners water every day, and we got to know each other over the months." Her tone was filled with awe. "He was the most beautiful man I would ever know and I thanked the gods that he actually loved me back. We got married right away and Tafari quit the mines so he could be my father's apprentice. He was to take his place as the village shaman one day. Our time together was cherished . . ." Leisha cleared her throat, her eyes fixed on Samantha. "You must understand, I wasn't considered very pretty in that area. I was different and people were still wary of me. Before Tafari, I had just assumed I would care for my father until his death, after which, I would either be offered up as a sacrifice or roam from place to place until my own end.

The possibility of sharing my life with another had never actually occurred to me.

"But Tafari was different. He had this depth to him that allowed him to see the real me. He made me feel desired, and we connected so well. You've read all the poems about true love? Well, that's how it was between us . . . And when we had Adanne, life seemed more perfect than I could ever have believed possible."

Leisha brushed her cheek, but not before Samantha saw a blood red tear slide down. She realized Leisha didn't talk about Tafari to many people, if any, and was touched to have Leisha take someone like Samantha into her confidence. It made her wonder if vampires were really as bad as legends made them to be. Leisha certainly appeared humane enough. Samantha hadn't known her long, but she already knew this woman was warm and compassionate.

"Anyway," Leisha said. "Ptah and his men had been mining in our village for just over a year when it happened."

"What happened?"

"No one knew exactly. There was some kind of accident in the mine and ten men were killed. A few days later, another tragedy struck the village. The chief's hut caught on fire, consuming his wife and children. The next day, a camel broke loose and trampled a woman in its path. There was this surge of random, fatal accidents with no explanation.

"My father was completely tense. I went to visit him; he was with the chief at that time. They both had haunted

looks on their faces. 'We've simply dug too deep,' my father told me. 'We have unleashed a chaos demon.'"

That wasn't something Samantha was expecting to hear. "A chaos demon?" she repeated. "So, a chaos demon invented vampires to wreak havoc on the earth?"

Leisha sighed. "Stop trying to get ahead of the story. Just listen."

"Sorry."

"So, where was I? Chaos demon. My father told me a demon from another world had managed to wiggle his way into ours. It didn't have a body, but it did have the power to influence bad things to happen.

"He said not to worry, and sent me away while he and the chief prepared to deal with the demon. He had an idea of how to get rid of it, but he wouldn't tell me how. Tafari left me and Adanne to help my father. But I was curious. I waited until after Adanne was sleeping soundly before sneaking out to see what they were going to do.

"I crept to my father's hut and peeked through a crack near the entrance. Ptah was tied up on the floor, surrounded by little bits of incense and magic sticks. My father and Tafari were chanting softly just outside the circle. Men I recognized from the village stood quietly in a corner."

Leisha's eyes glazed with vagueness, unfocused. "A strange sensation overwhelmed me. It was as if darkness had taken on some sort of unseeing form, like a mist creeping up my spine, embedding my body and soul with a feeling of dread. It felt like there was only despair in my future, like I was doomed to fall into a never-ending pit of darkness." Leisha hugged herself, shivering as if she were experiencing it all over again.

"Suddenly, the feeling left me and I saw what looked like a strange, dark cloud hovering above Ptah. I glanced at the men in the corner and suspected by the looks on their faces that they had felt the same despair that I had. As my father began to chant louder, the dark cloud lowered toward Ptah.

"He looked terrified as it descended closer to him. His skin was ashen, a gleam of sweat showed on his forehead. His eyes were so wide they looked like they could pop out of his skull at any time, but he did not cry out. He just watched as the cloud came closer and closer toward him. Then, just as the dark mist began to touch his skin, it disappeared.

"That was when Ptah screamed—a shrill, pain-filled scream. His body writhed on the floor, as if he were being tortured. The trauma continued for maybe five more minutes before it all stopped. Ptah's body now lay so still I thought he'd died. The men in the corner pulled out knives as they approached Ptah's body, but my father held a hand out for them to wait. He was watching Ptah intently.

"When Ptah's eyes opened, they did not resemble his anymore; they were shining pools of complete blackness. It was as if his eyes were the embodiment of what pure darkness was supposed to be, ready to engulf any light that approached." Leisha paused and looked at Samantha. "They are still like that, those eyes. I suggest not looking

directly into them when you meet him. They can have a disorienting affect on humans."

Samantha shuddered.

Leisha studied her for a few seconds. "My father gestured for the men to come. They made a circle around Ptah's body, raising their knives to kill him. Then, before they could even digest what was really happening, one of them went flying through the air through the wall of the hut. Ptah, already on his feet, grabbed another man's head—I can still hear his screams in my mind—twisting it until it snapped. The third man froze, completely terrified. Ptah lifted this man off his feet and bit his arm. The man cried out in pain but he seemed unable to move or do anything to stop Ptah from draining out his life. Then he looked at my father and Tafari. They were frozen under his gaze. I thought they were about to die in that moment, but Ptah just looked at them.

"'Thank you,' he said in a strange voice. It sounded like Ptah, but it also reverberated some kind of power when he spoke.

"With that, Ptah turned and looked directly at me. Somehow, he knew I was outside, watching through the cracks of the hut. He stared at me for what felt like an eternity, though it was only for a second. He broke the stare, leapt out though the ceiling, and disappeared into the night."

Leisha turned to face Samantha. "He was the first of our kind."

CHAPTER 8

Samantha shook her head. "But I don't understand. What did they do to Ptah?"

"You see, there was no way to kill the chaos demon while it was in its spirit form. We had no weapons to fight against something like that, so my father pulled its spirit into a human body to make it vulnerable enough to be killed." Leisha turned away, her face full of sorrow. "What no one realized was that the demon had wanted this to happen all along. Its powers would have been limited in spirit form, but when it was able to fully posses a body as its own, its potential to wield over humans became invincible."

"Oh."

Leisha just nodded solemnly.

"But why did you become a vampire? I can't imagine you would want to leave your family for a chance at immortality."

Leisha's expression turned bitter. "There is more to the story that you should know." Sighing wearily, she expounded. "Ptah had been openly interested in courting me as well. When he found out that Tafari and I were to wed, he was very angry with me. That was another reason Tafari stopped working for him." Leisha paused, looking pensive. "I think the real Ptah—the Egyptian who had desperately mined for all that gold—I think he died the moment the demon entered his body. We only call him Ptah because there was never any name for the demon that we know of. So, while Ptah was dead, I think the demon retained all of his memories, including his attraction for me."

"But you couldn't have left Tafari for Ptah!" Samantha was outraged, a feeling of fury bubbling up through her stomach. "You were just telling me what you had with Tafari was true love! If so, how could you do that to him?"

"You're jumping ahead of the story again," Leisha snapped. "Let me give you a little advice: Do not judge until you have all the information."

Samantha realized with shock that her accusation had hurt Leisha. She flushed red and quietly murmured, "Sorry."

Leisha regained her composure and continued in a detached manner. "Like I said, Ptah—the demon—seemed to have an attraction toward me. He would sneak into our hut in the middle of the night to seduce me, urging that I join with him. I always refused, but was scared to wake up Tafari and tell him about it. I was afraid Ptah would kill him if Tafari tried to defend me. But then, Ptah suddenly stopped coming into our hut, and I thought he had left us alone.

"But he was simply taking his death and destruction to other villages. The terror of having our blood sucked was horrible, and everyone lived in fear for months.

"One day, Tafari came home from a meeting with other shamans, more hopeful than I had seen him in a long time, and told me the shamans had figured out how to combine their powers to create a breed of immortals."

"Immortals?"

"Yes. The shamans had discovered that they could modify a complex healing spell to create immortality, which could make them strong enough to fight the vampires. If they became wounded, they would heal rapidly, even faster than a vampire can. Death was still a threat, but at least they had a chance of fighting the vampires. It sounded promising, and Tafari's excitement was contagious."

Leisha hesitated. "Then he told me he had been chosen to become one of the immortals. He was to go to a ceremony the following evening to take an oath—he would dedicate every fiber of his being to locate and destroy any and all vampires. After he pledged himself, they would proceed to make him an immortal. He was to be one of the leaders for the new order of immortals."

Samantha was about to vocalize more confusion, but Leisha cut her off with a gesture of her hand. It was

obvious this was truly difficult for her to divulge. Seeing this, Samantha forced herself to sit quietly.

"The night Tafari left for the ceremony was the night Ptah sent his men to capture me and my daughter. I fought hard, but they were too fast and too strong. They blind-folded me and bound my wrists, and carried us to a cave somewhere . . ."

SUDDENLY, THE MAN CARRYING LEISHA stopped, while the other one carrying her daughter continued on. Leisha tried to protest, to struggle to get to Adanne, but the man's grip tightened, taking the air out of her lungs.

"Don't worry about her, Leisha." The voice came from behind, but she immediately recognized it.

"What do you want with us, Ptah?" she gasped. The air was still not completely back in her lungs. He gave a soft, deep laugh and gestured for his man to release her. "I must admit, I don't care much about your daughter, but I do have a great deal of interest in you. There's something different about you, and it's more than just your fair skin." He walked around her until their noses almost touched. "There's a spark in your eyes I wish to ignite."

She shuddered in revulsion. "I do not understand what you mean. But if your interest is only in me, then why did you bring my daughter?"

Ptah looked smug. "She's my leverage."

"What? Leverage for what? You already have me here."

He began to pace casually in front of her as he spoke. "Ah, but that's not enough. You notice I have created beings that are like me?"

She nodded slowly.

"I can gift this to any human, but there is one condition." He came close and put his face next to hers. "They have to give me their permission"—his breath cold against her cheek—"They have to say yes to me. Otherwise, they simply die. Don't ask me why it works this way, but that has always been the way.

"What I want from you is to join me and my growing forces." He began to pace again. "You have a unique strength inside of you. I can feel it. If I have you at my side, then I truly believe nothing can stop us."

Leisha scoffed. "I would rather die the most painful death than join you. You have darkness and evil in you, and I will not be a part of it."

He turned to look at her, his cold, black eyes penetrating hers. Leisha tried not to squirm. "I thought you might say something like that." He smiled again. "This is where the leverage comes in."

Leisha felt an icy sense of foreboding work its way up her spine, filling her body. Blood drained from her face as she realized his intentions.

A torch lit in the distance and she could see there was some kind of lower level in the cave. Adanne was down there, her small wrists bound above her head as she looked at Leisha, terror in her eyes.

Ptah nodded his head at something below in the shadows. Suddenly, a whip flashed, and Leisha screamed out with her daughter. There was blood coming down the front of Adanne's shirt.

"I like to whip the stomach and work toward the back," Ptah's ugly voice said.

She closed her eyes, but the horrid image of little Adanne bleeding seared into her brain. "You win, Ptah," she murmured through stiff lips. "If you let her go and promise me she will not be harmed anymore, I will become one of your monsters."

"You gave in rather easily, did you not? I knew your daughter was going to be instrumental in getting to you, but I was expecting a lot more torture to be involved first." He released a breath of disgust. "Oh well, I will get what I want, and so will you. No more harm will come to her. Now, we shall commence the mixing of our blood to become one in body and soul."

Shaking, Leisha couldn't believe what was transpiring before her. "You have brought me to hell itself," she murmured.

Ptah pulled her out of her thoughts by grabbing hard on her hair. Leisha's neck was exposed and he didn't waste any time biting into her flesh, upon which she cried out her desolation to the gods she once believed were her protectors.

"You taste exquisite!" Ptah exclaimed, his tone filled with surprise and lust. As he threw her to the ground, she looked up to see him slicing his own wrist with his fingernail. He put his bleeding wrist in front of her mouth and ordered her to drink.

Leisha hesitated for a moment, but when she was reminded of her tortured daughter, she immediately put her mouth on his arm and drank.

Ptah's blood was thick and vile. Leisha could feel it oozing down her throat and into her stomach. It felt heavy, and she thought she would pass out before she drank enough to transform.

Pulling her off his arm, Ptah studied her intently. She felt disgusted by what she'd just done, strangely violated without physical harm.

Then it came. A cold, burning sensation rapidly snaked through her body all the way from her toes to her scalp.

Leisha arched her back and screamed. It felt like acid was eating her from the inside out. She writhed around on the ground, trying to rub the odious sensations out of her body, but it only made the pain worse. She stopped and tried to think past the agony, but it was no use. She had to make it stop. Suddenly, she realized she was on the edge of one end of the cave, and that she could easily roll over it. The fall would kill her and make the pain go away.

Leisha summoned the strength to roll onto her side, but the pain had drained every bit of her energy. She took a few ragged breaths and tried again. It worked. She just needed to roll over once more, and she would be over the edge.

A noise came through the throbbing; Leisha couldn't tell exactly what it was. The only thing she knew in that moment was that she was experiencing more affliction than anyone could ever endure. It should have killed her by now. But it didn't, and she was still beyond any measure of pain one could fathom.

Leisha tried valiantly once again to roll over—just once more, and everything would end—but couldn't. Her mind got fuzzy, she couldn't think anymore. As the blessed darkness of unconsciousness descended on her, she gradually gave into it . . .

LEISHA SAT QUIETLY. HER VOICE remained neutral while she recounted her story. Reliving it had made her close in on herself.

Samantha shuddered several times throughout the

story. She almost cried at the thought of Leisha having to watch her baby being tortured.

Leisha cleared her throat and continued, "When I woke, I was a vampire. Everything felt and looked very different. I could hear every little thing so clearly, like the water dripping in the cave. It sounded as if it were just next to my ears. I could see every crack, every speck of dirt. It was startling. It takes a while to get used to it. Some vampires can't handle it, can't learn to distinguish and ignore some of the sights and sounds."

Samantha was getting impatient. While hearing what it was like to be a vampire was interesting, she had to know what had happened to Adanne.

Leisha glanced at Samantha and read her face. "My baby girl was all right, considering what she had been through. I was unconscious the entire day, during which they fed her while waiting for me to wake. I always suspected that while they didn't touch her, they might have played with her mind." Leisha frowned; a haunted look conquering her eyes. "But I'll never know, because I wasn't able to talk to her about it."

"You mean you never saw her again?"

"I thought Ptah was granting me mercy when he said I could take Adanne home that night to say goodbye to her and my father. I carried her the whole way back—my daughter crying in her sleep in my arms. When I arrived at my father's hut in the middle of the night, I laid Adanne

in my old cot. I went to my father to explain to him everything that had transpired, when it hit me."

"What hit you?" Samantha prompted.

Leisha's tone turned grave. "The Hunger." She exhaled slowly before continuing, "When someone first becomes a vampire, he needs to drink blood right away. Ptah, of course, knew this, but didn't warn me at all. If a vampire doesn't eat when he needs to . . . The Hunger . . . takes over . . . It's the most primal instinct that exists. You act like an animal. You don't think, and you don't see anything as it is. It's like your brain just shuts down and The Hunger takes over your body. All you can see is what's food, and what isn't."

Samantha wasn't sure she wanted to hear any more, but stayed calm and tried to keep the look of abhorrence off her face. "So, you . . . ate your father and daughter?" she whispered hoarsely.

"Almost," Leisha answered. "I was a mere inches away from my father's neck, ready to bite into him, when my daughter's terrorized shriek temporarily brought me to my senses. She was extremely scared of me . . . terrorized." Leisha broke off, unable to face the memory of her daughter.

Samantha wanted to reach out to Leisha, to give her some sort of comfort, but she stopped herself. Leisha had more to tell, and would probably not welcome the comfort.

Leisha cleared her throat again. "I immediately apologized to my father and told Adanne I loved her, and then I ran as fast as I could. I wasn't paying any attention to where

I was going. I just wanted to run as far as my legs would carry me. Far away from everything. When I finally collapsed to my knees, a man—I guess, you could call him a good Samaritan—saw me and tried to help.

"At that point, The Hunger had paralyzed my sense of discernment. That poor man died a most horrible death at my hands."

Tears rolled down Samantha's cheeks. "Oh, Leisha, that's so terrible."

Leisha's smile was twisted with irony. "You think that's bad? Tafari was on that same path, and had come to see me sitting in a puddle of gore that used to be a man."

Samantha couldn't stand how depressingly wretched this story was—she could no longer tell if she was shedding tears of remorse or fear. "Were you able to tell Tafari what happened?"

Leisha shook her head, and turned to gaze out the window.

Samantha quietly got up and went to the bathroom. For a few minutes she wept on behalf of Leisha before splashing water over her face. Vampires do exist, and Leisha is one of them. Samantha couldn't believe she was able to accept it so easily. The mild shock had perhaps numbed her to this great revelation.

No, she thought. The existence of vampires was the easy part to accept. The hard part was going with Leisha and Nik to meet this cruel demon-man named Ptah—she would be face to face with Ptah in less than a day. Samantha wondered if she would live through this experience.

CHAPTER 9

Leisha stared out the window at nothing, working to keep her tears at bay. Talking about her past caused her emotional wounds to feel fresh and vulnerable, like a newborn baby exposed to the elements. She was surprised at herself for having shared so much with Samantha. She had only planned on telling her the bare minimum, but the words just came out of their own volition.

She sucked in a deep breath and held it for a few seconds before slowly letting it out. As she exhaled, she felt her shoulders release the tension they were holding. While divulging her story was definitely painful, it was also a relief to finally tell someone everything that had happened. Before today, she'd kept her story to herself, but now she found herself sharing the deepest parts of her life with a young girl she hardly knew.

What was it about Samantha that made her feel comfortable enough to open up so much about her past? She had started to tell the girl about vampires out of necessity, since they would soon surround Samantha, but there was something more to it. Leisha felt touched that this young girl would risk her life just to save her. It was obvious to her Samantha would still have risked everything had she known Leisha was a vampire.

Coming out of the bathroom, Samantha sat next to Leisha again. She could see the questions swirling through the girl's mind, so, Leisha just waited until she was ready to voice them. She didn't have to wait long.

"Why didn't you try to find Tafari and tell him what happened?" Samantha started. "I'm sure he would have forgiven you if he had known."

"I've wanted to do that so many times, but he wouldn't have believed it. It's easy for you to accept me as I am, because you didn't see what I did to that poor man. It may have been over two thousand years ago, but Tafari will never forget what he saw—that image of me stooping over the remains of an innocent man." She added, "Plus, the immortals believe that once we become vampires, our souls leave our bodies—that we are no longer the humans we used to be."

Samantha nodded. "I remember hearing that in the movies they've made about vampires. So, you're saying that it's not true?"

"As far as I can tell, I still have a soul. I am still the same person I was when I was human . . . well, maybe a little more on the cynical side of things, but you understand what I mean."

"Whatever happened to your daughter?"

Leisha's throat tightened at the mention of Adanne. She still remembered her guilt the day her daughter saw her as a monster. "She lived in the village with my father. I believe Tafari visited her often, but I don't really know. The last time I saw her, she was fifteen."

"How come?"

Leisha swallowed. "I was really depressed," she explained. "The first few years, I would sneak into my village and check on Adanne. I tried very hard to refrain from drinking any blood. But I couldn't fight it."

"So, when you finally gave in to truly being a vampire, you couldn't bear to see Adanne anymore?"

"Sort of. You see, I tried to live off the blood of animals for a time. It didn't last more than ten years though."

"Why?"

"When a vampire drinks from a life source, we take more than just blood. We absorb a piece of them as well. Some believe we drink in their aura, or their *chi*, but no one really knows. When I drank from animals, I started to lose my brain capacity. Literally. I was beginning to act and think like an animal myself, and it made me do some really embarrassing things, not to mention that I would eventually end up drinking human blood out of instinct, anyway." She shrugged. "So, I decided if I was going to drink

from humans, I should at least be fully aware of what I'm doing. It was hard, though, feeding off a human. I became so depressed I only functioned on the surface. I was too numb on the inside to try and keep my sanity. This lasted for three hundred years."

"Oh, wow."

Leisha did not respond.

"How were you able to come out of it? And how did you stay alive for so long if you were that depressed?"

Leisha's lips twisted. "Ptah kept me alive. He didn't like that I was lost in my own dim world, but he took what he could from me, and he liked me warming his bed. I was like a prize to him."

"I'm sorry, Leisha," Samantha said softly.

Leisha ignored the sympathy. "It was what I deserved. If I had been stronger, maybe I could have sacrificed Adanne's life as well as my own, but I wasn't, and that was the consequence of my choice."

Samantha shifted. "So, are you and Ptah still . . . ?"

Leisha chuckled. "No, we're definitely not. You asked how I came out of my depression. Well, it was when Ellery came along."

"Ellery?" Samantha took extra effort to pronounce the name, slowly.

Leisha smiled at the memory of Ellery. "Yes. I guess you could say she was kind of like a savior to me. Ptah had gotten sick of me after a time. I wasn't entertaining to him anymore. So, he went out to find a new mate, and he came home with Ellery."

"The woman who replaced you brought you out of your depression?"

"I know, it's pretty ironic. But she was kind to me, and I felt a kinship toward her. She would come and visit me every day while I sat in my room feeling sorry for myself. She was so full of life. I guess she started to rub off on me."

"Did Ptah trick her into becoming a vampire as well?"

"No, I was the only one he did that to. She wanted to be a vampire. She felt we existed for a reason, and that killing people wasn't exactly bad as long as you stuck to it for food. She didn't approve of torture or being sadistic like a lot of them. She just thought it was the proper way of the food chain.

"I never fully accepted her mindset, but it helped me realize that just because Ellery was a vampire, didn't mean she was completely evil. So, that's when I decided to make a real life for myself and to stop feeling sorry for my mistake."

Samantha gave a look of exasperation. "But you didn't make a mistake. You had no choice!"

Leisha's smile was rueful. "I can't use that excuse anymore. I did have a choice, and I can honestly say I made the wrong choice. But I can also honestly say if I had to do it all over again, I'd probably do the same thing. I do take comfort in the fact that my daughter was able to grow up, and hopefully be happy."

Samantha's brow wrinkled as Leisha spoke, and changed the subject. "Will I be meeting Ellery?"

Leisha grieved for a moment, but pushed it out of her heart. "No, you won't," she said. "Ellery died over three hundred years ago. She was burned as a witch in France."

"They still did witch trials in that time?"

"It was a smaller village that still held on to their superstitions. Ellery could have escaped, but she was watched all the time and didn't want to do anything that would expose us—our kind—to the public."

Samantha shook her head. "That doesn't make sense. They would just have thought it was some kind of witchcraft."

Leisha lifted one shoulder in a half shrug. "Maybe she was sick of living. I don't know why she didn't fight for her life, but I do know it broke my heart for her to go." Leisha paused, her face pensive. "But if she hadn't died, I never would have gone out on my own."

"What do you mean?"

"Ellery had been my best friend for hundreds of years, and I relied heavily on her emotionally. Once she died, I had to rely on myself. I became independent and didn't want to be with Ptah and the other vampires anymore. Over time, I convinced Ptah to let me go on my own."

"And he just agreed?"

"Well, there were some conditions. But I was setting a bad example to the others since I wouldn't listen to him anymore. I continued to show a lack of respect; he was compelled to let me go since he had no desire to kill me."

"But now you're going back to him."

"Unfortunately, yes. Like I said, there were some conditions. But you need not worry yourself over that. I promise I will do everything in my power to protect you, and get you back to your home as soon as possible."

Samantha shifted a little. "I . . . I don't know if I'll want to go back. It doesn't seem like there's anything to go back to."

"What do you mean?"

Samantha explained about her father. Leisha immediately connected the dots—her torturer was Samantha's dad.

"I am truly sorry, Samantha."

The girl nodded and looked away. They sat in silence for some time until Samantha fell asleep, her head tilted back, her mouth slightly open.

Leisha laid Samantha across the seats, securing the girl with a blanket. It had been so long since Leisha had acted in a nurturing way, and she was surprised at how naturally it came to her. She looked down in wonder at the girl's pale face.

Samantha was bringing out a side in her she thought had died. This young woman was truly destined for amazing things in her life. At that thought, Leisha worried about taking her to the vampires. There was only so much she could do to keep them from touching her, but she would die before any harm came to Samantha.

MASON ROLLED ONTO HIS SIDE in his cot and groaned.

He knew he needed to get some sleep, but he remained alert so he could find Samantha.

He felt a sense of protectiveness over Samantha he had never felt before. She would have had a better life without him—he'd encouraged Mary to take her when she left him—and now that Mary was gone, taking care of their daughter was one responsibility he'd failed. Samantha was only in his life for a minute before she was snatched away by the most dangerous creatures on the earth.

He wished he knew what his daughter was doing at the compound in the first place. Security cameras showed her wandering all over the place, and it looked too obvious she had aided that vampire's escape. But Mason wouldn't believe it.

He had to find her before it was too late. The idea of what she must have been going through at that very moment gave him a painful headache. He pinched the bridge of his nose. She had to be alive still. If they had wanted to kill her, they would not have gone to all that trouble to take her with them. For some reason, she seemed special to them, and he needed to find out why. He wanted to know how she had gotten mixed up in this mess. Maybe these creatures had emotionally seduced her. Samantha was in a vulnerable state with her mother's death; she was prone to do something outside of her character.

A cold chill slithered through his belly like a snake. What if they turned her into a vampire? He panicked at the thought and jumped to his feet.

The door opened to illuminate the room and Carter walked purposefully toward him. He matched Mason's six-foot-three frame perfectly, but that was the only similarity they shared. Carter had dark curls that took fifteen years off his forty. He was also skinny, making him appear lankier than he actually was. His skin was pasty pale, like the nerdy kids who sat in front of computers all day. They were not alike in personality either, but they got along just fine.

Mason read Carter's expression in the dim room as clear as day—he'd worked with Carter for fifteen years. Whatever Carter had to say, Mason was not going to like it. Mason sat back down on the cot, his panic forgotten as he prepped himself for the unpleasant conversation they were about to have.

Carter sat next to him, slumping in his usual manner. "How are you feeling, old buddy?"

"I've been better." He shrugged awkwardly.

He hesitated. "About your daughter—"

"She's not dead," Mason interrupted. "I know they wouldn't have killed her yet."

Carter put a hand on his shoulder in reassurance. "No, not that we know of. But I was able to track them to a small airport just outside of Vegas. They were somehow able to slip through security. Their flight plan checked out. They went to Madrid. I don't know if they picked up another flight from there or not."

Mason's mind swirled at the possibilities. "Let's get our

people out there now. Check to see if maybe they rented a car. It will take a while to check all the flights, but if they continued on from there, it would be on a private plane. The vampire woman can go out in the sun, but none of the others we've worked with could, making privacy of the essence."

Carter was slowly shaking his head.

Mason felt defensive. "It may be a long shot, but it also might not be. We could find them pretty quickly if we just jumped on this."

"Mason," Carter started. "I just came from a meeting with the big dogs."

"So?" Mason scowled.

"So, they have ordered us to let them go; we'll continue with the samples we already have." He paused. "You know, we have more than enough to work with now. They think it's a waste of our resources to try and get more."

Mason felt his heart exploding in a fury, not being able to contain his anger anymore. "*A waste!* My daughter's life is not important enough for us to tap into a couple of agents in the field? Spain has nothing going on right now, anyway. They would probably jump at the chance to stop sitting around twiddling their thumbs. How can they say that? It's my little girl in the hot seat and they just want me to drop her?"

Carter's tone hardened. "Mason, you know where the priorities of this company lie. Like everyone else here, you have agreed to make the necessary sacrifices for the greater good." He pulled a hand through his curls. "I think you and I have a mutual respect for each other, and I'd like to keep it that way. Just remember, if you begin to do anything outside of the norm, I'm going to have to report it." With that, he stood and walked into the hallway only to pause for a moment halfway. "You'll get a day to recover from your tragedy, and then it's back to work."

A cloud of despair engulfed Mason as he watched Carter walk away. Carter was right; the company had no feelings for its employees—they were expected to follow orders. Mason hadn't felt this helpless since he was a boy being locked in the closet. There wasn't anything he could do to save his little girl.

No, he couldn't sit and let his grief blind him. There had to be a way, but it wouldn't be through the help of the company—that was abundantly clear to him. He would have to use and push all of his connections to get the help he needed. He didn't care if he used up all the favors he'd collected over the years; all he cared about was setting Samantha free. Before it was too late.

CHAPTER 10

Samantha dozed off in the car. It had been a long trip—thirteen hours to Spain where they couldn't leave the plane, and over an hour of waiting time while the plane refueled. She wasn't sure how many more hours before they reached India; all she knew was that she was exhausted and never wanted to be in a plane again. The car was waiting for them when they landed that evening. She knew she should be awake and pay attention to her surroundings. She had never been out of the country before, and India seemed exotic and exciting, but she couldn't keep her eyes open. Different smells filled the air, some of them pleasant and some of them not so pleasant. But that was all Samantha identified before her head dropped to her headrest, falling asleep instantly.

The next thing she knew, Leisha was shaking her gently.

"We're here," she said. "Do you remember all of the protocol I taught you on the plane?"

Samantha numbly nodded her head. They were already there, and now she had to remember all the things she was supposed to do in order to be a proper human servant. There was so much to remember, it was like going to visit a king in a palace, making sure not to offend anyone by sneezing, or something.

She followed the vampires out of the backseat and walked with Leisha towards—"A catholic church? This is where you vampires live? A catholic church in the middle of India?"

"There are Catholics living in India, you know. And in case you are still wondering, no, we don't fear the cross or holy water. Or garlic. In fact, a lot of us like the taste of it in our cooking."

The last comment gave Samantha another pause. "Wait, you eat regular food, too?"

Leisha glanced at Samantha's shocked expression in amusement. "There are a lot of myths about vampires you'll have to put out of your mind. Yes, we can eat food just like anyone else. We don't actually need it, but vampires tend to enjoy gourmet foods. If you were hundreds of years old and have heightened senses, you will want to delight in all the finer things in life as much as you can."

They followed Nik and their driver into the church building. It was a regular size cathedral; not something that could house hundreds of vampires. Samantha wondered if they had coffins lined up in every room. She shuddered at the thought of having to sleep in a coffin.

They walked through the pews to the altar in the very back. Once there, Nik turned to the right and slipped through a backdoor, which led to a small entryway with stairs leading up to the second floor. Samantha was about to continue up them when she realized that Nik and Leisha were just standing in the cramped entryway. Waiting. Then, a red laser came out of the paneled wall and scanned across Nik's eyes.

One of the panels opened inward to show a modern staircase going down. Samantha was too absorbed in her surroundings as they descended that it was not until they were halfway down the deep stairway did she notice Nik was gone. She assumed he didn't want to go down the stairs at human speed, and was grateful that Leisha was being so patient with her. After all, she had seen how fast they could move.

The stairway was well lit and painted a soothing taupe. Various paintings, from modern to abstract to classical, hung on the walls. She had anticipated something more like stone steps instead of the cream colored carpeting, and she thought the atmosphere would have been more foreboding. Contrary to what she thought, this place was pleasant and invigorating, as if she were entering a five-star hotel instead of an underground base infested with evil vampires. It even smelled like vanilla and lavender.

Once they were at the bottom of the stairs, Samantha gaped. The room the stairs led to was huge. It had to have been the size of two football fields with high vaulted ceilings. Five large chandeliers hung from the ceiling to give off a warm, golden glow. Sconces matching the crystal chandeliers lined the walls, reinforcing the soft hues of the room. The floor was a dark cherry hardwood with several large rugs strategically placed, segmenting the room into different lounging areas.

The walls were covered with paintings of sunrises and gardens and exotic animals. And then there were the disturbing ones with women being chased by frightening creatures, pictures of snakes, spiders, bats, and other dark beasts. Quite a few of the paintings were of men and women in passionate embraces, which made her want to giggle and blush at the same time. It would take Samantha at least a year to study each depiction on the walls.

Once again, she was shocked that it was nothing like what she was expecting. It seemed so hard to imagine that anyone living in such a warm and grandly elegant place could be a real monster.

A woman entered from a doorway at the other end of the room. She became a blur before suddenly standing before them with a welcoming smile on her full lips. The first thing Samantha noticed was her icy blue eyes. They were of such a pale blue that they reminded her of the arctic. She had high cheekbones and a heart-shaped face. She wore a touch too much makeup—although it didn't look bad on her—and an old-fashioned light blue silk dress that complemented her voluptuous curves. She could not have

been more than five-foot-one, but she held such presence that Samantha felt like the lady was towering over her.

The brunette's gaze was on Samantha. "So you are the girl who found her way into Leisha's heart. My, you are just such a lovely little thing." She reached up and caressed Samantha's cheek. "Your skin is so pale and perfect." She closed her eyes and breathed deeply. "And you smell absolutely wonderful."

Samantha couldn't help but smile back. This woman was as pleasantly surprising as the room.

"No welcome for me, Annette?" Leisha asked casually. Samantha glanced at her. Leisha held herself rigid, her body language belying her tone.

Annette's smile dropped and her expression turned cold. Samantha could almost feel a frosty draft emanating from her. "You are welcome as long as I can tolerate you." One side of her mouth curved up. "Maybe if I enjoy my time with your pet, you will be more welcome than usual."

"She is not a toy," Leisha responded in a low, dangerous voice. "She's under my protection, and you will honor that."

"Nikita was telling the truth then? You do intend to make her your human servant. Last time I saw you, I believe you said you were above that."

Leisha kept her face impassive. "It has been a while since you last saw me."

"*Touché.*" Annette brushed back dark curls behind her ear

and changed the subject. "Be sure you are properly dressed for dinner. Ptah desires you to sit on his left side."

Leisha rolled her eyes, but said nothing.

Annette seemed amused. "You would not think of going back on your promise to our dear leader, would you?"

She bristled at the insult. "I'm much more honorable than you are, lowborn."

Squaring her shoulders, Annette spoke softly. "You would be wise to show the proper respect to me, as well," Her tone was frigid. "You are not revered as the 'magnificent warrior' that you once were." With that, she turned away and sauntered to a doorway directly to their right.

Leisha sighed and turned to the adjacent doorway. "Come on," she said.

Samantha didn't need the prompting to follow her. She'd been keeping up while trying to observe her surroundings. "Do you know where we're going to be staying?"

"Yes. The layout of this building is exactly like that of others we've had in the past."

They turned and wound their way through a few corridors in silence. Samantha had plenty of questions, but she thought it would be safer to ask them when they were in the privacy of their room.

Leisha stopped in front of a door at the end of the hall. It was more like an apartment than a room when she walked through. There was a front room that looked like an ordinary living room with a couch, love seat, and a coffee table dividing the furniture and a television. There was a door

on the left of the front room leading to the bedroom. The bedroom was spacious with a queen-size, four-post bed in the middle. It was draped with fake ivy and lace.

"I'll take the couch and you can sleep in the bed," Leisha said. "I don't sleep for more than a few hours, anyway." She walked into the closet and flipped on the light. The closet was a walk-in furnished with a full wardrobe ready for any occasion. "I'm a few inches shorter than you, but I believe you should be able to fit in my clothes."

"Your clothes? I thought you hadn't been with the vampires in a hundred years. This stuff is definitely modern."

"Ptah was prepared for my arrival. He'd already sent along most of my belongings before I was taken."

Leisha turned and pulled a rosy pink dress from its hanger. "This should look good with your complexion, and the bodice is adjustable."

Samantha held it up to the light. It was a silk dress overlaid with some kind of sheer material. "I don't think I've ever worn anything as nice as this."

Leisha was already pulling out a dress for herself. "Well, as they say, there's a first time for everything. Put it on and we can make sure it fits."

It was pretty loose in the chest, but Leisha made the proper adjustments. It felt like prom all over again. The thought brought an aching longing Samantha hadn't even realized she had felt until that moment. What would her life be like now? Would she go back to school and dating boys and dancing ballet? Or would she be stuck in this new world of vampires?

Her face must have shown some of her anxiety, because Leisha spoke up then. "Don't worry," she said. "No one here will touch you while you are under my protection. I'll try to get you home as soon as I can."

"What home? Where exactly should I go? I'm pretty sure staying with my dad isn't the safest option for me anymore."

Leisha seemed at a loss for words. Finally, she pulled Samantha in for a hug. "I don't know what the future holds for you, but I have taken you under my wing now. So, why don't we just take it one step at a time together, all right?"

The words flowed over Samantha like a warm blanket. *Together.* She wasn't alone anymore. She would always miss her mother, but she realized that her life would go on now that she had her vampire for comfort and support. The irony of her situation made her smile. She had not felt this hopeful since her mother was alive.

Leisha pulled away and started changing into her dress. "Now, I need to talk to you about Annette."

"Yeah, what's up with you guys, anyway?"

"We just have conflicting personalities." The zipper squeaked as she pulled it up. "She sees me as a threat since Ptah still holds an attraction to me, and I dislike the ruthless methods she uses to get her own way."

"So, she's Ptah's mate now?"

"Yes." Leisha straightened her dress along her thighs so it flowed in one elegant line. Then, she turned to hold Samantha's gaze. The dark green color of her dress set off

the emerald in her eyes, adding depth to her expression. "She is a lot more dangerous than she seems. Stay away from her."

"But she didn't seem so bad."

Leisha scoffed. "Wolf in sheep's clothing, and don't you forget it. Remember that about all vampires. You may be under my protection, but if you are naïvely lured into someone's apartment, I may not be able to help you. Do you understand?"

Swallowing, Samantha tried to calm the tempest that was suddenly raging in her stomach. "Yes."

"Do you remember everything I told you on the plane?"

Samantha closed her eyes as she tried to remember every detail. "I'm to stay on your right side at all times, except when you sit down to dine. That's when I stand behind you and wait until you are finished eating."

"Correct. Once I am done eating, you will be excused to the kitchens where all the humans eat. Don't worry, though, we vampires only eat a bite or two of each dish, so, you will not have to stand for too long." Leisha led the way into the bathroom on the other end of the bedroom. She picked up a brush and gestured for Samantha to kneel in front of her.

She brushed out her light brown hair, and continued, "Be sure to be courteous to everyone around you, but don't be too friendly. Especially with the other human servants. They are extensions of their masters, and will relay anything you say or do back to their masters."

Samantha shivered at the thought. This place was not as amazing as it had first appeared. How could she live in a place where she must be on her guard at all times, and never to trust a soul?

"I forgot to tell you what you'll need to do when we first enter and greet Ptah." Leisha was pulling Samantha's hair up into a French twist. "We will walk directly to Ptah and Annette when we enter the dining room. I will curtsy and bow my head, but you must kneel and touch your forehead to the floor. Don't stay down, though. As soon as your forehead touches the floor you can rise."

When Leisha was done, Samantha stood to face her own reflection in the mirror. Her hair now twisted up on the back of her head with a few strands hanging around her face—she looked like she was really getting dressed for prom, only she doubted this evening would be as fun for either Leisha or herself.

CHAPTER 11

L eisha took a deep breath before they entered the formal dining room. It was just off from the ballroom where everyone waited in a line to enter and show their courtesies to Ptah. When their turn came, Leisha could feel butterflies fluttering around in the pit of her stomach. She squared her shoulders and straightened her back as she walked gracefully toward Ptah and Annette.

Ptah had rid himself of the modern clothing she'd seen him wearing in Las Vegas for decorous Egyptian attire. He wore it only in the presence of vampires—it definitely drew attention—appearing regal with his black, gold-lined robe open to bare his toned chest. Abounding amount of jewelry adorned his neck—they were of pure gold studded with diamonds, rubies, amethyst, and other gems, emitting a spectrum of colors and sparkle. The black skirt wrapping his lower region was made of the finest silk, almost transparent, yet it didn't lessen his masculinity in any way. Instead of the typical pharaoh's headdress, Ptah's wore a gold and black viper coiled around his crown with moonstones for eyes; its head poised, ready to strike.

Annette was now in a deep scarlet gown with black and gold trimmings. The sleeves were long and flared out at the forearms, capturing a bit of a medieval style. Her V-shape neckline plunged down past her breasts, revealing her cleavage. The dress hugged her delicate curves to her knees, flaring out in the same manner as her sleeves.

Leisha gave a formal curtsy and bowed her head while she watched Samantha from the corner of her eye. Samantha's bow was supposed to express the greatest of humility to Ptah, and when the girl executed the custom flawlessly, as if she'd mastered the ways of the vampires, Leisha wondered if Ptah would be offended. But he seemed quite amused.

His thin lips were quirked in the slightest smile, appearing genuine. Leisha prayed he wasn't smiling about a secret he had yet to reveal. It was not like he'd never pulled a nasty surprise from up his sleeve before.

"You are welcome," Ptah said pleasantly in his deep voice. He was now smiling at Samantha, who was staring into his eyes.

Leisha had tried her best to warn Samantha about the cold depth Ptah's black eyes held, but she knew no one could truly understand what she meant unless they witnessed them themselves. Leisha nonchalantly stepped

closer to Samantha and grabbed the girl's arm. Samantha turned her head sharply and looked at Leisha. Blinking her eyes, the girl looked a bit unsettled, but forced a thankful smile.

Leisha turned to Ptah. "We are most grateful that you've allowed us the privilege of standing in your presence."

Ptah inclined his head ever so slightly. "It is truly my pleasure, Leisha. It has been some time since you were with us." His gaze fell on Samantha. "And I must say that you have brought me a pleasant surprise. Surely, she will prove to amuse me."

Leisha pulled Samantha with her into another curtsy before retreating toward the long table. At the head of the table was another that met it perpendicularly, forming a T shape. This was where Leisha would be sitting next to Ptah.

"You did well, Samantha," Leisha whispered. "Now, pull my chair out for me to sit, and then stay directly behind me. Try not to move too much. You are allowed to rest your hands on the back of my chair. It is symbolic of possession and therefore permitted."

Samantha looked slightly pale, but nodded and pulled out Leisha's chair for her. Leisha gave the girl an encouraging smile and took her seat.

Leisha felt a little more relaxed, but she knew things could still turn sour. She needed to think of a way to get Samantha away from here, but she would have to think on it later. Now was time for vampire politics, and she needed her wits about her.

Nikita sat just a few feet in front of her. He looked over her shoulder and nodded to Samantha, and then to Leisha. It was technically against protocol to acknowledge a human servant before their master, but Leisha didn't care. Ptah and Annette were taking their seats. Dinner was commencing.

The meal was delicious, even better than Leisha remembered it. She found out between courses that Ptah had turned a gourmet chef from Italy about fifty years ago just because his cooking was that amazing.

When everyone had eaten their dessert, it was time for Ptah to attend to business. He nodded to his right hand, Victor, and Victor, in turn, gestured toward two vampires standing by the door. They disappeared for a moment and returned dragging another vampire between them.

"Darshan is ready to hear your will, Great One," Victor intoned as the vampires forced the weakling to kneel before Ptah.

Leisha didn't know Darshan well; he had been newly turned when she left. She remembered him as a young man bursting with energy, excited to be in his new world. Now the handsome Indian could barely hold his head up. His lips were cracked and oozing pus, while the rest of his body was decomposing. Leisha knew all too well the symptoms of starvation. Ptah had probably allowed him to drink only vampire's blood. It was a way to keep one sustained, but barely. The worst part was that drinking the blood of a fellow vampire would actually exacerbate the gnawing thirst.

Ptah barely glanced at Darshan as he finished his last bite of dessert, focusing on his crystal goblet of fresh, warm blood. He took a sip and savored it before finally speaking, "Do you agree with me yet?" His tone showed boredom.

Darshan tried to wet his lips with his dry tongue, which stuck to his lips; he pried it away with his fingers, a layer of skin mixed with infected puss spurted onto his tongue. He nodded and croaked, "I yield to you, my master."

Ptah looked on him as one would on a dog. "As well you should. I believe that in the future you will remember to always obey me in all things. I do not care if you have a unique opportunity. I never gave you permission to stay in Thailand for an extended amount of time, and I do not care that you stayed to kill an immortal. You are not the one to strategize unless I give you permission. Do you understand this, pest?"

The broken vampire nodded slowly.

Ptah finished off his drink. "Good. Now you must pay the price. I have decided that your punishment shall be one filled with humiliation," he announced, smirking. "For fifty days and nights, you will crawl. You are not allowed to stand, sit, or lie down. You will be allowed to feed on human blood, but you are not allowed to hunt for yourself. You will have to rely on the kindness of your brothers and sisters to bring you a human to feed from. If they wish, they may give you their leftovers. Do you have anything to say to me, Darshan?"

Darshan bowed his head. "You are wise, and most merciful, my master. I worship you and your cunning."

Ptah nodded and waved for the guards to drag him away.

Of course, it was far from merciful—vampires delighted in the misery of others, and would taunt Darshan to make him do ridiculous things in exchange for his much needed food. It would be a long and miserable fifty days for him.

The human servants were being excused. Leisha caught Samantha's eye on her way out. The girl forced a smile. She seemed to be holding up all right, but Leisha would feel much better when they were back in her little apartment that night. Or rather, morning, since it was now past twilight.

Once all the humans had exited, the vampires turned to Ptah expectantly. Leisha realized something else was planned after dinner.

Ptah stood. He did not raise his voice very much, although it seemed to resonate clearly throughout the room. "As you all know, the signs of the prophecy child have come. We know the immortals are scouring the world right now in hopes of finding the baby. We have discussed at length what our course of action will be, but to no avail.

"I have had many conversations with Victor in private, and I agree with him that we must take action now."

Leisha remained stoically quiet as murmur of agreement and appreciation sounded around the room.

Ptah gestured for everyone to quiet down. "It will take some time before we declare war with the immortals. I

have conceived a strategy that will give us the advantage to win.

"Not many of you were present when we were at war with them five hundred years ago, but it was costly. Many of us died, as well as a good portion of our enemy. It seemed we were too evenly matched. We walked away in a stalemate, with no victors or losers. Looking back, I ascertained a key contributor to their success was one of their leaders. He instills a strong sense of duty and morale among his people, even though he is not on the immortal council, and I believe if we capture him, we will have a very good chance of wiping the entire population of immortals from this earth. If we succeed, then there will not even be any need for some prophecy child. *I* will be the one who will save us from those fools who think they are better than us!" He raised his arms with the last sentence, prompting the cheers and applause that followed.

Sitting perfectly still, Leisha stared up at Ptah. She fought to keep the trembling in her lips from showing, knowing very well he had to be referring to Tafari, who was one of the few leaders who'd survived the war.

"I need the war council to stay. Everyone else is excused to celebrate my declaration." As everyone stood to depart, Ptah turned to Leisha. "You will stay, as well." The men who stayed moved closer and took their seats at Ptah's table.

Leisha suddenly wished she were anywhere but here. She did not want to be a part of this scheme to get rid of Tafari. She'd rather be back in that nasty compound with Samantha's father, being viciously tortured.

Her thoughts were interrupted as a vampire she did not recognize stood and waited for Ptah to acknowledge him. He looked like he'd been in his early thirties when he became a vampire. He had sandy-colored hair and brown eyes. His shoulders were broad, giving his five-foot-ten height more presence.

"Pardon my ignorance, Great Master," the man started. "I was wondering the possibility of us capturing one of their leaders. They are well protected, and we have a hard time as it is just spying on their activities from afar."

Ptah smiled. "Superb question, Colum. The answer lies at the feet of our prodigal daughter, who has finally returned home." He gestured to Leisha, and her blood turned to ice. "Our beautiful Leisha here is going to use her wiles to make an assignation with the immortal, Tafari."

Colum's face shadowed with doubt as he promptly sat down. The room stirred, though no one was willing to voice their thoughts at the announcement.

"Not many of you are aware of the history between Leisha and Tafari," Ptah continued, "and I expect that would be why I see doubt written on your faces." Ptah glared at each man, and all vampires cast their eyes down at the table. "It matters not. I am your master, and this is the strategy I have adjudicated." His tone left no room for argument, and the discussion quickly turned to other topics of preparation for war.

As the night progressed, the vampires gradually gained confidence in Leisha's abilities to act as spy. Victor studied

her with an intense scrutiny throughout the planning; Leisha made an effort to meet his gaze, sending him a clear message—she was not affected by him.

He had been a military man—a Roman soldier—when Ptah turned him into a vampire, and she knew he would respect someone who could hold her own. She also knew it would be best to avoid him as much as possible. Victor was just as ruthless as Annette, and could make things more complicated if he decided to antagonize her. From her past experiences with him, he could be completely unpredictable.

When the meeting came to a close, Ptah turned to Annette, who stood waiting for him. "I would like you to go and enjoy the dance in my absence tonight, my pet." He kissed the inside of her wrist. "Leisha and I need to sit and talk privately for a while."

"Of course, my loving master," Annette said, shooting a sharp look at Leisha with the corner of her eye, "I will make sure everyone is celebrating accordingly." She turned and walked to the ballroom, her head held high.

"Come with me, sweet." Ptah grabbed Leisha's upper arm and hoisted her out of her seat. She tried to get her thoughts in order as he led her down the hallways into his apartment. His anteroom was large enough to fit a few elephants with a long table in the middle. He walked through the room and into his private chambers that housed a king-size bed on a dais.

Ptah pushed her into a chair, pulling up another and sat

directly across from her, their knees almost touching. He looked at her and waited.

Leisha barely contained the fury that had been pounding in her ears. "You had no right," she spat.

"I had every right," Ptah countered. "You belong to me, Leisha, whether you like it or not. You are a vampire, and it is your duty to serve me and my kind. What I command of you is a simple service to help keep us alive."

"Lies! You know I can't do this. I don't even know how to find Tafari in the first place. He could smell a trap long before I could snag him." The words tasted bitter on her tongue. She had already betrayed Tafari enough by becoming what she was, and now Ptah demanded she drive that betrayal much deeper.

Ptah took her hand in his. "My beauty, do you not see that this is the best way we could win? I know you probably think the idea of going to war again is fruitless, and I agree. That is why I have decided this will be the best course of action. Besides, I already have all the details worked out. I know Tafari sought you out while you were in Nevada."

A jolt of surprise shot straight down to her toes.

"I know a lot more than you'd like me to. But that is inconsequential. I believe Tafari may be confused over how he feels about you. There is a possibility that love still lingers somewhere deep within his psyche."

The very idea was too much for Leisha to try to contemplate. "No, he doesn't. He believes as the other immortals do. That I am devoid of a soul. He thinks I'm not the woman

he married." She kept her voice neutral, though she knew Ptah would still hear the pain coming through anyway.

Ptah reached up and stroked her hair. "Poor Leisha," he cooed. "Trying so hard to be strong. It has not worked for you very well, has it?" His hand moved to her jaw line, his thumb caressing her cheek. "I have a solution to your problems, sweet. You must trust me. If you do as I say, then you will finally be free of Tafari and all that he did to you."

"He didn't do anything to me," she protested.

Ptah's tone harshened. "He betrayed you, you imbecile. You keep thinking of yourself as the martyr who protected your poor little baby. I have a new concept for your cognizance, and it is time you listen to me." He cupped the other side of her face and forced her to look at him. "Tafari never bothered to question why you became a vampire. He accepted it as fact and then damned you for it. You have him on some kind of pedestal, and it is high time you abase him.

"I am the one who has stayed with you for better and for worse. I am the one who let you go when you needed reprieve. I will always be here for you, and *I* will always be the one standing at your side. If you do what the vampires need you to do, then you will see for yourself what I say is true. Tafari is undeserving of your affection for him. It is entirely wasted."

His eyes looked fierce, and Leisha felt as if she were falling into a volcano of black lava. She could barely think past what he was telling her. She knew she needed to clear her head before she responded. Otherwise, Ptah would bully his way into her mind and take what he wanted from her.

She stood and he let his hands drop. Leisha walked the length of the room to the foot of his bed, her mind whirling at the possibilities of Ptah's words. Had she put Tafari on a pedestal? Her memories of her and Tafari together were magical—she could not imagine their relationship not lasting if she weren't a vampire. Had Ptah not come into their lives, she and Tafari would have been happy growing old together, playing with their grandchildren, laughing together. Tafari had made her laugh so much when they were married.

But was all that just in her head? Would he have grown tired of her if they had grown old together? The thought of it was too painful to fathom. Ptah was trying to manipulate her, and it almost worked. She needed to think of some way to turn this situation to her own advantage.

She whirled to Ptah, her voice trembling slightly. "What exactly did you have in mind?"

Ptah's grin was vainglorious. "It's quite simple. I will deduce where he was last seen from our online spy network, and then you can pursue him from there. We will stay a good distance from you so he will not suspect a trap. Once he discovers you are looking for him, he will come to you."

Ptah had not realized his own inconsistency—how could Tafari judge her without any hesitation, and yet at the same time be willing to come to her without hesitation because he still had feelings for her. The very contradiction

gave her a sense of possibility that she could outwit the master vampire.

"Once he finds you," Ptah continued, "we will be able to capture him and bring him here. We will then torture him to get all the information about the immortals we need, especially their progress in finding the prophecy child. Then Tafari shall leave this earth." Approaching her, he wrapped his arms around her waist and pulled her in for an embrace. "You will then be able to conquer your inner conflict and stay with me. You have a much deeper strength than Annette now. Temporary enfranchisement has been good for you. I can see the fire in your eyes has once again come to life. We will be wonderful together. Absolutely invincible."

Leisha suppressed a shiver. "Your plan is too short-sighted," she said. "I think there is room for improvement."

He pulled her back and raised his eyebrows. "Such as?"

"You said you want information out of Tafari about the immortals, but I think you are underestimating how tenacious Tafari can be. You are right about his unyielding sense of duty. He would rather die than to betray his people."

"I think you've underestimated my methods."

Laughing bitterly, Leisha answered, "No, Ptah. I don't doubt your methods are the best, especially with the help of Annette, but I still think you are underestimating your enemy. And that is something you must never do. You must still remember all too clearly what happened during the last war."

She had said exactly the thing that would enrage and yet enrapture him. Ptah might have been a master manipulator, but Leisha knew him better than he realized, and was turning the tables now.

His expression turned wary. "What do you suggest, instead?"

She gave him a seductive smile. "I suggest something that will give you an even better edge. I suggest that I seek out Tafari and convince him to take me in. He'll do it if what you say about him is true. Even if he is really confused, he'll still take me in out of sheer curiosity. Then, I will be in the midst of the immortals, knowing every move they make. You would be three steps ahead of them."

His expression took on a mixture of lust and pride. "I like the boldness of your plan, but I fear it is too obvious. Also, there is always the risk of the immortals killing you while you are among them. Even if Tafari has a soft heart toward you, the others may not."

"I know the risks involved, but I am willing to bet that Tafari will make sure they don't harm me."

"You are willing to bet your life?"

"Yes." She paused. "Plus, with Samantha along, Tafari and the others should soften up a little. At least, toward her."

He seemed doubtful. "I did not say anything about your human servant going with you."

Leisha swallowed. If nothing else, she had to get Samantha out of there. "She will be an important part of

the plan. She can pretend to be some human on whom I have taken compassion in her time of need. It will be the biggest asset to ensure Tafari's confusion about me."

Ptah smirked. "So, you truly intend to make her your human servant. I was wondering if it was all a lie." He stroked her hair again. "Shall I set up a formal ceremony, or would you prefer just a small, informal one?"

She knew this was going to be the tricky part, and still had not come up with a good lie to put off making Samantha her human servant. "I would like to wait for a little while before I mark her as my own." Ptah tensed ever so slightly, and she rushed on. "She is only sixteen, and while I know she is perfect for me, I would prefer her to be just a couple of years older before she is officially my human servant."

Ptah chuckled at that. "I did not realize you were self-conscious of how your possessions were viewed by the others."

Walking back over to the chairs, Leisha sat. "I'm not ashamed to admit I am partially self-conscious; I would like her to be more mentally mature as well. You know better than anyone how vampire politics are these days. I need her exposed to all kinds of situations before I mark her. That way, I can be absolutely sure she can handle belonging to me."

"I agree with your caution." Ptah joined her in his own chair. "You understand, if she is not to be your human servant, you'll only have two options."

"Options?"

Ptah shrugged as if it were obvious. "She knows too much about us to go about on her own. She will either have to become a vampire, or we will need to dispose of her. Knowledge about who we are and how we live is too dangerous a threat to take lightly."

The muscles in her stomach clenched. "I am fairly certain she will become my human servant. However, if for some unforeseen reason she does not, I will make sure she is taken care of," she lied.

"Good," Ptah said, appeased with her explanation. "Once you have finished with spying on the immortals, you can assist us in following the signs to the prophecy child. Any information on the child will be a great asset to us. I want to know everything."

Leisha studied Ptah's face, but it was as unreadable as her own. "What do you plan to do with this prophecy child?"

"Kill him, naturally."

"But, why?"

"Because," Ptah explained as though she were a half-wit, "no one knows what this prophecy child will do. We only know we will be connected to him in some way. The immortals think if they can find him first, they will be able to exploit and manipulate him into giving them the upper hand in our little power struggle between our two races. If that is the case, then it will obviously be most advantageous for us to kill him off before he becomes a threat to us all."

"And what if he is actually being sent to help the

vampires become more powerful?"

Ptah looked away. "I am fairly certain he is not on either side."

Leisha raised an eyebrow. "You're certain because?"

"Because he will be coming from my world, of course. That is, the world from which my spirit originated."

Leisha was stunned into momentary silence. Ptah had never mentioned anything about the world he came from, and he wouldn't answer any more of her questions regarding it now. What would it mean for humanity—or vampire kind—if two beings from Ptah's world existed here?

CHAPTER 12

Leisha shut the door to her apartment and sagged against it. The night had been long and trying on her nerves. She never needed to keep up such a façade in front of Ptah and the other vampires before, and it proved to be truly exhausting. She was a good liar, of course, but it was different having to put on an act for vampires who knew just as much as she did about reading body language and detecting lies.

She pulled herself up and went into the bedroom. Samantha was sound asleep in bed. Peeling off her dress and changing into a pair of sweats, Leisha thought of going to sleep as well, but her brain was swirling with all the things she was about to face.

She already had more than she could handle. She knew spying on Tafari and the immortals was a terrible idea; but it was the best excuse to get Samantha out of there. Facing

Tafari was going to be hell. The odds of convincing him to take her in were pretty slim, but she hoped he would at least give Samantha his protection.

Leisha knew the immortals were willing to kill humans if they had to, but she had no choice but to believe Samantha would be safer there. Leisha cringed at the thought of making Samantha a human servant. She had never wanted one and felt it cruel to bind a human to herself in that way. But the ways of the vampires were set deep in their traditions, and breaking from it could prove fatal.

She heard Samantha stirring. Leisha grasped the distraction so she would not have to face any more thoughts of Tafari, and headed back into the bedroom. Samantha was still asleep, but was writhing on the bed, making whimpering sounds.

Sitting on the edge of the bed, Leisha gently shook the girl awake. After three tries, Samantha bolted upright and screamed in an anguished voice, "Mom!" It took her a few seconds of scanning her surroundings, and then Leisha, before realizing it had been a dream.

When Samantha met Leisha's sympathetic gaze, tears sprang into her eyes and Leisha caught her in an embrace.

"It was all my fault," Samantha sobbed. "I stayed late and it was all my fault."

"What was your fault?" Leisha asked.

Samantha choked out the words, "That she died." She sat back and wiped hastily at her eyes. "I was at ballet practice and my mom was supposed to pick me up. Ashleigh, my instructor, wanted to work on some choreography with me for an upcoming competition and I called my mom on her cell." She sniffed and again wiped at the tears that continued to stream down her face. "She was already waiting outside for me, but I really wanted to stay and work, so she went to get takeout and was going to come back in an hour."

She slumped forward, back into Leisha's arms. "If I had gone with her when I was supposed to, the carjacker wouldn't have been there to shoot her." Gasping for air in between sobs, she continued, "She was already dead when I found her. There was blood everywhere!" Samantha continued to mumble incoherently.

Leisha placed her hand on Samantha's back, massaging it lightly to hopefully soothe the girl. She doubted anything she said would make the girl feel better, but she tried anyway. "You know that there was no way you could have known how one innocent choice would change the course of your life. It happens to someone every day. In your case, what happened to your mother was out of your control. It was the carjacker, not you, who should be blamed. You didn't know."

Samantha laughed bitterly. "But I did." She wiped the back of her hand across her nose and continued crying.

Leisha held her until Samantha toned down to small sniffles. "What do you mean by that?"

"I guess you could say I'm psychic." She paused, the corner of her mouth lifted. "I've never said it out loud before. It's strange. That's why I tried to rescue you from my father. I had a vision about it."

"Really?" Leisha wasn't sure how to respond to that. "Did your mom know of your ability?"

Samantha nodded. "I always told her about my visions and we discussed them, and she would help me figure out what I could do about them." She closed her eyes. "When I dreamed of her death, I almost didn't tell her. But my mom knows me too well—*knew* me too well." She opened her eyes and looked into the distance. "So, when she asked, I told her what I saw—that she was going to be shot and would die on the pavement."

Samantha shuddered. "I wanted to figure out some way to stop it from happening, but I didn't know when or where it would happen. My mom was shaken up about it, but she slowly accepted it after a couple of days. She told me not to worry, and that she was grateful to know so she could make sure I was taken care of after she was gone." She looked at Leisha, blue eyes bloodshot. "I should have known, should have guessed when I had to stay late. I should never have left her alone."

Leisha took Samantha by the hand. "Have you ever been able to change what happens in your visions?" She already knew the answer, and Samantha didn't bother replying, but looked away.

"You see," Leisha said, "you gave your mother a gift—a glimpse into the future—so she could be ready for it when her time came. There is no reason to feel guilty. Nothing that happened was within your control."

Samantha nodded, but kept her lips pressed in a thin line.

Leisha pulled the girl to her feet and led her to the bathroom. Once there, she proceeded to fill the tub with warm water.

"I want you to take a warm bath. I will go and find some food for you when you get out."

Samantha complied, still looking miserable. Leisha wished there was a way to take the girl's pain away.

When Leisha finally returned with a plate full of cheese, crackers, and cookies, Samantha was sitting on the couch in the front room, her wet hair combed out to the tops of her shoulders. She seemed to be feeling better, but Leisha decided the girl might need more time before they discussed the loss of her mother again.

Samantha ate all the cookies and half of the crackers with cheese. After she drained her glass of water, she sighed and looked at Leisha. "Thanks." A flush blossomed on her cheeks. "I . . . uh . . . haven't talked to anyone about the incident before. It just kind of came out."

Leisha reached out and softly squeezed Samantha's shoulder. "Any time, sweetheart. After all, I did tell you all about my tragic past, didn't I? And did I tell you that you are the only one who knows my story? I never told anyone before you."

Samantha's eyes warmed considerably at that. "Wow, really? I'm honored, Leisha."

She patted Samantha's knee, sitting back. "I think things might be a little easier for you, now that you have talked about it. It always helps to be able to share your burdens with those whom you trust."

Samantha grinned, her innocence obvious. "I do trust you."

Leisha felt a warm sensation move through her heart and looked away. "I'm a murderer, Samantha. You should never trust one who takes lives." Pausing, she changed the subject. "So was everything all right last night? You didn't run into any problems while you were left alone?"

"It went just fine. I made sure not to talk to anyone for too long, but it was kind of hard. All those people I ate dinner with were loaded with information about their masters and their origins. It was like gossip central!" She was getting more animated as she spoke. "Is it true that human servants can live up to three hundred years?"

"Yes. When a human bonds with a vampire, it slows their aging process. It also makes them stronger and they can heal more quickly, as well."

"Cool!"

Leisha shook her head. "That is the only good part. There are drawbacks, as well."

"Like what?"

"Your very existence as a human servant is devoted to helping your master. If you were my human servant, and I wasn't able to get to blood, then you would have to drink it for me. Until you drank, I would draw from your energy and make you weak. Plus, if your vampire master dies, so will you.

"I would also have to feed more often in order to maintain a strong link between us. That was one of the biggest reasons I never liked the idea of having a human servant."

Samantha tucked her legs under her. "I can see that. Anything that requires taking more lives really bothers you. This is why I don't see you as a monster, Leisha."

Leisha met Samantha's gaze. "But that doesn't take away the fact that I am still a monster, Samantha. Don't ever forget that. I'm usually in control, but I have my moments of cruelty. You should never ever trust any of us."

Samantha let the subject drop. "I did have some questions, though."

"Like what?" Leisha relaxed a little.

"Well, I thought all vampires were supposed to be pretty, but I saw a lot of chubby ones and some were really plain," she said sheepishly, suppressing a smirk.

Laughing, Leisha explained, "When someone becomes a vampire, everything that they already had becomes perfected. But even the magical power that makes us vampires can only work with what it is given. I look pretty much the same as before, when I was a human, minus the scars and blemishes."

"So, when you become a vampire, it just heals you fully? It doesn't do anything else."

Leisha shrugged. "Sort of. It also corrects small imperfections. For instance, your left eye is just a tad smaller than your right eye. Becoming a vampire would fix that, making your face perfectly symmetrical."

Samantha huffed, changing the subject again. "So, what happened after I left?"

As Leisha filled her in on everything, Samantha looked more incredulous. When Leisha was finished explaining, Samantha asked, "So, are we really going to track down Tafari and the immortals, or are we going on the run?"

Leisha shook her head. "We have little choice here. Going on the run would be incredibly difficult, and Ptah would not stop until he found me." She paused. "Ptah would not kill me if he ever found me. He'd just keep me alive to feel misery and pain for as long as he could."

"You think Tafari will really take us in?"

"Yes. He will at least take *you* in. If he won't have anything to do with me, the worst I can do is go back to Ptah and receive my punishment for failure."

"How can you say something like that so casually? He would hurt you just because what you tried didn't work? That's not fair."

Leisha smiled sardonically. "It is part of the price you pay to become a vampire." She waved the issue away with her hand. "Besides, we all heal rather quickly. Yes, I may be in pain for maybe a few months, but I also know the pain is going to go away. Why worry about it when we don't even know what will happen?"

As soon as Leisha finished her last sentence, Samantha suddenly sat straight up, her eyes completely unfocused, staring directly ahead. Leisha called her name a few times with no response. She could hear Samantha's slow, but steady heartbeat as she waited anxiously. Ten minutes had passed, and she still had no idea what to do.

Then, Samantha's heart rate began to normalize. The girl studied her environment, a little puzzled. "I've never had a vision quite like that one," she murmured.

"What did you see?"

"I'm not sure," she whispered. "It was like flash after flash of all kinds of images. First, I saw this thick, almost black blood pouring out of someone's neck, like he was decapitated or something. Then I saw a bunch of images, but they went too quickly for me to identify them. Some of them had weird symbols I didn't recognize. You might have been in one of them, but I'm not sure. I think you were arguing with a tall, dark man." She rushed onward. "Then, I saw myself. I was helping deliver a baby boy . . . Somehow, he was very special, and I was determined to protect him." She put her hands to her temples. "I have never been in one of my own visions. It was strange."

"Do you need to lie down?" Leisha cradled Samantha in her arms, heading for the bedroom.

"I get headaches after the visions," Samantha said, her eyes squeezed shut.

Leisha tucked Samantha into her bed and pulled the covers over the girl. "Most do."

Samantha's eyes opened wide. "You mean there are others like me?"

"Both vampires and immortals have the gift of premonition, but no vampires with that gift are alive today. Many suspect that these abilities are our potentials when

we were human; we just did not know how to use that part of our brain yet."

Leisha turned to go, speaking over her shoulder, "Go ahead and rest now. You can ask me questions later when you feel better."

CHAPTER 13

Samantha walked alongside Leisha with a spring in her step. Leisha looked mildly irritated that Samantha was so happy, even when surrounded by bloodsucking monsters—Samantha knew Leisha would keep her safe. She was too excited at the idea that there were other people out there who could do the same thing she did. She'd always had her suspicions, of course—it had been lonely not knowing anyone else with the gift of premonition.

Though she couldn't actually think of anyone like her, she knew they were out there. According to Leisha, the immortals had at least one person with the gift of premonition. To think she might be meeting them soon put a large smile on her face.

Samantha felt beautiful, especially in the pale blue evening gown she was wearing to dinner. This time, she

let down her hair—Leisha had helped put large, soft curls in it.

She couldn't begin to describe the deep bond she felt with Leisha. Since they first met, there was some kind of connection between them. But after today, Leisha felt like a sister now. A two thousand-year-old sister.

Studying the people around her, Samantha noted that these vampires acted like humans. They talked and gestured just like anyone else, and Samantha had yet to find someone with actual fangs. Last night, a human servant informed her that Leisha was the only one who could go under the sun without getting burned, which was intriguing. Vanessa, another human servant whom she'd sat with, had told her how most vampires got severe burns when they were exposed to the sun. It wouldn't usually kill them, unless they were exposed for too long. The strangest part about it was that they did not heal quickly from sunburns. If a vampire was in the sun for five minutes, they would return with second degree burns that took a couple of weeks to heal. But with the invention of sunscreen, according to Vanessa, it wasn't as bad now, although they would still burn.

Samantha was having a hard time regarding her life before all this as real anymore. Being among vampires seemed to make everything else surreal, and she was glad for Leisha's company to keep her grounded.

They did the same formalities as the night before, Ptah wearing his same attire that made him look like a genuine

Egyptian pharaoh. Samantha was careful not to look directly into his eyes this time. The last time she looked into those eyes, she was falling mentally, getting lost in the oblivion that was his gaze. If it had not been for Leisha nudging her, she would have been swallowed in the darkness of his eyes. Samantha hated to think what would have happened next.

She stood behind Leisha's chair as the vampires ate, and observed everything with continued curiosity. While not all of the vampires were beautiful like Leisha, they all held a certain grace and elegance that was incredibly alluring.

She squeezed Leisha's shoulder when it was time for the human servants to eat—a sign of reassurance. Vanessa walked with her and chatted about a few of the vampires, clearly loving to have someone new to share gossip with.

They were sitting at one of the four round tables, visiting with the other diners when a young man pulled a chair to their table, taking his seat next to Samantha. He was large and burly, with very broad shoulders to accommodate his equally impressive frame. His light, moss green eyes met Samantha's and bore into her.

"So you're going to be Leisha's new human servant, then?" he asked in a baritone voice.

Samantha found she couldn't meet his stare. "That's right," she said as nonchalantly as she could, though it sounded weak. His forearm was the size of her calf, and she reminded herself Leisha would protect her.

The man smiled pleasantly at that. "Great. We always

love getting fresh blood." He leaned in close and smelled Samantha's hair. "Mmm, yes. I think you'll be most welcome here."

Samantha suppressed a shiver. He seemed genuinely pleased she was going to stick around, and for some reason, that felt threatening. He was practically leering at her even though he had barely moved. "Thanks," she said, avoiding his face.

"Don't you worry about a thing, sweetie," he whispered in her ear unsuspectingly, causing her to jump. He chuckled, putting one hand over her shoulder. "I will be sure to make sure you are well cared for. It will be a great pleasure." He sniffed. "I'll bet you're a virgin."

Samantha's cheeks turned bright scarlet as she tried to redirect her attention back to the conversation around the table.

"Yes, I really do like fresh blood," he chortled.

Samantha jerked her shoulder out from under his grip and pierced him with her eyes. "Good for you, but I don't like you, so you can just back off." She was shocked at herself for speaking so forcefully, all the while trying to keep a stern demeanor.

"A feisty one, huh? I would not have guessed." He leaned back, an amused smile on his face. "Yes, I think I really am going to like you." He stood. "Enjoy your dessert, sweetie. See you again soon."

Samantha guffawed as he walked away, mentally shaken. Vanessa leaned in and said, "That would be

Jonathan. He is Victor's human servant. Be careful around him. Since Victor is Ptah's second-in-command, Jonathan has a lot more sway than the rest of us."

"You don't think he would try to . . . force me, do you?" Samantha could barely get the words out.

Vanessa shook her head. "Don't worry about that. He likes to boast that he is one of the best lovers since Casanova. He would never try to force himself on a woman. It would taint his precious reputation, not to mention his ego."

Samantha exhaled, a little relieved.

"But plan on him trying to seduce you every way he can," Vanessa warned.

Laughing nervously, Samantha pulled strands of hair behind her ear. "I think I can handle that. I have no problem saying no."

Vanessa giggled with her. "Apparently not, my virgin friend."

"Come on, I'm only sixteen!"

Her companion chuckled and was about to continue the friendly banter when she looked up over Samantha's shoulder. "I think you're being summoned," she said.

Samantha looked behind her to see Annette staring at her and waiting, as if Samantha was supposed to have known Annette's desire to speak to her. She swallowed the lump of anxiety in her throat and left the table without bothering to say goodbye to the others.

Annette smiled warmly at her when she approached.

"Come along now, girl. Ptah would like to see you in his chambers."

Samantha felt herself pale at the words. "What about Leisha?"

"Leisha is in a meeting of her own at the moment. But you have nothing to fear, young one," she cooed. "Leisha has placed her protection over you. That means that we cannot touch you unless we want to challenge her in one-on-one combat." Annette turned and began walking down the hall. "She is an incredible warrior, our Leisha. She has studied many different cultures and their fighting techniques. It came to great use when we were at war with the immortals."

Annette's words should have been consoling to Samantha; even so, her anxiety continued to escalate. What did Ptah want with her? He created the vampire race and all the rules, so he could easily break them without worrying about the consequences. Samantha was so lost in nervous thoughts that she hadn't paid any attention to the many turns they had taken as they went deeper into the earth; the air felt oppressive and chilled.

Suddenly, Annette stopped to open a set of double doors leading into what looked like a spacious living room. Directly in front of her were a large conference table, and a couch and love seat to its right.

Walking to the left, Annette opened the door to Ptah's chamber. Samantha hesitated briefly, then decided she had no choice but to enter; she might as well put on a strong front like Leisha did. The girl straightened her spine and walked in to see what Ptah wanted with her.

He was sitting in front of a gas fireplace in a comfortable looking chair. Smiling warmly, he showed off a set of perfectly white teeth against dark brown skin.

Annette walked over to the large bed that was elevated on a dais and laid on her side, propped up by an elbow. Her black dress flowed provocatively around her figure, the devil's temptress.

Samantha was unsure of what she should do, so she just stood in front of the door, waiting for someone to say something. She noticed the large oil paintings around the room and tried not to show her disgust and fear. Several paintings showed gruesome details of women being raped and mutilated. Some by regular looking men, while others by monstrous creatures resembling loathsome dragons. The rest were portraits of Ptah and other vampires. The artist had painted them to look menacing, and it wouldn't seem at all impossible for them to jump out of the canvas and attack.

The floor and walls were made from stone rather than the hardwood and plaster like the rest of the building. The room seemed ancient, emitting a cold, foreboding ambience.

The room was lit only by the fireplace and the weak illumination of a few scattered lamps.

The awkward silence lasted for a brutal five minutes. Samantha fidgeted under Ptah's stare, trying not to stare

at the pictures around the room. It felt like he was caressing her with his eyes. As uncomfortable as it could be, Samantha was drawn to him at the same time. When she couldn't take the tension anymore, she finally said, "You wished to see me?"

Ptah's smile curved on one side of his mouth. "Why, yes, I did. Will you not come and sit with me?" Though phrased as a question, it was spoken as a command.

His black eyes impaled on her as she strode toward him, her gaze focused intently on the chair she was to occupy. She sat directly in front of him—only five feet away—and looked at his nose.

Sitting back with his hands clasped beneath his chin, he spoke. "I am surprised that someone as young as you could change Leisha's mind about human servants. She can be quite stubborn about certain beliefs sometimes."

Samantha sat, her posture rigid. "You mean her appreciation for human life? Maybe that's why she chose me. I share the same values as her."

"Is she aware that it was your father who captured her for his experiments?" he asked.

Bile rose in her throat, and she swallowed it down. She tried to remain composed, but she knew he had not missed her flinch. "Yes, she knows." She hesitated. "And how did you know about my father?"

"I know a great many things. Leisha was not the first of us to be captured by that American government, but that is neither here nor there. So, little one, you really do plan on becoming her human servant?"

This was why she was here. Ptah knew Leisha too well, and must have suspected something was off when she had brought Samantha along with her. "Yes," Samantha answered, her voice slightly trembling.

"And you are comfortable with that idea? You would be tied directly to Leisha on an intimate level for the rest of your life. Are you truly that fond of her?"

Samantha mulled over the question as if she really were to become Leisha's human servant. "I know we have just met," she said slowly, "but I feel as though we are kindred spirits in some strange, mystical way. It's hard to explain, but I do trust her with my life and know we'll do well together."

Ptah appeared more than pleased by her answer. "That is good, because until she does officially bond you to her, you are quite vulnerable."

Oh no, she thought. She knew Ptah could see her body shake as clearly as he could hear her heart beating wildly. "But I am under Leisha's protection," she whispered.

He laughed as if she had just told a great joke, sending foreign vibrations through her core, which she tried to ignore. "Yes," he said, still smiling. "No one is allowed to touch you while you are under her protection. But until you are bonded to a vampire, you are not protected from everything." He gestured to Annette, who was still lying comfortably on her side, watching them with a smirk on her face. "For instance," he continued, "Annette has a certain psychic ability that does not require any touch. She

can simply enter your mind in a most unique way. We refer to it as *mind raping.*"

He kept his gaze on Samantha while speaking to Annette. "Would you care to demonstrate for us, dear? Make sure you only use a fraction of your power now. I will not have her damaged."

There was no time for Samantha to fully process what Ptah was saying before she experienced it. There was no way for her to describe the filth that she felt. It was as if some rotten, oily mist was traveling inside of her brain, entering all the corners of her mind, even into her subconscious. She was being violated in a way no one should have to undergo. While there was no physical pain of any kind, all she could discern was the black slime seeping through her, invading her very essence.

When she was finally aware of her body again, Samantha was gasping for air. Her lungs felt like exploding. The muck that had been in her mind was gone, although she could still feel the taint of its residue. She was left with the feeling of being emotionally defiled and broken.

"That was just a small taste of what Annette can do," Ptah said pleasantly.

She couldn't look up to acknowledge him; she could not move at all. The only thing she was capable of in that moment was breathing. Tears streamed helplessly down her cheeks. She did not think she would ever get over the vile feeling she was imposed with in the most private corners of her mind.

Ptah continued as if he were teaching a small child. "Now, if you were Leisha's human servant, then Annette would not be able to reach your mind at all. You see what I mean now when I speak of your vulnerability? Anyone with an aggressive psychic power can harm you."

"Wha-what do you . . . want?" she choked; her voice rasped as if she had been screaming for hours. Maybe she had.

"It is quite simple, really. I do not trust anyone. But you can help me have a little more faith by making sure Leisha does as I see fit."

"Huh?"

Ptah stood and strolled slowly around her chair as he talked, "First, I want to be assured you know where your loyalties lie. You have now committed yourself to the vampires, and therefore, you have pledged yourself to me. I expect you to be made Leisha's human servant within the next two years. If not, well, you know what can happen to you if you are not bonded to her." He caressed her shoulder and down her arm with his hand. "You may rest assure that what you felt tonight will seem like sleeping on a feather bed compared to what will happen to you if you betray me."

Samantha shuddered violently as Ptah smiled and continued, "Additionally, I want detailed reports of everything when you and Leisha are with the immortals."

Samantha's voice still trembled. "But Leisha—"

"Leisha is Leisha," Ptah interrupted. "She has just

returned to us, and is presently used to thinking and choosing for herself. I need to be sure she is truly dedicated to me."

Ptah stood in front of Samantha and motioned for her to stand. He pulled under her chin until she was staring directly into his obsidian eyes. He was four or five inches taller than her, but he easily made her feel so much smaller, and helpless. "I know when you are lying and when you're telling the truth. You are easy to read, and I am most knowledgeable in how to cause such great pain that you'll be begging for me to end your life. You may as well do as I tell you before I have to torture you into doing it anyway. Leisha would also suffer most grievously if you do not comply with my wishes. Since she does have the capacity to heal quickly, her punishment would have to be much longer and more painful than you can ever fathom."

Samantha saw herself falling into the endless depth of his gaze, fighting with all her will to tear her eyes away. But she could not. Instead, she forced out an answer that barely made it past her lips. "All right."

Ptah smiled again and turned his attention elsewhere. Samantha blinked several times to clear her mind, but she still felt like she wasn't fully herself.

Ptah stroked her cheek lightly with the back of his hand, traveling sensuously down her neck. Samantha was disgusted with herself; she couldn't believe this monster was actually turning her on.

"I am glad we could so easily come to an understanding

with each other. I believe it will make our relationship flow more smoothly throughout the future." Ptah leaned down towards her, and Samantha knew she should pull away— she knew she would regret standing there like a mindless bimbo—but her brain and her body did not seem to be in synch with each other. Ptah's lips were on the thin side, and yet they were soft, stroking her own lips with such erotic expertise that she couldn't help but kiss him back.

She was vaguely aware of the door opening behind her—it would not have registered if Ptah hadn't pulled away.

Samantha turned numbly to see Nikita with an attractive woman following behind. The woman's brown eyes widened at the sight of Samantha, and she looked somewhat miffed.

Ptah walked up to the woman as he slipped on a pair of sunglasses. He put his arm around the woman's trim waist and led her towards the bed. "I told you I had interesting tastes, my dear."

The woman seemed to accept it, glancing back at Samantha. "Will she be joining us, then?" she asked in a thick Portuguese accent.

"Not this time. I want to have you all to myself tonight," Ptah purred as he pulled pins from her black hair. He turned to Annette, pointing at Samantha. "See that she memorizes all of my personal directions before handing her off to Nikita."

Annette smiled, a cat about to eat a mouse. "We shall

see how well you are with your memory. I hope it takes a while, because I do love to dole out punishment when you do poorly."

Samantha gulped as she followed Annette to the outer room of Ptah's apartment. As the door closed behind her, she heard the Portuguese woman moaning in delight. She jumped when an agonized scream echoed from the bedroom.

"Don't worry about her," Annette said. "She'll be dead within the hour." She gave a predatory smile. "But you and I are just getting started, *oui?*"

CHAPTER 14

Leisha was walking back to her apartment after she had spent what was hopefully an appropriate amount of time on the dance floor with the other vampires. It had felt odd socializing with them. She'd enjoyed catching up with a few, while putting on a pleasant façade for the rest of them as they boasted of their new strategies for beguiling humans into their bloodthirsty arms.

A few new faces also graced the scene—the younger ones had apparently put her on a pedestal. They had heard about her and knew she was one of the oldest and more powerful vampires. The thing they were most impressed by was the fact that she'd had been living on her own for so long.

Independence was not something Ptah allowed, and these vampires were awestruck that she had somehow

obtained it. Of course, vampires lived all over the world, and not everyone stayed with Ptah at the exact same time— modern day technology had made that possible. Vampires could travel around in groups and check in every day via their secure website. Though it made a lot more opportunities possible for the vampires, they were still constantly monitored, not truly independent.

"Leisha," Victor said from behind, interrupting her thoughts.

She stopped and turned, waiting for him to catch up with her. "I should like to speak with you, if you will permit me?"

That surprised Leisha. Victor had never paid much attention to her before. He used to only acknowledge her with politeness, occasionally complimenting her on her fighting skills, nothing more. Out of curiosity, she agreed to talk with him.

He led her in the opposite direction, toward his own apartment. She stopped short when they walked in to see his human servant, Jonathan, lighting candles in the dim room. A large red circle big enough to fit two people was outlined in chalk on the floor. A silver goblet stood in its center.

Victor turned to Leisha, closing the door behind her. His demeanor was serious and intent. "I require a blood oath from you before we can go further."

An eyebrow inched up her forehead. "What exactly

would I be promising?" She wished she hadn't followed him now. This could only lead to trouble.

"I only ask that you promise not to discuss what I will speak of to you tonight."

"There is no need for a blood oath, Victor. I will give you my promise. You know that I always stand by my word."

He shook his head grimly. "It does not matter whether I can trust you or not. What I have to discuss with you could lead to my destruction, and I will not take any chances."

Considering briefly, Leisha nodded. "All right, I will accept the oath."

Victor relaxed slightly. "Good." He walked to the circle on the floor and knelt on one side of the goblet. Leisha followed him and took her position opposite him inside the circle.

Jonathan sat on a couch facing them, watching with reverence.

Victor held his wrist out above the goblet and sliced open a vein with the nail of his thumb, letting his blood pour into the cup. When the goblet was a quarter full, he pulled his arm back. Leisha followed suit, repeating the same ritual.

When the goblet was more than halfway full, she took her bleeding wrist to her mouth, licking off the blood until the cut healed.

Victor picked up the goblet, swirling it gently to mix their blood. He nodded to Leisha and waited.

Leisha nodded in acknowledgement and began speaking,

"I, Leisha, one of the first of the vampires, who came from the land of Africa, do hereby give my oath to you, Victor. I swear that whatever I hear tonight will not be uttered to another soul as long as I walk this earth." He handed her the goblet. "I drink of our blood to unite and bind us in this oath, so that you may feel my true intent running through your veins as well as my own." She gulped down three big swallows and felt the cold, lifeless liquid trickle down her esophagus.

Victor took the goblet from Leisha's hands. "I, Victor, one of the older vampires, who came from the land of Rome, do accept your oath, Leisha. I know that as I drink our blood, I can entrust you with what I am about to reveal." He proceeded to drain it. The ceremony complete, Leisha waited patiently for Victor's next move, knowing very well what she'd gotten herself into. Leisha was now bound to her word. If she were ever foolish enough to break a blood oath, she'd find herself under the power of the one she betrayed—Victor. Having no will of her own, she would have to comply with her new master's every wish. This went the same for Victor.

Once Victor placed the empty cup on the floor, Jonathan got up, flipped on the lights and blew out the candles he had lit only moments before.

They got off of their knees to sit more comfortably on the couch. Jonathan picked up the goblet and exited the room.

"Ptah has become weak in his old age," Victor began. "He

is bound by traditions and rules he could easily break if he wanted to."

"He holds to his traditions to keep all of the vampires in a stable environment," Leisha said. "Can you imagine what would happen if they no longer trusted in Ptah as their leader? It would be madness. Surely, none of us really want to see vampires in a panic, running around slaughtering humans everywhere. Ptah gives them a sense of order and peace. We all need that."

Victor gripped his hands into fists on his lap. "I would be better at it," he said with more conviction than she had ever heard from him. "I would lead us all to more glory than Ptah could ever imagine. He is just a demon who is content with having a body and a few followers to worship him. He cares not to let us grow and expand as a race on this earth."

"What are you saying, Victor? Are you going to pull a Brutus on him?"

He ruefully shook his head. "Not exactly. I would never be able to kill Ptah. He is too aware of everyone around him." He held her gaze. "Except you."

Leisha's stomach sank.

"I don't think he even understands what it is he feels for you; but whatever it is, you are his one weakness. His Achilles' heel, if you will. I have my pride, Leisha, and I do not come to others for help very often, but you are our only hope of helping the vampires to truly prosper. Ptah has been a hindrance to us for centuries; he is stuck in the old ways."

Shaking her head, Leisha protested, "That is not true, Victor. Look around you; he has updated everything to the latest technologies, even the latest fashions. He knows we all must change with the times to keep a low profile."

"That is not what I mean, and you know it," he snapped, reaching for her shoulders. "He only allows a couple hundred vampires to leave at a time, and they must constantly check in with him."

"But the immortals—"

"Exactly. Don't you see? He could have wiped them out a long time ago. He is using the immortals as an excuse to keep a tight net on us all. Ptah enjoys making us subservient to him. He likes keeping our power reined in when we could be so much more. He only allows each of us two or three kills a week. If I could drain a life source every night, do you know how much more powerful I would be? If he was not so concerned about drawing attention to us, we could be dining like the gods we are. We would be powerful enough to stomp down any threat that comes our way."

Leisha felt sick at his perspective, but kept an impassive face. "There is nothing I can do about it, Victor. Ptah is still just as wary of me as he is anyone else. Besides, it is good for us to keep a low profile. What if our existence was out in the open? We would be hunted down by all kinds of fanatics."

He tightened his grip. "That is not true. You're like a blind spot to him. All you have to do is become his mate again, prove your loyalty to him for five years or so. Then, you could cut off his head in his own bedchamber, and he would never see it coming. As for your fanatics, you give them too much credit. They wouldn't be able to handle our power. They will more likely worship us as gods."

"So, you want me to kill him, and then what happens? You rule the vampires while I do your bidding?"

Victor's hands began to slowly trace down her arms. "*We* will rule the vampires. Together. You'll become my mate, and we will be unstoppable."

This was sounding too close to what Ptah had said to her the night before. Victor had become too arrogant. She had been so focused on being wary of Ptah that she did not realize the existence of a bigger threat than him. Victor had proven to be much more formidable than she'd expected.

She brushed his hands away. "Save it, Victor. You and I both know you have no physical attraction toward me."

He smiled. "But you are definitely my match. You do not even realize the influence you carry over the others. They respect and fear you. If you acted as my mate, we would create the strongest race to ever walk this earth. Humans would revere us as gods."

Talk about a God complex, Leisha thought to herself as she suppressed the urge to roll her eyes. "Victor, I just want to go back to being independent. I have no wish to rule over anyone. I want to be left alone."

He readily agreed. "Then, that shall be your reward for helping me. I promise to leave you be; you would never have to come back. You could live out your existence in absolute privacy."

Victor would, of course, prefer it that way, so he could take all of the glory himself. She had to play this out carefully. She could not agree to any of his plans, but if she baldly rejected his proposition, she would be making herself an incredibly dangerous enemy.

She was quiet for a moment or two before sighing, "I will have to think on it, Victor. I must focus on my duty to infiltrate the immortals first. They are a more immediate threat to the vampires."

Lips twitching, he looked pleased. "That will be perfect. When you have successfully completed that task, Ptah will become even blinder to you," He stood. "We shall meet and discuss this again when you have returned from spying on the immortals. You may be with them for some time, which will give you plenty of time to decide on your course of action."

"Exactly." She decided to push a compliment, just so Victor wouldn't see the disdain she felt for him. "I must say, Victor, I had no idea how clever and ambitious you are. You have truly made an impression on me tonight."

His lips twitched as he opened the door for her, stopping her just before she crossed the threshold. "You were wrong, you know."

Her brow rose in question.

His gaze traveled down her body appreciatively. "I do find you physically desirable." With a coy smile playing over his mouth, he shut the door behind her.

SAMANTHA FELT AS IF SHE were drowning in a sea of muck and oil. *So filthy. Dirty.* She could not seem to think beyond the rancid pit that had invaded her mind.

A familiar voice broke through her haze. "I believe Ptah said she was supposed to be undamaged," Nik said.

She felt Annette's shoulders rise and fall under her arm. She hadn't realized that Annette was supporting her weight. "She'll get over it," Annette said. "I went easy on her. It's not my fault if her mind is too fragile."

Nik picked her up, carrying her. "Dirty," Samantha murmured as she squeezed her eyes against his chest.

He stroked her hair. "Yes, I know," he said gently. "It will pass. I promise."

She started to shake her head, but it only seemed to thicken the refuse in her head. She gasped at the feeling.

"Shush," he whispered in her ear. "We are almost there." Nik laid Samantha down on a soft bed.

"I can make it go away, Samantha. All you have to do is open your eyes and the muck will be gone."

He must have been insane. This scum was cemented to her memory. It was more than just the residue from the first time Annette raped her mind.

Annette had ruthlessly possessed Samantha's mind at any excuse the vampire could think of. Samantha was forced to memorize five cell phone numbers, three fax numbers, and ten email addresses—memorizing them wouldn't be a problem for her if she were given an hour. Instead, Annette had quizzed her immediately after

Samantha was able to glance at the list only once. Plus, the screaming coming from Ptah's bedroom distracted her with an immense amount of guilt. In her mind, Samantha knew there was nothing she could do to save that woman, but just sitting outside the room and trying to memorize phone numbers as if nothing was happening proved too much.

Each time she got something wrong, Annette would fill her mind with the smut that only someone as evil as she could create. And each time that happened, Samantha found it harder to memorize the information. She had no idea how long the session had lasted; it seemed at least a week, possibly longer.

If she already had a week's worth of slime coursing through her mind, how could Nik possibly think she could be rid of it by her merely opening her eyes? In answer to her thoughts, he said, "You must trust me in this. You have nothing to lose by simply opening your eyes, do you?"

Unable to fight with the logic, Samantha opened her eyes. All she saw were Nik's hazel irises. Then, suddenly, the muck *was* gone. Nik was all that existed in that moment. She felt the compulsion to touch him, to be with him, encircled by his arms. She needed him more than she needed anything else in her life, and he needed her as well. She was his; she would give herself over to him completely. Nik was—

Samantha felt a tremor of loss surge through her whole

body, her vision blurry. She blinked in confusion for thirty seconds before she was able to see where she was.

She was lying in a canopy bed she didn't recognize. A man stood over her, watching her intently. No, not just a man, it was Nik. He had carried her from Ptah's chambers. The dirt, the slime, it was gone! She was clean.

"How?" was all she could muster.

"I used a little mind trick on you to rid your brain of what Annette did," he explained as if it were no big deal.

But it was a big deal. "Thank you, Nik," she whispered, tears leaking down her cheeks.

He just shrugged and sat on the edge of the bed. "There was no reason for you to suffer any longer."

Laughter bubbled up into her throat, a hysterical laughter. Her body must be releasing the tension it had been holding all night. She did not even try to stifle it. Sitting up, she and gave Nik a fierce hug, high-pitched squeals escaping her mouth.

Nik sat perfectly still for a long time, his arms slowly encircling her. She felt safe and warm, and never wanted to leave the security of his arms again. How she could go from feeling complete despair to pure joy in so short a time?

"I think I might've used a little too much of my power on you. You should not feel so comfortable with me."

Sitting back, Samantha grinned at him. "You know what, Nik, I think that there's a lot more to you than what you show people."

He grimly shook his head. "You would be wise to show

caution with all vampires. We can turn on you in an instant."

The memory of Annette and Ptah flooded her vision, and she immediately became more subdued, though not entirely backing off. "You helped me when you did not have to. You showed a moment of compassion."

"A moment is all that it was. Do not read into things where there is nothing to be read."

She sat quietly for a moment, openly studying him. His expression was still dour, his eyes giving nothing away. But Samantha somehow knew she was right about him.

"Do you know what I did when I was human?" he asked. Maybe he was able to read her expression after all.

She shook her head.

"I was an assassin—a very good one at that—with an enormous amount of wealth to show for my great success. As a vampire, I continue to care little for human life. I have no scruples about killing, unlike your beloved Leisha."

The words chilled her, just as he had intended. "It doesn't mean that you have no compassion within you. People are allowed to change. You could decide to take on the same kind of lifestyle Leisha has anytime you like. It's your choice."

Nik looked at her with little enduring affection. "You are even more of an idealist than I thought." He cocked his head to one side, studying her just as intently as she him. "What is it about you, I wonder? You are young and innocent and definitely naïve, but there is something about you. You have a subconscious ability to lure people to you. Or maybe you are always trying to find the good in people, even when they show you their darker sides."

Samantha blushed under his praise. "That's not true at all." Her face darkened a little. "I don't think I can ever see any good in either Ptah or Annette." He took her hand in his and squeezed lightly. "Not everyone can be perfect, I suppose. They actually do have good traits, but they just use them for their own selfish—what you'd probably call evil—purposes."

"That's an interesting way to look at it." She tried to say it with Nik's objectiveness, but the horror of what she had just experienced was too fresh. A woman she had only seen briefly was probably now dead. Suddenly, everything that had transpired—all the stress over her mother's death, and who her father really was, having to remain composed in this strange and dark world of vampires and immortals, and of course, whatever happened with Ptah and Annette—came rushing to her with an immense impact.

She had been pushing off dealing with everything for far too long, and now the reality of her life in the last few weeks was forcing its way into her consciousness. The burden of it all was too much, and she felt herself crumbling under it.

"What am I doing here?" she asked, her voice shook. "I'm not strong enough to deal with all this. I have a hard enough time just dealing with high school! Now, I'm in the middle of some kind of political plot between vampires

and immortals, and not to mention my dad has probably assigned someone from the government to find me." She inhaled. "It all just seems too unreal. I keep waiting for myself to wake up and find my mom alive and well, waiting to put her arms around me and tell me it was all just a dream."

She broke off from her rambling as sobs took over.

Nik gathered her into his arms and caressed her back, murmuring something inaudible in Russian.

"I'm sorry, Nik," she said, reigning in her emotions. "I don't know what's wrong with me. I usually have better control over myself." Sniffing, she added in an attempt at humor, "Maybe I'm about to start my period or something."

Nik just held her. "Well, first of all, I can smell it if you are ready to start your period." She stiffened in his arms at the thought as he released a snigger. "Secondly," he continued, "you have every right to be overwhelmed by emotion. You have been through so much in such a short time. Annette messing with your mind makes you more prone to being emotional. It is the mind's way of dealing with trauma."

His straightforwardness reassured her as she relaxed against him, crying a little more. After quite some time, she pulled back and smiled triumphantly. "See? You really are capable of showing a healthy dose of compassion."

Smirking with one corner of his mouth, Nik inclined his head. "I'll admit, you bring out a side in me that no one ever has." He looked her over. "Do you think you are ready to face Leisha now? You mustn't act strangely around her.

She cannot know what happened to you tonight."

"Why not? Leisha promised she would protect me." She certainly did not like the idea of keeping something so big from the only friend she had.

The Russian held her gaze with a sudden intensity that was very unlike him. "Because," he explained, "if she found out, then she might lose her temper and try to kill Annette."

"I wouldn't mind it in the least."

"Think about the outcome, Samantha. Either Annette will kill Leisha, leaving you helpless in a place surrounded by vampires who will gladly take advantage of your presence."

Samantha shuddered.

"Or," he continued, "Leisha kills Annette, returning to Ptah's side as his mate until he grows tired of her again."

"What? Why does she have to be Ptah's mate if she kills Annette?"

He half shrugged. "It is part of our tradition. If another female challenges Annette and then defeats her, they must fill her place as Ptah's mate. It is a large responsibility with many duties, including fulfilling Ptah's sadistic sexual desires."

"You vampires are impossible!" She burst out in frustration. "Don't you see, all these rules are only making you people more miserable! Is being a masochist part of the requirement to becoming a vampire or something?"

"I know it is hard to understand," Nik said patiently. "But Ptah made things this way for a reason. He knows how to

keep things in his control, and he makes sure everyone follows his rules and stipulations so that he can maintain that control. He has been doing this a long time and it has worked well."

Samantha took a deep breath and held it for five seconds before blowing it out. "All right, so everything here is for Ptah's purposes. I don't like it, but I think I understand what you are saying." She paused. "Yes, I think I can face Leisha now. I will make sure she doesn't know a thing about what happened." She smiled at him. "You were right to warn me. I would not want anything to happen to Leisha. I haven't known her for more than a few days, but I would feel absolutely lost without her now."

CHAPTER 15

Leisha turned to look at the back of her outfit in the mirror. It was quite simple: black slacks that flowed elegantly down her long legs, and a faux wraparound white cotton long sleeve shirt. Her hair was swept back into a French braid, and she wore a simple silver necklace to dress up the outfit a little.

She was trying her best to look sophisticated. The last time Tafari saw her, she wore heavy makeup and a tacky clubbing outfit. If he saw her today, she wanted to look her best and as innocent as possible. It probably would not make a difference—he saw her as the monster that he always saw, no matter her attire.

Samantha strolled into the bedroom with a suitcase and paused to look at Leisha in exasperation. "Again? That's the fourth outfit you've tried on. Please don't tell me you don't like this one, either."

Leisha felt sheepish and young at the admonition. "I suppose it will have to do," she conceded. "We only have a couple of hours until we leave, and Ptah wanted to see us off in a grand ceremony." Rolling her eyes, she added, "He likes to do everything ceremoniously. It tends to get old after a while."

Samantha stiffened slightly at the mention of Ptah, but didn't change her expression at all. She had been acting like that for the last three days. Leisha had asked if everything was okay—if anything had happened—but Samantha insisted everything was just fine, that everyone had been treating her with formal respect. But the girl was having nightmares, murmuring in her sleep about drowning in blackness, and Leisha could not help but wonder if Ptah's eyes were the source. Those eyes were absolutely terrifying, and she could never blame the girl for being frightened.

"Do the immortals do everything in ceremony as well?" she asked.

Leisha shrugged, trying to be nonchalant about the fact that she might be seeing them soon. After all, these immortals had all sworn to kill her, and many had tried to do so. This would prove to be an interesting, if not deadly, experience. "I would assume so," she said. "But I know nothing of their ways. Just that when Tafari was made an immortal, the ceremonies lasted for about three days."

"Well, I'm sure they'll be less intimidating than these vampires."

"I wouldn't count on that. They are just as prideful as we are. Some of them more so." She paused. "Do you find me intimidating?"

Samantha smiled warmly. "Actually, yes, but not in the same way as the other vampires." She started to blush. "I kinda look up to you, Leisha. I find you intimidating, because I don't know if I can ever be like you."

Stunned into silence for a second, it took a moment for Leisha to find her voice. "Samantha, I don't ever want you to be anything like me. You are impressive just as you are. I'm not sure if I have ever known a human quite like you. You should value your uniqueness."

Samantha waved it off with her hand. "I think it's getting way too sentimental in here." She glanced back at the closet. "Have you packed yet?"

"No, but it will take fewer than five minutes."

Samantha cocked her head to the side. "I didn't know you are a light packer."

Leisha grinned. "I'm not. But I do have super speed, so it doesn't take long to get everything I need packed up."

"Right. I keep forgetting about that kind of stuff."

"Just leave your suitcase by the door. Someone will carry them to the car for us. Did you make sure that everything you packed fit you all right?"

"Of course." Samantha smiled. "I may not get flustered and change my outfit ten times, but I do like to look decent."

Leisha laughed, hoping to hide the raw nerves throbbing inside her.

Saying goodbye to everyone was not that big of a deal. Everyone gathered in the ballroom to watch them go. Leisha and Samantha both gave their formal courtesies to Ptah. He kissed their hands and wished them a safe journey, quite pleased with all the arrangements, although Leisha thought otherwise; unlike him, she wasn't as confident.

Victor barely spoke to her since the night they met in his apartment, but he squeezed her hand in parting. "I look forward to your return, Leisha," he said, his tone somber. "Have a safe journey; we can't afford to lose you." Leisha simply nodded.

They followed Nikita up the steps after saying good-bye. He was going to see them off at the airport. In the car, Samantha seemed in fairly high spirits. Leisha noticed how well Samantha and Nikita were getting along. She was surprised that Nikita was indulging the girl in conversation. If Leisha did not know any better, she would assume Nikita was fond of Samantha.

Samantha was obviously attracted to Nikita. When they parked in the lot at the airport, Samantha asked him to see them off inside.

"Sorry, but I can't. The sun has just come up, and I need to stay in the car. These windows protect me from getting burned."

Samantha looked down at her feet. "Right." She leaned across the seat and gave him a hug. "Well, thanks for everything, Nik. I'll miss you!" With that, she jumped out of the car and grabbed her suitcase, waiting for Leisha to follow.

Leisha turned to Nikita. "You haven't been working your mind tricks on the girl, have you?"

Nikita shook his head in complete nonchalance. "I suppose it must be because she knew me longer than anyone else, with you as the exception."

"I suppose that makes sense." She met his gaze. "You just make sure you don't get too close to her. She does not realize the dangers that lie in befriending vampires."

"I bet she knows more than you think she knows. Besides, she has already befriended you."

"Yes, but I am surrounded by humans all the time, and I don't let my appetite get in the way. I'm not sure you would be able to control yourself if you were around her for too long."

"It will not matter much now, with you leaving. I believe this conversation is a little moot."

He was right, and she knew it, but she could not stop feeling the need to protect Samantha. The last time she felt like this, she was a mother. "Thanks for the ride, Nikita. I'm sure I'll be seeing you again."

He smiled and nodded goodbye.

"What was all that about?" Samantha asked, trying to catch up with Leisha on the way into the airport terminal.

"What?"

"When you were saying goodbye to Nik. You looked like you wanted to put him into a meat grinder. He's been kind to us; you should be more grateful to him."

Leisha decided to let the issue go. There were many

things the girl did not understand. Samantha did not realize she was playing with fire. At least from here on, she was no longer surrounded by vampires. Leisha hoped the immortals would be less dangerous for her.

MASON PACED RESTLESSLY BACK AND forth in the small waiting room. He sat in each one of the four chairs available in the room for about five minutes before deciding to walk off his anxiety. He could only take six long strides before he had to turn around again.

Mason knew, of course, they were doing this on purpose. The confined space and the wretched chairs were all part of the psychology his superiors used to manipulate their employees. If he wanted to show them he was unaffected by it, he would have to just stay put in the first chair and sit without moving until they called him in.

Though he had nothing to prove, the pacing helped him keep his mind clear and his goal in focus. A low buzzer sounded, signaling him to enter the room.

He walked in the dimly lit room to see his three superiors sitting at one end of the conference table. Henderson was smoking a cigarette, as usual, his tie slightly askew from the rest of his nicely pressed suit. A small lamp sat on the table in front of him.

Doyle had his pipe in his mouth, the smell of tobacco practically overwhelming in the room. That, too, was deliberate. Doyle wore a charcoal gray Gucci suit today. He seemed to wear a new one every few weeks.

Sampson was the only one who never smoked, though he got enough secondhand smoking to guarantee lung cancer. Sitting perfectly still, his hands rested on the laptop on the table, his light gray suit immaculate. He gestured Mason to take a seat.

"We want to keep this as brief as possible," Henderson started, his bushy silver eyebrows dominating the glare he was giving. "We have noticed that your productivity has increased by about twenty percent since the disappearance of your daughter. We've also just received your request to take some personal time. The two actions don't seem to fit well with each other, wouldn't you agree?"

Mason allowed his face to show just a hint of anxiety through a twitch of his lower lip. "Actually, sir, I believe it fits perfectly. I was hoping to lose myself in work to help deal with my grieving, but it has only backfired. This was the last place I saw Samantha. I feel I need to get away for just a couple of weeks, so I can truly say goodbye to her, and then jump right back into work when I return."

Sampson leaned back. "How do we know you won't just try to track her down as soon as you get your personal time? If we lose you to those disgusting creatures, all of our research would come to a standstill. It would take us several months to accomplish what you can do in just a few weeks."

"I feel that you give me too much credit, sir," Mason grimaced. "My team and I all work together to accomplish all that we have so far, and they will continue to do so in my

absence." He paused to look each one of them in the eye. "It wouldn't be logical for me to track down the vampires myself. I have lost my daughter; there is no need for me to end my life as well. I only ask that I have time to recover from my loss."

"She'd barely been living with you for a week," Doyle pointed out. "Why should you be grieving for her so much? You didn't need time to recover from losing half of the men in your sect when we were trying to recapture the female vampire."

"Samantha is of my own flesh, and she was the last link to my ex-wife. Even if she and I were never close, she was going to continue my legacy. And now, that is lost."

All three nodded slightly as if they understood. This grief was more about losing a part of one's self. They could certainly relate to someone who was as self-absorbed as he. Mason knew it was the perfect thing to say.

They agreed to give him one week of personal time off. It wasn't what he had planned, but it would have to do.

As soon as he was in his car, he flipped the switch to an encrypting machine, scrambling signals emitted by his cell; he didn't want anyone listening in on his calls, or even knowing who he contacted.

He dialed a number and waited for three rings before someone answered. "We don't have much time," Mason said without preamble. "I will book a ticket to India and should be in the air by tonight."

"You better change that. I have verified several reports

of two women matching the descriptions you provided. According to the images captured by security cameras, they flew out early this morning on a direct flight to Batal, Brazil."

"Matching descriptions of both the females?" His heart fluttered with newfound hope. Samantha could still be alive. "What was the percentage?"

"The one matching your daughter was seventy-five percent, and the other woman's match was eighty-seven-point-nine percent." The man paused to check his computer, the sound of keyboard clicking incessantly. "Wait, I see two other females on route to Chile. Their images yield a sixty percent match in our facial recognition program."

"I'll get a flight over to Batal right away. If they're not the ones we want, we'll track down the ones in Chile. Meet me there at the usual hotel."

The voice chuckled. "You mean what used to be the usual? You have been out of the game for a while, old man. Things have changed."

"You can never stop change. I'll see you in a day or so."

CHAPTER 16

The flight was long, but Samantha slept peacefully almost the entire way. Being surrounded
by vampires had probably made sleep somewhat
difficult for her. Maybe Nikita was right. Maybe Samantha
knew the danger ahead—she was certainly brave to be able
to keep her spirits up if that was the case.

If Samantha could go through all of that with a smile
on her face, the least Leisha could do when they met with
Tafari was to follow through with her plans. At this point,
she was not even sure if Tafari would come.

All she could do was go to the location he was last seen by
the vampire spies and ask around, seeing if anyone knew
where to find him. She had no doubt someone would know,
but she couldn't trust anyone; Tafari's men would just alert
him, causing more problems. That was why Leisha would
have to wait for him to seek her out.

She just hoped he didn't send a patrol to kill her. Seeking him out like this made her vulnerable. She was a sitting duck. But it would be the fastest way to get in contact with him.

Even if Tafari did agree to take them in, Leisha was not sure exactly about her next step from there. Should she stay loyal to Ptah and the vampires, and spy on the immortals to give them an advantage in the upcoming war? Or should she just stay there for a while for the sake of pretense, and then return to report her failure? If she did that, Ptah would no doubt dole out a horrendous punishment—that would be worth it. But she could not leave Samantha to her own devices among the immortals. Once they discovered her gift of premonition, they would surely try to exploit her. No, she wouldn't let that happen; she couldn't. Leisha knew what she had to do.

She was a vampire, after all, and had accepted the consequences of becoming one long ago. Sometimes, she admitted to herself, it was hard to accept. Becoming a vampire had taken away her free will. For the last hundred years, she'd been fooling herself into believing she was free and independent.

The truth was, Leisha would never be free; Ptah forbade it. In that moment, Victor's proposition seemed tempting to accept, even if Victor was never a good choice to lead the vampires. Of course, as Ptah's second-in-command, everyone would turn to him if Ptah were to die.

Leisha sighed and looked out the window. She had no

idea what she was going to do. She needed to stay focused on the task in front of her, and deal with everything else when the time came.

They landed in Batal, Brazil, after what seemed like over twenty hours. But Leisha knew it was less. Her nerves were messing with her internal clock, and she needed to get herself under control—the closer she got to finding Tafari, the more frayed her nerves became. "I don't know if I can do this," she murmured to herself as she unfastened her seatbelt and stood to get their luggage from the overheads.

"I'm sure it will be fine," Samantha said, her eyes still sleepy. "He will come and at least talk to you. You know he'll be curious about why you're seeking him out."

"What makes you so sure? You've never met him."

"I know a small part of him from what you've told me." They stood to retrieve their luggage. "I guess I'm being so optimistic because I really want to meet him, and you know how they say you should send positive energy in your mind to get what you want."

"Is that what they're saying these days?" Leisha chuckled. "I can hardly keep up with anything in the world anymore. It seems to be changing every day."

They left the plane, maneuvering their way through the terminal to find the car rental kiosk where they had made their reservation. Samantha stayed alert on the crowd as she continued their conversation. "I thought the world has always been like that. From what I see of vampires, you adapt to change pretty well."

Leisha smirked. "It's sort of a survival skill if you intend to live a long life. When you can't blend into a crowd, immortals can find you pretty easily. But it feels like everything is so much more fast-paced now than it used to be."

"It's because of technology today," Samantha said. "I'll bet that even though you guys have Internet and stuff, you probably don't even know what an iPhone is, huh?"

Leisha rolled her eyes. "We are not that bad. We're always perusing online to stay up to date with technology. It helps us just as much as anyone else."

It took them a while to get their car since Samantha really wanted to upgrade to a nicer car, like the convertible Mustang she saw, but Leisha said it would attract too much attention.

"We may be seeking out the immortals, but there is still wisdom in keeping a low profile."

Samantha reluctantly agreed when Leisha promised to get a Porsche when they were safe enough to drive around.

Samantha seemed to have all kinds of surprises up her sleeve, Leisha thought. From their short time together, she already knew Samantha was a serious ballet dancer and loved her mother very much. The girl had also been brave for the past couple of weeks. Samantha might be many unexpected things, but Leisha never would have guessed her to be a car fan.

Leisha suddenly realized how nice it was to be able to have a companion and . . . a friend. She had been alone for so long, and now that she had Samantha—a teenager so

full of life and free of judgment—Leisha marveled at the very idea. Samantha was the sister she never had.

SAMANTHA PULLED ON HER NEW swimsuit in anticipation. They had been in Batal for four days doing nothing but work. They went from place to place in the area, questioning people if they had seen a man with Tafari's description. Leisha did the asking, while Samantha studied their faces carefully. Leisha had taught Samantha a thing or two about reading people's faces to see if they were hiding things. Simple idiosyncrasies and unconscious gestures like the scratching of the face, or a sudden shift of the body could all be used to decide if the person was telling the truth.

She couldn't believe how much people gave away once she knew what to look for. Even the man who owned the café had given himself away. He had kept his face carefully blank, and his body too still, when Leisha asked if he had seen Tafari, but it was too obvious he was hiding what he knew. Samantha felt like a detective from television, and she enjoyed it.

Of course, no one would admit it even if they knew Tafari, but Leisha was convinced he was in the area in the last year. They exhausted all the places they could think of, and now they could only wait. Leisha suggested a day at the beach, and Samantha jumped at the opportunity. Earlier, she spotted several beaches that looked inviting with their crystal blue water and white sand.

They didn't pack swimsuits, so they spent the morning shopping. Samantha found a cute light blue bikini that helped her bust look a little larger. Leisha bought a dark red one-piece swimsuit cut low over her cleavage, which made her look like she belonged in a Victoria's Secret catalogue.

Samantha stared at her own pale skin and wished it had Leisha's golden glow. Though she lived in Florida for the majority of her life, she could never tan. Whenever she tried, she just got freckles, so now she put on lots of sun block and tried to accept her porcelain complexion.

The drive to the beach was not very long. They found a decent spot amidst the many sunbathers and swimmers to lay out the new beach towels. It was a beautiful sunny day, and the sun was high in the sky, bearing down waves of heat.

"So, do you burn at all?" Samantha was curious.

"Only if I haven't fed for a long time," Leisha responded. "So I had better use some sunscreen as well, since it's been almost a week."

"I thought you said you could go for a whole month."

"I can as long as I'm . . . snacking in the meantime. I haven't had anything besides regular food for six days, so it makes a bit of a difference."

Samantha didn't realize Leisha had been sacrificing so much. "How do you snack, then? Is it something you can do here?"

Leisha explained how she picked up on men and made out with them in dance clubs.

"So, why don't we go out dancing tonight?"

"No, I won't be able to watch you the whole time, and this city can be dangerous. Besides, you're underage."

"You may be right. But that shouldn't stop you from going. I can just stay in the hotel while you're out."

Leisha did not take much time to decide. "I'll go after you have fallen asleep."

Samantha closed her eyes and reveled under the warm rays of the Brazilian sun. She sensed someone standing over them. "Hi," a deep masculine voice greeted.

When she opened her eyes, she jolted into an upright position. The first thing she noticed was these rich, deep-blue eyes that shined with a silvery iridescence accentuated by the sun. The man's ebony skin barely contained the hard set of muscles across his torso and arms. Something about him oozed a fierce presence.

Samantha felt another jolt as she remembered this man in her vision. He was the man Leisha had been arguing with. Samantha tried to remember that portion of her vision, but couldn't quite do it. She only remembered that it was a very heated argument, and that they were in an ordinary looking house. She must tell Leisha about this later.

"Tafari," Leisha breathed, taken completely off guard. Neither of them was expecting him to show up so soon, and Samantha certainly never envisioned their meeting to take place on a sunny beach with hundreds of people around.

As if he was reading her thoughts, he said, "I figured

this would be a safe and neutral place. No vampires can ambush me with the sun so bright right now."

"But I'm sure there are plenty of immortals around just waiting to ambush me," Leisha reflected.

"It would be foolish of me not to bring backup, no?"

"Be honest, Tafari, are any of them within hearing range?"

"You should be able to attune yourself to them if they were."

Standing, she sent him a competitive glare. "Not if they were using long range devices."

The corners of Tafari's mouth quirked. He continued to stare at her for what felt like infinity, touching his ear with his right hand at intervals as if giving out a signal. "Now no one will hear what you have to say. Satisfied?"

Leisha did not appear too pleased; she could only trust Tafari's word that no one was listening and gestured for him to sit with them on the towels.

"I assumed that since you were searching for me so obviously, you must want my attention. What is it that you wish to discuss?" This man was completely cold and closed off.

Samantha wasn't sure what to expect. After all, according to Leisha, Tafari considered Leisha a monster now, although he might still hold some kind of softness towards her.

Leisha remained composed, mirroring Tafari's diplomacy. "I have a request. Quite a large request. If you do this for me, then I would be in your debt, Tafari."

The man sat and waited for her to continue.

"I ask for . . . for your protection."

Tafari scoffed and then started to laugh, his face lit up—borderline playful—in a way that made him appear incredibly warm.

Before he could get his chuckling under control, Leisha continued. "Not for me, you idiot! You should know that I can take care of myself. I am asking you to promise your protection over Samantha."

Tafari stopped laughing at that, turning his sober attention to Samantha, who blushed at being the subject of their conversation under his prodding scrutiny.

"What does the child need protection from?" he asked.

Leisha sighed. "I must have your oath not to tell a soul what I am about to say. No one can know. Will you promise me that?"

"I can only promise if what you tell me does not compromise my cause with the immortals."

Leisha mulled that over in her head for a brief moment. "Samantha got mixed up with me and the vampires. She'd helped me escape from this compound, one thing led to another . . . and she sort of got dragged to our lair."

Tafari interrupted before she could continue. "She helped you escape? Not the other way around?" He glanced back and forth between the two women. "What kind of a compound would you need escaping with the help of a little girl?"

Leisha clenched her jaw. "I would rather not go into

details. All you need to know is that a division of the U.S. government is looking for both of us at the moment."

Tafari's lips twisted. "U.S. government, huh?" He didn't bother to hide his skepticism.

"Anyway, she got pulled into my world. I had to lie and say she is to become my human servant so she could stay under my protection while we were there. Ptah has since taken a special interest in her." Determination shone in her eyes. "She has to go into hiding so she isn't forced to either be my human servant or be killed."

Tafari searched her face as she met his stare with a defiant set to her jaw. Samantha could feel the tension coming from them like the spraying mist of the ocean—there was more than just animosity. Samantha could see their attraction to each other, as if a magnet was trying to pull them together. Tafari's gaze traveled down Leisha's bare shoulders to her cleavage and then down her long legs. Leisha quivered as if he were caressing her. Glancing away, Samantha suddenly felt like a third wheel.

Just as she was about to make some excuse to go in the water, Tafari turned to Samantha. "Is what she is saying true?"

Samantha swallowed. "Yes, it is. But she is leaving a few things out."

Eyes narrowing on her, Leisha shook her head in warning.

"I think it is all right for him to know, Leisha," Samantha said. Leisha was as still as a stone, waiting to see what she

had to say. "Leisha will be severely punished if I disappear. I know she's too proud to show her vulnerability to you, but she also needs your protection."

Leisha's eyes looked like they were about to pop out of her head, and her face was so red it was nearing purple.

Tafari was watching Leisha, his lips twitching.

"I told you I would handle it," Leisha said, her lips tight. Her color was returning to normal, and she was now staring at Samantha as if she was going to strangle her.

Samantha knew Leisha did not like her telling Tafari about it, but it was also the only way for Tafari to agree to take them both in for a short time.

"I wonder, what kind of punishment is in store for you should you lose Samantha?" Tafari asked.

Leisha raised her chin. "Nothing I haven't already lived through. Samantha just doesn't understand our ways, and she feels protective over me like a sister. Actually, I think she is *over*protective of me."

"I think that's hypocritical, Leisha. You treat me the same."

Tafari glanced between them again and shook his head. "What are you trying to pull here, Leisha? Some bloody con to make me believe you have feelings? It does not work, you know. I know what you are." He turned to Samantha and took her hand in his. "Whatever web she has woven around you, it is dangerous. I do not know how you got mixed up with her and her kind, but I warn you to get out of it. Now."

"You are making a mistake, Tafari," Leisha said.

"Samantha is completely innocent."

"I know she is, I can see it in her eyes. But I also know you are far from innocent. You have the ability to wrap just about anyone around your dainty little finger. I will admit you had almost convinced me there, but I think Samantha overplayed your little 'sisterly bond.'" He paused. "You and I both know you do not have a humane, nurturing bone in your body."

Leisha's lips thinned slightly.

With anger bubbling up through her chest, Samantha was on her feet before she knew it and got right in Tafari's face. "You know nothing, you self-righteous jerk! This woman was once your wife. How dare you treat her that way! I can't believe she is so quick to forgive you of everything even after how you treated her." Samantha breathed hard. "I know Leisha better than you ever will, and you want to know why? It's because you're blind! You see only in black and white, while there are shades of all different colors staring you in the face"—turning to Leisha—"We don't need his help, Leisha." She started gathering their stuff. "Let's get out of here. We'll figure out a way to get out of this mess without begging these heartless immortals."

Leisha appeared stunned by Samantha's outburst, saying nothing, and proceeded to walk away with Samantha, leaving Tafari speechless, his mouth hanging open.

CHAPTER 17

Leisha had a strange sense of satisfaction brimming within her as they entered their hotel room. In all her many years, no one had ever stood up for her like that. And this little wonder named Samantha did just that, burrowing her way even deeper into Leisha's heart.

Samantha went into the bathroom to change and came out wearing a tank top and pajama bottoms. She was looking rather glum when she sat next to Leisha on the bed. "I'm sorry I lost my temper like that, Leisha," she said. "I don't know what came over me. I'm just a little nobody, but there I was, yelling at a two thousand-year-old immortal who is probably connected to all kinds of power." She chuckled.

Leisha grinned. "I have to admit, it was quite the sight. The look on Tafari's face was priceless. He looked like he'd just been dropped into the Twilight Zone or something!"

They laughed together for some time, but when it died

down Samantha took on an apologetic look. "I wish I had thought more clearly, though. I killed any chances of us going to the immortals. That means Ptah will punish you." Samantha paused. "Is it going to be worse than what my dad did to you?" she asked softly, her eyes wide.

"Well, it will probably be more painful," Leisha admitted. "But it won't be as bad, because unlike your dad, I know Ptah's purpose." She shuddered. "That was why it was so frightening when I was strapped down in the compound," she whispered. "I had no idea why your dad was hurting me, or how long it was going to last. I only knew the pain."

"I'm so sorry, Leisha," Samantha's voice trembled.

Leisha shook off the memory and gave her a side hug. "It was not your fault, and it's over now. There is nothing to be sorry about." She pulled Samantha's chin up to meet her gaze. "Don't let any of it trouble you, all right. It's in the past now."

"That may be in the past, but whenever I think about what my dad may be doing this very moment, or what he will do to someone else . . . I get nightmares knowing that I'm related to someone as frightening as him." She paused. "I need to tell you something. When we were with the vampires . . . I spoke to Ptah about—"

A knock at the door interrupted Samantha. Leisha instantly stood as she sensed the heartbeat of an immortal.

"It's an immortal," she alerted Samantha. "I can feel his heartbeat."

"How do you know it's an immortal's heartbeat?"

Samantha whispered curiously.

"They have a slower heartbeat, a steadier rhythm. Human heartbeats tend to go up and down more frequently." Leisha explained, approaching the door. She looked through the peephole and saw Tafari looking very grim.

Leisha wished she had changed into something more sophisticated; she was still in her swimsuit with her loose beach pants on. Stifling a sigh, she opened the door. He always saw her at her worst, it seemed.

Leisha didn't say anything, but just looked at him, waiting for him to explain why he had followed them home.

Tafari cleared his throat. "While I am sure that there are things you are hiding from me, I am positive that Samantha was not acting back at the beach."

"Why thank you *so* much," Samantha called sarcastically from the bed. "Your trust in your fellow beings is overwhelming."

Hiding a smile, Leisha held the door wide. "Come in, Tafari," she said coolly. "We can continue the conversation if you like."

He nodded and entered the room. There were two chairs and a table next to the window. He pulled one of the chairs to the wall and sat. Leisha rejoined Samantha on the edge of the bed.

It was awkwardly silent for a minute, until Tafari finally broke the restrain. "I apologize for allowing my anger to overrule my logic on the beach. I must admit I do not entirely understand what it is you want of me, Leisha. Just to take Samantha to my home indefinitely?"

Leisha sighed and shook her head. "Not exactly. She needs to be protected, and I do believe that you are best suited for the duty, but I don't want her to stay for long." She paused, trying to find a way to explain without being offensive. "Samantha is quite unique as she is, and I want it to stay that way." She held his gaze. "I don't want her to become an immortal any more than I want her to be a vampire. Do you understand?"

He smiled ruefully. "I cannot promise that my people will not try to convince her to join them. If she truly is as special as you say, then they will want her for themselves." He glanced at Samantha, who was looking mildly irritated. "Just what is so special about her anyway?" he mused.

"I don't think you'd understand even if I tried to explain it to you." She hesitated. "So, what do you say, Tafari? Will you take care of Samantha until I can be sure that I have an even safer place for her to stay?"

"You expect me to answer you now? You have not explained very much to me about this situation. What about the government looking for you? Are you going to explain that to me?"

Leisha had no desire to tell Tafari about that. Instead, she kept herself composed. "I don't believe it is anything you will have to deal with. What happened last week is on a need-to-know basis, and you don't fall into that category."

Samantha piped up, "I don't think it needs to be all that confidential, Leisha. Besides, you don't know my dad." She grimaced. "Well, I don't know him either, really. But from

what my mom told me—and from the look in his eyes when I left him—I'd bet there is a possibility of him trying to find me. If that is the case, then Tafari needs to know anyway."

Leisha did not like Samantha's upfront honesty at the moment, and communicated that with a hard look and a shake of her head.

Samantha returned the stare, before turning to Tafari and explained everything that had happened at the compound. Leisha felt completely mortified under Tafari's scrutiny when Samantha explained how they had tortured her to test her pain threshold.

"So, you knew where Leisha was because your father told you about all this?" Tafari asked.

Samantha dropped her head. "No, my dad would never divulge something about his work like that." She looked up and squared her shoulders as if she had come to some kind of decision. "I knew Leisha was there because I had a vision about it."

"No!" Leisha's shout came out too late. She did not think to warn Samantha against telling people about her ability, because she thought Samantha needed reassurance that she was still normal and could be accepted for what she was. Now, she sat horrified, staring at Tafari's stunned expression.

Leisha stood, closing the gap between her and Tafari. "Tafari, if you tell anyone else, so help me, I will hunt you down and anyone else who knows, do you hear me? I will not have the immortals use Samantha as a tool!"

Samantha gasped behind her. Tafari stood and pierced Leisha's eyes with a cold stare.

"Has she seen anything about the child?" he whispered.

"Get out," Leisha said through clenched teeth. "You will not touch one hair on her head."

He studied her for a long while, searching for something—what it was, Leisha did not know. Then his thumb brushed across her lips, leaving a tingling sensation. Leisha sucked in a breath of air, but did not move.

"You are very protective of this girl," he murmured. "I wonder if your motives are entirely pure." He cocked his head to the side. "Does Ptah know about her?"

Leisha shook her head, still taken aback by his soft touch. What was he doing to her?

"Interesting," he said as he stepped back and sat down again. "You can relax, Leisha. Her secret is safe with me."

Leisha exhaled and sagged her shoulders.

"I have seen the prophecy child," Samantha said, unexpectedly.

"Samantha!"

Samantha looked at her and shrugged. "I don't see the harm in telling him since he promised not to tell anyone else."

Leisha put a hand to her temple. "You are too trusting."

Samantha shrugged again.

"What did you see?" Tafari asked, excitement laced in his tone.

Samantha explained the vision to him, omitting the part of him and Leisha arguing. When she was finished, he looked at her in awe.

"You are going to be present at his birth? Extraordinary! No one else has seen any visions like that. You are indeed special, Samantha."

The girl blushed slightly at his praise. Leisha just sat there.

"I don't know about that," Samantha said. "It's probably just by pure luck that I'll be there to witness it."

Tafari did not comment but still looked at her with a newfound respect. Then he turned to Leisha. "So, it seems you do not have much of a plan at the moment. You just want me to watch over her, and that is it?"

Leisha opened her mouth with the intent to convince him to take her along as well, but seeing his eyes alight in wonder like that caused her heart to beat a little faster. She saw so much life and passion in him that she simply could not bring herself to lie to him. In that one moment, she didn't care about the consequences if she decided not to spy for Ptah.

She closed her mouth and then opened it again. "I just need to know that she is well cared for while I figure things out. If you can just give me a way to contact you, that will be fine. You can buy a prepaid cellular for me to call." She paused. "But you must give me your word that you will take good care of her, and that nothing will happen to her while I'm away."

"Wait," Samantha said before Tafari could respond, confused and almost panicky. "You have to come, too, Leisha. It won't be safe if you don't come." She turned to Tafari. "I won't go with you if she doesn't come along. There will be absolutely no negotiating around that."

Tafari looked puzzled. He seemed torn, sitting there arguing with himself. Leisha wished she could read his mind.

Before Tafari could respond, Leisha became distracted by someone's heartbeat out in the hall. It was beating quickly in either nervousness or anticipation, she was not certain. The person paused in front of her door before continuing on again.

She went to open the door to see if he had put something there. She looked down and saw an object—a stainless steel cylinder—slipped under the door. The top suddenly opened and white gas poured into the room.

Leisha cursed and rushed to Samantha. She pulled the pillowcase off a pillow and put it over the girl's nose.

"Window," called Tafari. He picked up Samantha and went to open it. Leisha had been holding her breath the entire time and thought it odd when she started seeing doubles of everything. Shaking her head to clear it, she hurried to the window. Tafari was already on the ledge with Samantha in his arms. She could see two of him narrowly gazing on her with eyes that seemed to question if she was all right.

She moved in slow motion to pull herself up to the ledge, but could not seem to find the strength for it. She tried again but toppled forward, falling toward the ground six stories below.

She vaguely remembered Tafari swearing some illicit profanities, and realized that she was no longer moving toward the ground. She looked up to see the immortal holding her ankle in a firm grip. She tried to shake her head again, but stopped when it made her dizziness worse. Her mind felt clear, but her body had failed to function.

Before she could reach up to the ledge, Tafari swung her effortlessly up to the ledge where she landed in a heap. Her brain and mouth coordination was lamed as she tried to muster a word of thanks. Nothing came out except for a slur of inaudible sounds. It took her an entire ten seconds to look up at Tafari and Samantha. They seemed fine. Samantha was looking down at her with worry lines creasing her brow, while Tafari was glancing back through the window into their room.

"No one has tried to enter yet," he said. He surveyed the building, looking first down and then up. "The ledge below us is at too steep of an angle. We should climb up to the next level. From there, we'll take the elevator to my car."

Samantha nodded and gestured to Leisha. "Why is she like this? What was in that gas?"

Tafari seemed puzzled. "I am not sure. I can only assume it was something that absorbs into the skin. I assume only Leisha was affected because she was closest. I do not think the gas had time to reach us before we were out the window."

Looking down at Leisha, Tafari said impassively, "She appears to be incapacitated. I will have to carry her. Will you be able to climb up on your own, or do you need help?"

Samantha looked down and swallowed. "I think can manage," she said breathlessly.

Tafari picked Leisha up and cradled her with his left arm. "I will go first and let her rest on the ledge. Then, I will climb back down and make sure you do not fall."

Leisha moved her hands to grip Tafari so he did not need to hold her, but they moved too slowly. He was able to work his way up from one ledge to the other using only his right hand. Once he was on the higher ledge, he laid her down, a gentle tenderness in his expression.

She rested her eyes as Tafari went back down to help Samantha. When they were both up on the ledge, Tafari picked Leisha up again, walking along the ledge until they found a window to an unoccupied room and went inside.

Tafari set Leisha on her feet. She was able to keep standing on her own. The drugs were starting the wear off, but she was still moving slowly. At least, her vision was normal again.

"Can you speak yet?" Tafari asked.

Leisha opened her mouth, but nothing came out.

"That would be a no," he said. He walked to the door and opened it slightly. "I do not see anyone in the hall. We will go to the parking garage at once."

Samantha put her arm through Leisha's and guided her behind Tafari. Leisha felt frustration burning through her.

They walked warily to the elevator. Leisha knew it would have been safer to take the stairs, but she also knew Tafari had chosen the elevator because of her weakened condition. She pointed to the door that led to the stairs and Tafari shook his head slightly.

The elevator doors opened and they walked into the empty awning. Leisha was feeling better by the minute and smiled reassuringly at Samantha.

Tafari turned his back on the door to face Leisha and Samantha as the elevator began its descent. "Would anyone like to explain what all of that was about?"

"I'm not sure," Samantha said timidly. "It could have been ... maybe ... my dad?"

At that exact moment, the doors opened to reveal Mason with another taller brown-skinned man, waiting impatiently for the elevator. They looked surprised to see them.

Leisha immediately pulled Samantha behind her and crouched in a defensive position.

Tafari, who was a little behind since he did not recognize them, was pushing the button to close the elevator doors when Mason and his partner pulled out their guns. Leisha recognized them as tranquilizer guns they had previously used on her.

The men stood there with their guns pointed, but did not shoot, uncertain of what to do.

Before Mason was able to come to a decision, the doors

closed on their dumbfounded expressions and the elevator continued its course.

"I imagine they will not be far behind," Tafari observed.

"No," Leisha said hoarsely, her throat as dry as parchment. She needed to feed very soon, especially after the stress her body had to go through from the drugs, but she pushed the thought away. First, they needed to rid themselves of Mason and any other agents around.

Leisha glanced back at Samantha as they waited to get to the garage. The girl was trembling. She caught Leisha looking at her and forced a small smile. "I won't let him take you again," she said in a shaky voice.

Huffing, Leisha smirked.

The elevator doors opened and Tafari quickly checked their surroundings before turning to the women. "As far as I can tell, it is clear, but there are too many cars to be sure."

Leisha strained her ears. "I can hear three different heartbeats, but they are all beating normally. I'd assume if someone was waiting for us already, their heartbeat would increase at least a little."

Nodding, Tafari proceeded to lead them to his car. They tried to hurry, crouching between cars, hoping to remain unseen. The garage appeared empty, and they made it to his vehicle without incident.

The drugs now almost wearing off, besides the lingering thirst, Leisha felt like herself once again.

They pulled out of the garage, their tires screeched as they turned a corner. For about five minutes, everyone

remained quiet in the car, staying alert to make sure they did not encounter any more unpleasant surprises.

"We have a tail," Tafari said, looking at the rearview mirror. "The black Lincoln four cars back."

Leisha looked back and recognized the passengers in the Lincoln. They were Mason and his friend.

"Now what should we do?" asked Samantha.

Turning around, Leisha put a comforting hand on her shoulder. "They can't do much with so many people around. It's a Friday night and we are in the downtown area. We're safe for the moment."

Samantha didn't seem comforted by that, but there was not much else Leisha could do for her. A torrent of emotions flitted across the girl's face, and Leisha knew no words would make her feel better.

CHAPTER 18

Mason silently cursed to himself while Andres followed the blue Honda. Before today, he had been so sure their plan would work. Andres had been following Leisha and Samantha closely, and they knew it should not be a problem immobilizing Leisha and getting Samantha out. They even put a tracking device in their car just in case Leisha somehow escaped with Samantha.

What they were not prepared for was the man who helped them escape.

"Have you thought of something yet?" Andres asked.

Mason growled with frustration. "I'm still thinking." He figured they would try and stay in the busy part of the city to keep safe among the tourists. He needed to think of which weapon in his arsenal to use on that creature in such a public setting. Plus, he would probably need to use

something on the black man who was with them. Most of his weapons were specifically designed for catching vampires, and he wasn't sure if the man was a vampire or not. Even if he wasn't, it could still work on him, although it might also kill him.

"I think maybe we could . . ." Mason didn't finish his sentence when the blue Honda pulled to the curb in front of a movie theater. "They think they can lose us in the movies?" Mason scoffed. This may be easier than he'd thought. He and Andres had worked together for years doing all kinds of covert operations. They knew how to move through a crowd, but a movie theater would be even better. With most people seated, they could make quick searches and eliminate possibilities.

Andres shared a knowing look as he pulled into a parking spot on the side of the road. "We'll have your daughter back in no time," he said with a predatory smile.

LEISHA AND TAFARI WERE STILL arguing over their impromptu plan while he bought tickets to a movie. "It should be me," Leisha said emphatically, trying to keep her voice down. "I am faster than you and can lose them more easily."

Tafari shook his head and ushered her and Samantha into the dark theater. "No," he said firmly. Leisha knew that tone too well; he had made up his mind and was not willing to negotiate. "You are still not at your full strength, but you are right about running faster than me. That is why you need to take Samantha to the boat. I will divert them so they are unaware of where you go. I will meet you there in a few hours."

They had been arguing about whom Samantha would follow ever since they decided that it would be easier to lose their pursuers on foot. Leisha could move faster than a car, and would be able to maneuver more easily on foot. Tafari told them of his boat that was docked near the same beach they went to earlier that day. Once they lost Mason and his cohort, they could sail to Puerto Rico before flying out from there.

Leisha was almost grateful for Mason—it appeared that Tafari would now be taking them with him to the immortals. She pushed away the guilty feeling and focused on what was at hand.

"They do not know me," Tafari was saying. "They are after you and Samantha. Even if they did catch me, they would have no need of me. You just get Samantha out of here as fast as you can." He gave her a little push to the back exit, with every expectation of her complying. "By the way, my boat is called *The Seeker*. I do not think you will have a hard time finding it."

Tafari took a seat and waited for Mason and his associate.

Grabbing Samantha's hand, Leisha turned to leave. "Let's get out of here," she mumbled. Samantha had a small smile on her lips but remained tactfully quiet. They walked out the exit and into an alley between buildings. "Get on my back, Samantha. And hold tight. You may need to keep

your face down. The wind will be very strong."

Samantha looked a little nervous. "You promise this won't hurt?" she asked.

Leisha shook her head. "Just keep your head down and tucked into my back. That should prevent any damage to your skin from the high winds."

Samantha nodded jerkily, clearly not happy about this, and climbed onto Leisha's back, piggyback style.

Leisha heard a noise and looked to the entrance of the alleyway. The man who had been with Mason was pulling something out of his jacket, heading toward them.

Not wanting to discover what other surprises they had for her, Leisha squatted down before jumping high into the air, soaring for about a hundred yards before lightly landing on the roof of a tall building. She was jumping high and leaping from building to building, enjoying the freedom she always felt when she coasted the sky. Samantha had a death grip around her, panting hard.

Leisha stayed on the roofs for as long as she could to avoid having to navigate through the crowd, which was thinning considerably. They were at the edge of the city now. Leaping, she landed by the freeway and immediately ran along the road, while keeping a good distance from it to avoid running into anyone. It took only twenty minutes to get to the docks. Once there, she stopped to let Samantha down to walk on her own.

The girl was sweating and shaking almost violently, her head tucked against Leisha's shoulder, her arms still locked around them. Leisha reached up and gently pried her ankles apart. They stiffly came off her waist. Samantha let go with her hands to slide to the ground.

Leisha crouched next to her. "You all right?" She knew her vital signs were just fine, but was not sure if Samantha was able to handle the shock of going that fast.

Samantha jerked her head up and down, and then said through clenched teeth, "I don't want to do that again. Ever."

Leisha smiled. She was just fine, indeed. "I thought you liked fast cars and whatnot."

Samantha opened and closed her hands, which were no doubt cramped from her tight grip. "It's different when you are sitting comfortably with a seatbelt behind a windshield!"

Laughing, Leisha directed Samantha to stretch out her tight muscles. After ten minutes of stretching, the girl seemed ready to move on. She had stopped shaking, but was beginning to shiver, her sweat turning cold under the sea breeze.

"Let's get you out of those sweaty clothes and let you relax on the boat, shall we?" Leisha took the girl's arm and guided her to the docks, looking for the *The Seeker*. She found it in no time. *The Seeker* was a large yacht that looked like it could carry twenty people comfortably. Leisha was impressed, and a little excited. The last time she sailed was when she first came to America, and with all of the modern technology available now, sailing would be a much more pleasant experience.

They were twenty feet away from getting on the yacht when she saw someone lean over the side, watching them. Leisha realized too late that there were other immortals on this boat. Tafari had brought backup. She stopped, her hand still on Samantha's arm.

Leisha forced a smile she was not even sure the immortal could see in the fading light. "Tafari sent me ahead of him," she said. "He will be meeting us here in about three hours or so."

The man on the boat scoffed and jumped over the side, landing a few feet away from them. "You think me a fool, vamp?" his tone dripped with disdain.

This man was tall, about six foot five with wide shoulders to support his brawny muscle. His jaw was angular, and his face somewhat puckish; his sensual lips and prominent nose made him look relatively handsome. He glared her down with sage green eyes, as if he was ready for some gruesome murder.

Leisha could feel Samantha tense, her heart beating rapidly. Leisha squeezed the girl's arm. "It's okay," she said. "He won't hurt you." She looked pointedly at the menacing immortal. "Will you? You wouldn't harm an innocent, young girl, right?"

"If she's with you, then she is far from innocent." A slight Scottish brogue in his speech, he must be a highland warrior of some sort—he held himself as superior and noble. And with a strapping physique to boot, he was not an immortal to trifle with.

"Look," Leisha said patiently, "all you have to do is wait for a couple of hours for Tafari to show up and confirm my story. If he doesn't, then you have plenty of men aboard to take me down and kill me. I hold no threat to you at the moment."

His scowl could have turned her to stone. "I'm not an idiot. I know you killed him. I warned him that you were just luring him into a trap!" he growled. "He wouldn't listen to me. Well, at least I can claim vengeance for him." With that, he lunged forward.

Leisha pushed Samantha to the side and met the charging immortal with a swift kick to his gut. The air whooshed out of his lungs, but it did not stop him. He swung his arm and gave her a blow, nearly taking her head off. Crouching on the ground from the blow, she shot out her leg to trip him. He fell with a big thud, and Leisha flipped herself up into the air, landing on her feet over him. "I don't need this now, so don't make me hurt you. I'm trying to be gentle."

Rage flashed in his eyes as he moved like the wind to grab her swimsuit and tug her down. Before she could react, she was on her stomach with him sprawled atop her, yanking her head back at a painful angle.

Leisha was trying very hard not to fight back; she would have to be on the same boat with these people for a while, and wanted to get along as best as she could.

"Get. Off. Now," she gasped. It was hard to sound intimidating with her head pulled back so far she could barely speak.

"I think not," he said in her ear, spraying spittle on her neck.

Leisha bucked him off her and spun before he could topple her again. As he charged toward her, she brought up her foot to kick him again. This time, he was prepared for it, jumping up above it to land directly on her. She spun out of the way and brought herself up into a defensive crouch.

"I don't want to fight you," she all but seethed. "You have enough immortals on the boat to outnumber me. Why don't we just sit tight and wait for Tafari, so he can clear this up for us?"

One of the men watching from the side of the boat spoke up. "Listen to her, Sean. She speaks logically."

"It's a trick, nothing more!" Sean growled.

"What if it is not," another argued. "What if you are defying Tafari's orders by trying to kill her?"

That seemed to catch Sean's attention for a moment. His brow furrowed in thought for a few minutes before speaking again. "You give me your word that you will not raise any violence on that boat?"

"I promise that I won't, except in self-defense," Leisha said.

Sean stood, watching her for a minute longer before straightening himself. "I will allow you to come aboard if you will allow me to bind you in chains. Just as a precaution, you understand."

He was trying to sound reasonable, but Leisha saw the mockery in his eyes. He wanted to humiliate her, and she grudgingly admitted to herself she would need to be docile with this Sean until Tafari came back. She could not keep herself from glaring at him; but, she nodded her agreement.

Smiling smugly, Sean gestured for her and Samantha to climb onboard before him. She turned her back on him and kept her hand protectively on Samantha's shoulder as they walked up the plank.

Once they were onboard, six of the men surrounded them, some holding Uzis, and others machetes. Samantha gasped, backing up into Leisha, who squeezed her shoulder in reassurance. "They won't hurt you," she said. "They just have to be cautious. I'm the threat here, not you."

Samantha nodded but still stayed as close to Leisha as she could.

The man who had called over to Sean approached Leisha, carrying chains that looked like they had been in the water. Leisha assumed the chains must be connected to the anchor. *Oh great,* Leisha thought, *not only do I have to be humiliated by wearing shackles, I also get to smell like fish and seaweed, too.*

"My name is Ian," the man said. "Would you mind sitting over there while I get you situated?" He had the same accent and build as Sean, though not quite so tall—about six foot three—his hair lighter. The two men were definitely related; they shared the same sage green eyes and angular face.

Leisha nodded and walked to the seat he had gestured,

toward the stern.

Ian worked the chains from her shoulders all the way down to her ankles, pulling tight to leave no wriggle room. Leisha gritted her teeth as the chains pinched against her skin. It almost felt like a form of torture, but Ian was being polite, and she did not want to push her luck. It was going to be a long voyage.

"At least someone on this boat is nice," Samantha muttered, watching Ian.

Ian glanced at her as he put a lock over the chains on Leisha's ankles. "Don't you be thinkin' anything good of me, lass. I would be more than pleased to decapitate your friend here, but I respect my leader and I'll be waitin' on his orders."

Leisha hoped Samantha would say no more. If the girl continued to offend him, he would lose more than control over his accent. Samantha crossed her arms and glared at all of the men as she sat next to Leisha, saying nothing.

The men drifted off to different areas on the sailboat and waited in silence for almost an hour. Samantha continued to look to the docks, biting her nails all the while. Leisha studied the men as they worked. All of them seemed to be in low spirits, probably because they thought Tafari was dead. Even so, they continued with their work as a team alongside each other, each man understanding exactly what his duty was.

Sean murmured something to one of his comrades, and then sauntered over to Leisha, putting his foot up on the rail, resting his elbow on his knee. "Looks like he's not going to show." He smiled cruelly. "I knew you to be a liar. All of you vamps are the same. I am sorry for Tafari, but I must say he was a fool to think he could trust you."

"He doesn't trust me, but he knows a good opportunity when he sees one."

Sean scoffed. "I cannot imagine what you have to offer him. He's not into slut vamps who whore themselves for blood."

Leisha's blood rose to a boil, and it took all of her effort to restrain herself from breaking the chains so she could beat the man to a pulp. She knew there was no use in trying to defend herself to him, and kept her mouth clamped shut.

He chuckled and then gave another one of his smug smiles. "What's the matter there, vamp? Don't like it when I call a spade a spade?" He straightened. "I am going to enjoy slaughtering you. It is going to be a long and painful death. That's what you deserve for killing Tafari. He was one of our best." He had positioned himself so close to Leisha that she had to strain her head to keep eye contact. "First, I think I'll start with the skin. I'll peel it off one layer at a time all over your entire body. Then I'll poke around with your ligaments. That, I hear, is supposed to be excruciating."

Samantha made a gagging sound and bent over the rail.

Leisha glared at Sean. "It has not been three hours yet, moron. And even if the time is up, the least you could do is

spare the girl. She doesn't live the way we do. She is completely innocent."

He was studying Samantha, who was now sitting back against the rail, her eyes watering, her lower lip quivering. "You may be right about her," he admitted. "But I don't care if it has not been three hours yet, it's been long enough and I know he's not comin' back."

He grabbed a fistful of chains at Leisha's chest and hauled her up. "You are nothin' but scum to me," he growled before pulling his head back slightly and spitting in her face.

Leisha's temper came to an all-time high. She closed her eyes and mustered all of the strength in her to push against the chains with her arms. They finally broke from her strain, though it taxed heavily on her energy, her body shaking from the effort. She had no time to free her legs since Sean was standing so close to her.

The immortal looked stunned when the chains broke. Leisha seized the moment and punched him in the nose with the heel of her hand, cramming fractured bones into his brain. The blow would have killed a human, but not an immortal. It only detained him a little.

She stooped, sliding the chains down her legs and off her feet. Sean was coming to as she crouched over him and flipped him onto his stomach, yanking her right arm firmly around his neck while bending his left arm behind him at a painful angle.

Leaning close to his ear, she said, "I have put a lot of effort into being civil," She enunciated each word precisely.

"But you have done everything in your power to antagonize me. So, what should we do about it? I have no problem killing you since you're just begging for me to do it, but I'm still willing to forgive you if you will just let me be until Tafari arrives."

"Why would Tafari be comin'?" He rasped through the blood that poured into his mouth. "I know you killed him just like you're going to kill me. You are what you are, demon monster, don't pretend anything else with me."

"Leisha!" shouted a voice.

Leisha looked up to see Tafari standing at the entrance of the boat, his silvery blue eyes sparkling, his nostrils flared. Immediately letting go of Sean, she backed up. "It's not what you think," she started.

"I do not want to hear it." His body was shaking with contained violence.

Leisha looked away from his gaze and kept her face expressionless. She did not want Tafari to keep seeing her at her worst, but his timing seemed impeccable for it.

Sean got up to his feet, swaying slightly. "Tafari," he grunted. "I thought you were dead."

Tafari took a long breath and exhaled, tension building in his lungs. "Far from it, Sean. I hope you were not provoking our temporary ally here."

As Sean stopped and looked back at Leisha—she suppressed a smile. He turned back to Tafari. "She really is to come with us, sir?"

Tafari sighed, suddenly appearing quite weary. "Yes. We

will be sailing to Puerto Rico tonight, and from there we head home."

"Home? You mean to take them there with us? She'll tell all the other vamps where we are! We may as well hang up a sign saying, 'All vamps come and get us here!'"

Tafari gathered himself, his face intensely dark and forbidding. "I will not have you questioning me, Sean. You do as you are told, and when we get back, maybe we should discuss with the council about trusting the elders to know what they are doing."

Sean's back stiffened with the admonition. He did not look back at Leisha and Samantha, but withdrew himself without another word.

Leisha and Tafari stood for a moment staring at each other. She could see some blood spots on his clothes, but knew he was fully healed from whatever wounds he had gotten. She had the craziest urge to walk up to him and kiss all the wounds inflicted on him—she clenched her fists against the feeling. Tafari had just witnessed her attacking one of his men, and at the moment, he did not appear incredibly friendly. Neither one could think of anything to say.

Samantha jumped up and ran to Tafari, giving him a huge hug. "I'm so glad you're all right, Tafari! I was so worried that they would capture you and do horrible experiments to you."

Tafari laughed easily, and Leisha felt somewhat jealous.

"They did not follow you?" Leisha asked.

Tafari fixed his gaze on Samantha. "No, but I daresay, they will be needing a few days of recovery time." Before Samantha could ask any questions, Tafari put a reassuring hand on her arm. "Do not worry about your father, he will be just fine."

Samantha immediately eased. "Thank you so much for all that you're doing for us. I know we'll never be able to repay you."

Tafari smiled again. "Come," he said, "let me show you where you'll be staying for the trip." He led Samantha by touching the small of her back, glancing back at Leisha to make sure she was coming. Leisha quickly veiled her eyes with her lashes so he would not see her apparent envy. How many times had she wished for him to be at ease with her like that? He had once looked at her with so much tenderness and adoration that it hurt deeply to see the loathing he now had for her.

Stop feeling sorry for yourself, Leisha gave herself a mental nudge. Squaring her shoulders, she followed them below deck with all the pride she could exhibit.

MASON WAS DEFINITELY GETTING SLOPPY. Andres had been studiously observing him since he arrived in Batal, and it was obvious that Mason was wrought with emotion instead of his usual cold, unquestionable logic. Although Mason tried to pretend he still had it, Andres could see he had lost his cool exterior. Mason looked disappointed, and that did not happen often.

They did not speak as they walked through their hotel. "It will be all right," Andres started. "At least now you know your daughter is still alive."

Mason's face turned bitter. "She may be alive, but I have no clue what they've done to her. She might've been brainwashed. But at least I don't think she's one of *them* yet," his voice dripping with disgust. Sighing, he turned to open the door to his room. "We'll be moving early in the morning. I'm hoping my contacts will have something for me in a few hours. They're watching the airports, trains, and bus stations. I'm sure we'll catch up to them soon enough." His voice hardened. "Next time, we will be prepared for any scenario."

Andres nodded. "I will only need a few hours rest to recover from the tumble, *mi amigo*. Just knock when you hear something."

Mason nodded and closed the door behind him.

Andres shook his head as he walked into his own room. Mason was gone, and there was no getting him back. It was so strange to believe that the man who had been standing before him moments ago was once his mentor when he first joined the CIA's most elite team of assassins. A lot of men had lost it somewhere along the road, but Mason had always held it together—he'd been the strong one, dedicated to his duty to the American government, never allowing anything to disturb his conscience. Andres did not know what to think of him now.

Pulling out his cell, he dialed Sampson's direct line. It connected on the second ring.

"We just got back from the attempt to retrieve Samantha," Andres reported with no preamble. "We failed. They had an ally with them, but I am positive he is not a vampire."

"Do you know what he is? Is he just human?"

"No. He didn't move as fast as the vampires, but he healed at an astounding rate." Andres kept his tone cool and withdrawn as he recalled the black man he had fought just a few hours ago. "I shot him at least twice; his body seemed to heal instantaneously."

"Really?" Sampson sounded surprised, which said a lot. "Those vampires do not heal so fast. I wonder what he is? You don't suppose he could be a werewolf? I didn't think they existed, but after the discovery of vampires, maybe werewolves are roaming the earth as well."

"I doubt he is a werewolf. He did not remotely look like a wolf at all. He fought well, though. Even with Mason and myself against him, he was able to best us."

"That is saying a lot now, isn't it?"

Andres did not bother to respond.

A pause. "Continue to help Mason with whatever he asks, and report to me every forty-eight hours unless something pressing needs to be reported before then. And if you can capture this man who is with them, I would love to add him to our specimens in the lab."

"Understood." Andres hung up.

CHAPTER 19

They had been sailing for five days, and Samantha enjoyed every one of them. She was able to push aside her anxieties about her father, and everything else with the vampires, as she sat on the deck soaking up the sun and the saltwater breeze.

The immortals were finally warming up to her, and they all became somewhat protective, watching out for her safety—it was a touch on the overwhelming side. When she slipped on some water, Ian rushed to her side to help her up, insisting on escorting her below deck and wiping up the puddle of water before she returned.

On a different occasion, she had merely mentioned her embarrassment of having to wear the same pajamas in front of everyone the entire time, and within the hour, one of the smaller built men named James had given her a pair of his pants and a t-shirt. She had to cinch a belt over the pants and roll them up, but it was nice to have clean clothes to wear. But upon reminding him that Leisha would probably also need a change of clothes, he lost his smile and quickly insisted he had no other clothes to spare.

Samantha sighed thinking of Leisha, who'd been confined in their room for the duration, avoiding everyone, including Samantha. Tried as she might to not think too much about it to prevent herself from feeling hurt, Samantha convinced herself that Leisha might just be recuperating from her injuries. But even that did not fully deflect her from being surprised by Leisha's sudden change of behavior. In a normal day, Leisha's pride would take over, forcing her to show nonchalance.

This whole hermit business had gone on for far too long—Leisha must be hurting more than Samantha could decipher. She had to seek out Tafari and talk to him.

Tafari was a busy man. Samantha was only able to catch him at dinner in the evenings. He told her he'd been busy communicating with the council, a group of people, as he explained, who lead the immortals and make sure everyone was doing their duty. Although she was curious as to why he was not a part of the counsel, she did not pursue the question. As stressed as he'd appeared, Samantha had decided it best not to pry.

She found him below deck in the kitchen, talking to the cook. Samantha waited patiently for him to finish up. When he did, he smiled at her. "I did not notice you there. How are you?"

She could not help but smile back. "I actually wanted to talk to you about Leisha."

Tafari's smile faded. "What about her?"

"Well," she hesitated, "nothing, really. I just thought that . . . that maybe you could talk to your men about being a little more . . . well, polite with her?" She rushed on. "I can't imagine that she's very comfortable in our small room this whole time, and if we're going to be on this boat much longer, I think it would be good for her to come up on deck every once in a while."

His warmth was gone entirely by the time she finished, his eyes shuttered. "She is allowed to go wherever she wants on the ship, but I cannot speak to my men about actually interacting with her." Deep shadows cast on his face. "It is hard enough for them to have a vampire on board let alone not being able to lift a finger and kill her. I will ask no more of them."

Samantha frowned. "Do you all have to hate them so much?" She pushed out the memory of Annette before it could surface. "I know they can be cruel, but I have met a select few who are actually pretty decent."

He steered her along with him as he walked toward his bedroom. "Let us talk in here," he said and shut the door behind him. He gently ushered her into a chair and sat before her on his bed, his elbows resting on his knees.

"Samantha," he began, "you are young, and very sweet. I must say, in the short time I have known you, I have actually become quite fond of you."

His compliments might be flattering, but Samantha knew he was only preparing her for something she didn't want to hear. "What is it?" she asked.

"Vampires and immortals have developed all kinds of different talents over the years. They are all very different and unique, but I have noticed that a lot of vampires have the capability of luring people to them. They somehow brainwash you into thinking that you like, possibly love them."

"Yes, I already know that. In fact, Nik tried to lure me, but Leisha stopped him in time. Besides, Leisha said it was only temporary—only in their presence—so you needn't worry about me being . . . bewitched by them."

"Nik?" Tafari inquired.

Samantha waved a hand in dismissal. "Just another vampire. I'm sure you don't want to hear much about them."

"Actually, I would not mind, if you are willing to share with me your experiences," he said.

Samantha opened her mouth and then closed it. He had said it a little too pleasantly. She searched his face and saw that he was keeping it blank. "Tafari," she chided, "why would I divulge information to you when I am not supposed to give any information about the immortals to the vampires?"

Tafari smirked. "I like you, Samantha. You have wisdom beyond your years."—standing—"How about some dinner?"

They dined with the rest of the crew as usual—low-key,

easygoing. Samantha was laughing over some of the crude jokes they told, laughing even more whenever Tafari made a face at every punch line. But upon realizing that she was supposed to spy on these people, she took on a more serious demeanor.

She didn't think she could possibly spy on them anymore. They were so nice to her, thinking she was innocent. How could she betray them like that? But she also didn't like the idea of sacrificing Leisha to Ptah for her failure of reporting to him.

Tears of frustration threatened to surface, but Samantha forced them away. She could have easily confessed that whole sordid night with Ptah to Leisha back in their hotel room, but Tafari had interrupted. Now, however, nothing was stopping her. Her mind made up, Samantha headed toward her room to talk to Leisha. Maybe the vampire could help her figure out what to do.

Samantha's determination faltered when she opened the door to see Leisha huddled on the bottom bunk in the darkness. Samantha turned on the light, but when Leisha gave a weak moan in protest, she quickly turned it off.

Approaching Leisha, she put her hand on the vampire's shoulder. Leisha flinched and moved out of her grasp, but not before Samantha felt her trembling like a newborn puppy.

"What's wrong, Leisha?"

Leisha had kept her eyes closed all this while, but opened them to look up; Samantha gasped and stumbled two steps back. Leisha's eyes were dilated and bloodshot, but that was not what scared Samantha. What used to be a woman she knew now resembled an animal with eyes that projected no intelligence, only violent hunger. In that very moment, Leisha could very easily drain Samantha's life within seconds.

"Keep away from me," Leisha choked. "Stay on the other end of the ship, and keep one of the men with you always." Even to whisper seemed to take up every ounce of her being. Her strength dissipating, Leisha struggled to maintain control, gasping in pain, and then turning on her side, away from Samantha.

Samantha stood there, staring, not sure of what to do. How could she help? "I'll give you a little of my blood," she offered.

Leisha bolted upright, her head colliding with the bunk above her. "No! Stay away!" She was frantic, on the verge on panic. "If you don't . . . I'll lose control." She swallowed. "Have Tafari barricade my door, and have men ready to kill me if I try to get out." With that, she lay back down and curled in a ball, shaking so vigorously Samantha wondered if she was going to hurt herself.

"Go!" Leisha screamed.

Samantha needed no more incentive. She fled to the door and closed it, dashing above deck in search of Tafari.

CHAPTER 20

Leisha's body was on fire, The Hunger moving restlessly in her mind, waiting to be sated. She strained to keep control, not letting The Hunger take over—she'd been fighting it ever since they came aboard. It had struck even before Mason and his associate showed up; combined with the drugs they had used on her and with the energy put out to brake her chains, her body demanded to be fed, and soon.

How much longer before they made port? Even if they were to port soon, there was no guarantee her mind would be sound enough to find a murderer or rapist to kill. She couldn't deal with the guilt of killing someone innocent again.

Between now and then, Samantha must stay away from her—the smell of Samantha's sweet blood caused her to almost lose control. She'd exhausted everything she had to remain immobile on the bed when Samantha touched her. The Hunger was getting restless, and she was getting weaker. It was only a matter of time.

Leisha tensed even more when she sensed one of the immortals approaching. She cursed as the door opened, a whiff of the intoxicating scent of blood and musk permeated the room. "Get away, Tafari," she rasped. She would never be able to live with herself if she killed him.

"No." He walked right up to her bed and rolled her over to face him.

Leisha screamed and pushed herself into the wall as much as she could. "I c-can't c-c-c-control . . . it." She clenched her teeth, afraid to open her mouth for fear of biting down on him.

Tafari studied her with intense curiosity. "Samantha told me that something else takes over your will if you do not feed. Is that true?"

Leisha nodded as best she could, her body practically convulsing.

He continued to stare down at her, a sense of pity in his expression. But she was too occupied to savor the warmth on his face, trying hard not to leap on him. She squeezed her eyes shut tight, hoping he would leave immediately.

But he didn't. After what seemed like an eternity, he sat on the bed next to her.

Leisha cried at the top of her lungs, trying to turn her back, but he grabbed her arm. The pulse in his hand was like a Siren's song, begging to be taken. The Hunger overcame

her immediately and Leisha lost all control, lashing out at him.

He pushed her back, hard, the floor cracking beneath her weight, but it didn't matter; all The Hunger wanted was his blood. Bolting with insurmountable speed and strength, she toppled him to the floor. She clenched her thighs around his torso and pinned his arms to his sides, clamping his thighs down with her feet.

Tafari was now practically helpless, ripe for the taking. With her hands free, Leisha easily pushed his head to the side to expose the jugular. It beckoned, and she was more than willing to comply. She could feel him wrestling beneath her, making her urge to feed more irresistible. Too hungry to bask in the moment, she lowered her mouth without reserve.

As her lips touched his skin, Leisha's true self fought to the surface. The memory of snuggling into Tafari's neck and smelling his spicy, musky scent brought her back. She remembered how she had once felt so safe and secure in his arms, knowing that their love was endless.

Mustering all her strength to move her head back, she only managed to pull it back an inch. The Hunger was like a caged tiger, roaring and clawing at her mind, battling to possess her body. "Get out. Now," she ground out. "I don't know if I can contain it any longer. I'm going to jump off," she croaked, her throat parched. "You must leave as soon as I do."

Exerting her body to jump to the side felt like moving

through heavy molasses. Once on the side, The Hunger attacked her mind. Leisha felt her sanity strip one excruciating layer at a time. She screamed in agony and pulled herself into a fetal position to keep her body from doing something she'd regret.

"Listen to me," Tafari shouted—he might have already said it a few times. "You know how quickly I heal, that I can easily recover from blood loss. What if I gave you just a quart or more of my blood? Would that curb you enough to regain control?"

It took Leisha a couple of minutes before comprehending what Tafari was saying. It was difficult enough warring with the demon in her, let alone pay attention to her surroundings. It could work, but if it didn't . . . "I don't know if I can keep control while feeding . . ."

"I will keep you in line," Tafari reassured. It was a big risk, and Tafari knew it. Why was he allowing this? It went against everything he believed.

Leisha decided she was too desperate to worry about that. She needed blood, and Tafari was offering. She gasped out, "Okay."

"I will cut very deep into my wrist so it will bleed for a long enough time. You will only drink until I have healed. No more." Pulling out a knife, Tafari cut a deep gash on his arm. He grimaced at the pain, but it barely registered with Leisha. As soon as his knife left his wrist, her mouth was pressed to it. She drank quickly, sucking in as much as she could before his cut closed up.

Leisha slowly became more aware of herself, the tension in her body eased, her mind was her own again. She could feel Tafari's blood pouring down her throat, and it felt amazing. His blood was slightly cooler than a human's, and a lot sweeter. There was less of a coppery taste and more of a rich flavor that almost reminded her of chocolate. His memories did not bombard her while she drank.

Unknowingly, Leisha had been moaning in pleasure at the exquisite taste of Tafari's blood. Even when she realized it, she still could not seem to immediately stop herself from moaning; it was just too good. She could feel the veins closing up, and finally the skin. His cut now healed, Leisha leisurely ran her tongue along it. Nothing was going to waste.

When she finally looked up at Tafari, she saw that his eyes were filled with a look she was once familiar with, a look she had not seen in a long time—heated passion. His eyes shimmered with intense hunger and desire. Leisha's stomach tightened, a wave of heat circulated through her body, it had nothing to do with his blood.

Reaching out, Tafari slowly pushed her hair off her face. Her cheek tingled where he touched; she shivered with desire, and Tafari's body responded to it.

His head moved in slow motion, taking his time before leaning down and touching her lips with his. She knew if they could just have one kiss, it would ignite the unyielding fire and passion they had once shared. Her heart fluttered at the thought. Parting her lips slightly, she was ready to receive the man she loved.

Then, a little voice inside her brought her back to reality. She was a vampire, a demonic monster he was supposed to kill. If he was really going to kiss her, he needed to be aware of what she was and accept that.

"Tafari," she whispered.

"Leisha," he breathed.

"Thank you for giving me your blood," she said just as his lips were a hair away from hers, knowing that all it took as just one sentence to remind him of her true identity.

He paused, hovering painstakingly close, his warm breath tickling her lips. But he did not get any closer. After a long moment of gazing into each other's eyes, he straightened. She could feel a magnetic pull as he backed away from her, causing her body to ache and feel incredibly empty.

"I am glad it worked," he said, rather hoarsely. He cleared his throat, and then swallowed, a blank expression on his face. Leisha had an urge to wrap her arms around him in comfort, but that would only make him more confused. Suddenly, his eyes narrowed on her.

"Do you have the ability to lure humans?" he asked, his voice abruptly cold.

Startled by the rapid change, she only shook her head.

"Is this something that all vampires can do? They make it feel pleasurable to their victims while they suck their blood?"

"It felt good when I . . . drank?"

He only nodded curtly.

"That is very unusual. I mean . . . when I fed at the clubs, I know it didn't hurt them, although I'm pretty sure it wasn't gratifying either."

Tafari seemed to almost believe her as he leaned closer to her for a brief moment, but then closing his eyes, he sat back stiffly in a crouch. "Lying whore that you are, why should I ever believe you?" His voice became unguarded, raw. "Why should I believe you when you left me for *him!* Standing in a fluid movement, he walked to the door. It would probably be a good idea if you stayed here for the duration. No one really wants to deal with your presence." With that, he was gone, the door falling closed behind him.

Leisha blew out a breath at his exit. Tafari was not the only one feeling confusion at this turn of events, but Leisha decided to do her best not to dwell on it. Tafari was not one to follow impulses, and she doubted he would allow himself to be tempted by her again.

THE REST OF THE TRIP went by rather quickly. Leisha no longer needed to avoid Samantha and they had long talks to pass the time. Plus, it was quite entertaining vexing Tafari and the other immortals by going above to absorb the sun and feel the wind. When Tafari confronted her about it, she nonchalantly told him that since all she had to wear was her swimsuit, she had to make the best of it.

The next day, he gave her a pair of his sweats and a white

t-shirt that practically drowned her. She put them on and went above to sit with Samantha. Tafari glared at her with such intensity she thought he might actually force her to spontaneously combust.

The nights were the longest, with Samantha sleeping peacefully and Leisha having nothing to do but smell the scent of Tafari on the clothes he'd lent her, reminiscing his warm breath tickling her lips.

When they finally made port, there was a sigh of relief in everyone's mind. Once the yacht docked, the next step was to make arrangements for the flight to England, to Leisha's surprise. Though she wondered about the exact point of destination, she didn't press Tafari on the subject. He only spoke to her when he had to, and she was not feeling too enthusiastic about seeing him much either.

Leisha and Samantha went shopping, and were told to meet Tafari in a few hours at the airport. They were not worried Mason would find them—people don't generally think of checking the docks for an escape route, but Leisha still remained alert to their surroundings while they picked out clothes and shoes.

Still feeling incredibly energetic from drinking Tafari's blood, she was amazed her high lasted so long. She thought her hunger pangs would return by the time they reached Puerto Rico. To be safe, she should probably visit a dance club upon arriving in England. She would never let Tafari see her in her weakened condition ever again, especially during her stay with the immortals—she must not allow

any of them to see any sort of weakness, and not just because of her pride. Samantha's safety was her priority.

Leisha knew she would not be able to stay with the immortals for more than a few days—if that. The immortals would, of course, try to kill her; it was the only reason the counsel would even let her come with Tafari. Whatever came her way she was ready for it. She'd escape. Knowing that she'd have to eventually report back to Ptah, she decided she wasn't going to tell him much. After what Tafari had done to save her, she could not possibly betray him now.

There could never be anything between Tafari and her again, but it didn't mean she had to betray him. She might belong with her people, but she refused to do their dirty jobs—spying being one of them. Leisha was fully prepared to face Ptah. Her only concern was Samantha's safety. It was crucial for Leisha to be able to leave the immortals with a certainty that they would protect her as their own, and that they would *not* make her an immortal. She wanted Samantha to have a full, mortal life filled with love and happiness.

Her mind back in the present, Leisha was pleased to finally be wearing something else besides her swimsuit and Tafari's baggy clothes. When they reached the airport, she was also very glad to finally be wearing something that looked a little more adult in front of Tafari. Her gray pinstripe slacks and hunter green blouse gave her the sophistication she wished to show him before.

She walked with great confidence toward Tafari, Samantha in tow. Tafari handed her a ticket in lieu of a greeting.

"You will want to check in your suitcases," he said glancing down at their new luggage filled with newly purchased clothes.

"Thanks," Leisha said. She and Samantha did not have to wait very long to get their bags checked in; the airport was sparsely populated at the time.

Glancing at her ticket as they walked back to Tafari, she noted that their flight was leaving in just over an hour. "Will the rest of your men get back here in time?"

"Yes," he said, unconcerned.

As they sat waiting for the rest of the immortals to arrive, Leisha and Tafari barely spoke to each other. Samantha, on the other hand, was telling Tafari all about her new clothes Leisha had bought for her. The immortal seemed to listen with a certain enduring affection. He truly liked Samantha, which boosted Leisha's mood considerably. Tafari was a hard man to penetrate, but once he allowed someone into his heart, he could be incredibly protective over her. Maybe Leisha need not worry so much about Samantha's welfare anymore.

Ian and Sean arrived first, and they did not so much as glance in Leisha's direction, which was an improvement compared to the looks of raging murder they had given her on the yacht. After assembling everyone, Tafari led them to the gate where they boarded the plane without

incident. It seemed Tafari was not the only one who re-garded Samantha with a bit of affection—it appeared the girl was already on her way to win over most of the men's hearts.

The flight was half full; the group spread out on the plane after takeoff. Leisha sat toward the front just to ir-ritate the rest of the immortals—having to look at her was enough to offend them. She had nothing else to do on their long flight, and grating their nerves would help pass the time.

Samantha and Tafari sat six rows back, and Leisha caught the tail end of Samantha relaying her mother's death to Tafari. Leisha was glad Samantha could see Tafari as someone to confide in.

They were silent for a time. Leisha assumed Samantha was trying not to cry after speaking of her bereavement. Then, Samantha spoke up, sounding just fine.

"Why do you hate Leisha so much?" she asked Tafari.

"Why do you love her so much?" he countered.

"That's easy. It's because even though she has been sur-rounded by death and darkness, and even though she lost everything she ever loved, she came out on top. I just can't believe how strong she is to survive so much. I thought I would never be able to recover from losing my mom, but when I see what Leisha has been through, I know that life will go on for me, too."

Leisha felt her heart stir at Samantha's praise.

"You do not see her as you should," Tafari was saying.

"She did not lose everything she loved, she gave it up. And of course she is surrounded by death because she brings death to those around her. She is no longer human, Samantha, and you need to remember that."

Samantha huffed. "You're not human, either, Tafari, and I still trust you to do the right thing. Why does Leisha have to be so different?"

"I may not exactly be human, but I still have my soul. I will not go to hell when I leave this earth."

"Leisha has a soul, too," she said hotly without raising her voice. "You know she does believe she's going to hell, don't you? She knew that when she decided to become a vampire, but she didn't care because of what she was saving."

There was a lengthy pause before Tafari spoke again. "Just what exactly did she think she was saving?" Every syllable was greatly enunciated.

It was Samantha's turn to hesitate. "It's not my story to tell," she finally said. "Maybe you should ask her sometime."

Tafari sighed. "I did not need any explanation. My little girl told me, through a lot of tears, every detail of what happened. She had vivid nightmares about that night for years. It took her a long time to overcome the terror, and the grief."

"I don't understand. If Adanne told you what happened, then why are you condemning Leisha for it?"

"Excuse me? Why would I not be? She made a choice and when she made it Adanne lost her mother, and I lost

my wife, forever. There is not even any hope that I will get to see my Leisha in the next life!" Leisha heard him stand up and walk toward the bathrooms in the back.

She shook her head. Now she was glad she had never tried to explain herself to Tafari. He knew the whole story already. Tafari and Adanne might hate her for what she did, but she stood by her actions, not regretting a single thing. What she did had saved her daughter, and that was all that mattered.

Pressing her lips together at the thought, Leisha felt hard pressed to keep tears from sprouting. The truth was, she was tired of having to stay practical in the face of grief and pain, feeling bitter resentment for all the sacrifices she had to make.

CHAPTER 21

It was an hour's drive from the airport, and Leisha saw all the signs pointing to Oxford University, but she still did not believe it.

When they finally pulled into a parking lot near some of the dorms on the very south side of campus, her jaw dropped. "The immortals are staying in dorms on the campus of Oxford?" she asked.

Tafari smiled. "I know. The perfect place to hide. No one ever thinks to look out in the open, do they?"

"How long have you been here?" Samantha asked.

Tafari thought briefly about it before answering, "We have been here for about four hundred years. We contribute quite a handsome sum every year in exchange for our accommodations. Plus, each of us attends every fifty years, just so we can keep up on the latest studies. Some of us have even been professors here."

"Were you a professor?"

Tafari smiled again. "Why, yes. I taught history."

They both laughed and got out of the car. It still blew Leisha's mind that the immortals had been there for so long "hiding out in the open," as Tafari had said, all these years.

They walked through the lobby of the first dorm building closest to the parking lot. Tafari motioned for Leisha to put the suitcases down on the floor by the stairs before leading them left toward the double sliding doors.

There were a few immortals sitting around on the couches of the lobby when they came in. They stopped whatever they were doing to stare at the intruders. Samantha looked around nervously, her face a little on the pink side. Leisha stood tall with a stoic expression.

Two men outside of the double doors searched everyone, including Tafari, before admitting them. Inside, ten men sat around a round table. They were dressed in various styles, most of them in suits of one kind or another, although a few of them wore jeans or slacks with casual shirts.

The ominous council looked very ordinary, indeed, but Leisha knew all too well that looks could be deceiving. Each one of them glared at Leisha for a long time. She met their stares defiantly, realizing she was as close to death as she had ever been, surrounded by her enemies. She would not let them intimidate her, and she would not die without a fight.

But they did nothing. After the "stare-down," the members of the council turned their attention to Samantha, and then to Tafari.

Tafari bowed his head in respect, Samantha following suit. Leisha just stood, waiting.

One man seated in the middle nodded his head to Tafari. "We're glad to see you and your men have returned home in safety. It appears that you have proven your word." He spoke in a British accent, though he looked like he was of Spanish descent, with his long dark hair and dark brown eyes. His build was slight, but his frame powerful when he shifted in his seat.

"Thank you, Esteban. You already have my word that they will be no trouble while they stay with us."

Another man with light brown hair and hazel-green eyes spoke up. "That is not all that concerns us, Tafari. We cannot be sure that all of our people will leave them be. The human child should be safe enough, but we do not know if that *vampire* should even leave her assigned room while she is here. There are many here who wish to see her die painfully, and to be honest, I do not have much incentive to stop them."

Tafari nodded. "It is a valid concern, Arthur, and I agree, Leisha should not leave her room for the duration of her stay. My men have already grown fond of the girl during our trip, and I believe they will help the others know that she is to be protected."

Arthur nodded as if he had already known that. "Show

them to their room, and then report back to us. We have much to discuss."

Their room was on the third floor, toward the back of the building. It did not look like anyone else was staying on this floor. Leisha was sure they had arranged it like that. The room had two small beds, a dresser, and a desk. It felt small and cramped, with hardly enough space for anything else. There was a bathroom attached to the bedroom, which was unusual for a college dorm room, but she was grateful.

Leisha let out a sigh as she dropped the suitcases to the floor.

"I think it would be best if you two stayed here for the rest of the evening. I will bring dinner up to you later." With that, Tafari closed the door after them to rejoin his meeting with the council.

"I don't know if I can stay in here all night," Samantha complained.

Leisha shrugged. "So, go out," she suggested. Samantha would be safe around here, and Leisha did not mind unpacking for the both of them.

Samantha gave a halfhearted protest as she made for the door. "I really should stay in here with you."

Leisha grinned. "But you're not going to. Just don't wonder off too far, though," she called after her.

SAMANTHA ENJOYED HER WALK, EVEN though a small part of her felt guilty for not heeding Tafari. But being in the plane for so long—not to mention the sailboat before that—made her feel restless. Just the thought of walking around the beautiful campus was too tempting to ignore.

The campus was extensive and beautiful. Large trees surrounded the grass and walkways, with the leaves changing colors in anticipation of the fall weather. Even the vines that covered a good portion of the dorms were turning vibrant shades of red, orange, and brown, yet the grass was still green from all the moisture in the air. The brick buildings were old—she didn't know exactly how old—but they looked like they had been standing there for centuries, enhancing their character through each generation they housed.

She should have been in school by that time, and wondered if she would ever have the chance to go back. But would she want that? To try and live a normal life with normal kids her age while she held all this knowledge of an entirely different reality?

Looking around the Oxford campus made her realize that, yes, a part of her did want to go back to school. She wanted to go to prom, graduate, and dance ballet. She wanted to be able to go to college, too. As of now, all she could do was hope, at least.

A few raindrops splattered on her forehead; it was time to go inside. Not paying close attention to where she had wandered, Samantha was not exactly sure how to get back to her room. The building closest to her was unlocked, so she walked in, hoping to find someone to give her directions.

The spacious lobby was filled with Victorian style furniture and the crystal chandeliers above her looked to be the original ones. It was a magnificent building, and all she had to do was look around for a while before she found her way back to Leisha. She walked for about fifteen minutes, enraptured by the old portraits of Oxford's deans, dating back to the seventeen hundreds. Growing up in Florida, Samantha wasn't exposed to many historical buildings. Standing amid so much history, these structures emitted characters that modern buildings could never imitate.

She wandered upstairs, but decided it was time to head back. As she turned toward the stairs, she noticed someone sitting in the window seat at the end of the hall. She decided to approach the woman for directions.

Samantha could not see her well; she was sitting in shadows with the storm as the only illumination through the window. The woman had long blond hair that fell in lovely layers all the way to the small of her back. Her profile looked attractive enough, with a small straight nose and slightly pointed chin. She had her arms wrapped around her leather-clad legs, lost in thought.

"Excuse me," Samantha said. "I think I may have gotten a bit lost, do you think you could help me?"

The woman looked over at her, but Samantha could not see much of her face in the shadows. "You're the human that brought that thing in our midst," she said in disgust, clearly English judging from her accent.

Word must have gotten out fast. "If you mean Leisha,"

Samantha responded in a friendly manner, "then, yes, we came here together. Though, to be fair, Tafari is the one who brought us."

The woman sneered in the dim light. "You have no right to blame Tafari for her presence. I know she was the one who sought him out."

"That's true, but I know Tafari well enough to say that he makes his own decisions. No one can bully him into anything."

Laughing, her tone was laced with affection. "Yes, that is quite true. That's why he will never be on the counsel, because he thinks too independently from the rest." She shook her head and pulled on a pair of sunglasses, even though it was not bright at all.

She walked up to Samantha and held out her hand. "You can call me Rinwa," she said.

Surprised by the change in her attitude, Samantha hesitated only for an instant. She put her hand in Rinwa's. "I'm Samantha."

Rinwa pulled her hand to yank Samantha's face close to hers, towering over the girl by at least three inches; Samantha had to look up to meet her gaze, spotting her startled reflection in Rinwa's sunglasses. "If you betray us, and especially if you betray Tafari, I will personally tear you apart limb from limb." She let go of Samantha's hand, her demeanor once again polite. "Do you understand, Samantha?"

"I have no intention to bring any harm to anyone here."

Rinwa's full lips curved up a little. "I'm glad to hear it. Now as long as I see it followed through, I think we can get along just fine."

"Rinwa," came Tafari's voice from behind Samantha. "You will be nice to our guest while she stays with us."

Samantha turned to see Tafari looking at Rinwa in warning, his arms folded across his broad chest.

Rinwa smiled warmly. "Good to see you, Tafari. I was getting worried that you were avoiding me. After all, you usually come to see me as soon as you get back from your missions."

Samantha stared at Rinwa. She was Tafari's girlfriend?

"I had business to attend to with the council as soon as I returned. But I am here now." He walked forward and gave Rinwa a long hug. Tafari stroked his fingers through her hair with the woman snuggling her head into the crook of his neck comfortably, and intimately so.

Samantha studied Rinwa as she cuddled into Tafari. She was quite beautiful. The teenager couldn't see her entire face, but could tell that it was pretty with high cheek bones and an incredibly full, lush mouth. Her skin was exotically tan in color. Samantha could not blame Tafari for being attracted to the woman, but was surprised that they were a couple. Rinwa's whole attitude seemed tenacious, like she was determined to prove something to the world around her. She could never have thought Tafari would be attracted to such a woman, but maybe she was assuming too much. She might not know the real Tafari at all.

Tafari pulled back and looked her over, caressing her face with his hand. They looked into each other's eyes for a few tender moments before either one spoke. "You look good," he said. "I missed you while I was away."

"Are you going to let me meet *her?*"

"You already know what my answer is." Gripping her shoulders, Tafari met her gaze. "Do not defy me in this, Rinwa. Trust me."

Rinwa looked annoyed, and Samantha thought she probably rolled her eyes beneath her sunglasses.

Tafari turned, putting his arm around her waist and pulling her into his side to guide her as they walked toward the stairs. Samantha followed. "I do have a task for you."

Rinwa brightened and looked up at him.

"You are to administer punishment to Sean, as decreed by the council. He disobeyed my orders while we were in South America."

Nodding, Rinwa gave a feral smile that made Samantha wonder exactly what the punishment would be. Rinwa seemed tough, and by that grin Samantha could deduce Rinwa liked action. Perhaps violence was a more appropriate word.

With those thoughts about Rinwa, Samantha was surprised when the woman defended Sean.

"You know he is loyal to you, Tafari," Rinwa said.

Tafari nodded. "That was part of the problem. He thought he was being loyal to me when he assumed I was dead. But he did not wait long for me to return to the ship.

I almost thought he wanted me dead so he could take over."

Rinwa shook her head. "Sean would never want that. Whatever happened, I know Sean meant well. You know how he thinks with his heart too much sometimes. It makes him act rashly, but it's always with the best of intentions."

They descended the stairs. "That may be true, but thinking with your heart is not wise in our lifestyle. We have pledged ourselves for a higher purpose and must push away those tendencies. A cool head will keep you alive."

Rinwa chuckled a deep, throaty laugh. "I don't think I can count how many times I have heard you give this speech."

"Sorry, I did not mean to repeat myself. I suppose it gets more difficult with the years. One cannot always remember exactly when they had a specific conversation." They were at the bottom of the stairs when Tafari kissed the tip of Rinwa's nose. "Sean is waiting for you, dearest. Report to me when you have finished reprimanding him." Rinwa smiled with great enthusiasm as she walked away.

Tafari finally addressed Samantha. "I thought I told you to stay put."

Cheeks flushing, Samantha pushed aside her guilt. "I got restless and needed to go for a walk. You can't really expect us to stay cooped up in that small room for who knows how long."

"No, I was not planning on making you a prisoner here, Samantha, but you could have waited for me to finish speaking with the council. We had much to say."

"About me and Leisha?"

"More about Leisha than you since I am keeping your secret from the others, for now. We will not allow her to bring the other vampires here to destroy us."

Shaking her head, Samantha protested. "She won't do it, I promise. Tafari, she has more honor and integrity than that. She'll not betray you, I'm sure of it."

He gave her a sad smile that made him look weary and years older. "You truly are young, Samantha. If Leisha does have any loyalty, it will be with the vampires. She does her duty, as I do mine for the immortals. It is the way of things."

Samantha's memories suddenly opened to the night when Ptah and Annette made her promise to report back to them. She shuddered as the pain and fear came flying back to her in full force. "If she does her duty to the vampires, I doubt it is because she really wants to." Her tone came out unsteadily.

She blinked and saw that Tafari was right in front of her, peering into her eyes, worried. "What exactly do you speak of?"

She cleared her throat. "Nothing that I can tell you. Just know that the vampires are vicious and Ptah will do anything to control Leisha."

"You think I do not know that already? I have been dealing with Ptah and the vampires for over a millennium."

It was time to change the subject. "Does Rinwa always give out punishments to the immortals?"

Tafari blinked. "Usually. She has a certain talent to distribute enough pain to make an immortal remember for a long time. When she was promoted to the position, a lot of the more 'rebellious' immortals started to behave themselves."

"You guys seem so organized," she exclaimed. "I wouldn't think you would have problems with people obeying the orders around here."

"It used to be different. In fact," he smiled broadly, "Rinwa used to be the one who gave us the most trouble. Ever since she became one of us she has been very willful and passionate. It took many years for her to learn discipline, but I believe that is why she is so talented with chastising the immortals now."

"She definitely has that intimidation factor, I'll give you that."

"She is truly a rare gem in this world," he said, an undercurrent of awe in his voice.

Disappointment sank to the pit of Samantha's stomach. She hadn't realized it until that moment, but she had believed Leisha and Tafari could still work things out. Now, after seeing the beautiful Rinwa and listening to the way Tafari spoke of her, she knew it was not going to happen.

Tafari turned to the exit. "Come, Samantha. I left your dinner in your room and it is getting cold."

CHAPTER 22

Samantha walked into her room to find Leisha pacing restlessly.

"They are going to keep me in these confines indefinitely!" Leisha growled as soon as she saw Samantha.

It had been two weeks since they arrived at Oxford. Samantha was allowed to wander where she pleased, though she knew Sean and Ian were taking turns following her, but Leisha was not allowed to leave the room at all. The immortals would not allow her to return to the vampires.

At first, Leisha had been her usual self, cool and collected, making witty and snide remarks to any immortal that came to interrogate her, which were not many. But she gradually grew agitated, and it looked like it was about to come to a head.

"Why don't you do your tai chi again," Samantha suggested.

Leisha huffed. "I already finished it. I have been doing all kinds of stuff like yoga and kick-boxing and anything else I can think of. I am still feeling on edge." Leisha paused. "Plus, I can feel The Hunger coming back."

Samantha stilled. "Do I need to stay somewhere else for a while?"

The vampire sighed in frustration. "You would have no need to if I could just go out to a club for one night. They're lucky Tafari's blood has sustained me for so long. Normally, I would have had to do some serious snacking to ward off The Hunger for this long."

"So, why doesn't Tafari just donate some more of his blood?"

"It was not the most pleasant experience for him," Leisha said, her face expressionless.

"Okay," Samantha said slowly. She remembered that Tafari had not spoken much on the boat after he had given Leisha his blood, but didn't think much of it. "I will talk to Tafari and see what we can do," she said after a few moments, smiling. "I can even talk to Arthur. Remember, he's one of the people on the council? I've gotten to know him a little and I think he likes me."

Samantha had certainly enjoyed talking with him. "Did you know that he was *the* Arthur? Of the Knights of the Round Table? I couldn't believe it when he told me. I thought he was pulling my leg! Then he started speaking this crazy language that he told me was Old English. I asked him all kinds of questions about what really happened with Lancelot and Guinevere, but all he would say is that legends grow to unbelievable proportions over time." She could not help but to stifle a little giggle.

Leisha smiled, but Samantha could tell it was forced. "Yes, I did know that. I hope you don't call him King Arthur. The man doesn't need his ego stroked any further."

That made Samantha laugh. "He wouldn't let me. He said he never was actually a king, and that he preferred it that way." She hesitated before continuing, "I think he's a really good man, Leisha."

Nodding, Leisha's face maintained that same tolerant smile.

"I'll go see what I can do for you." Samantha turned and went down the hall in search of either Tafari or Arthur. She wasn't sure which one to seek out. She had avoided bringing up Leisha with both of them, but Tafari was already familiar with Leisha's needs. She figured even if Tafari did not want to donate his own blood again, he could probably convince the elders to let Leisha seek out a donor for one night.

Samantha couldn't believe she was all right with the idea of Leisha going out and hunting down someone as food. Why had she condoned murder so easily? Her own mother killed in a gruesome way, Samantha knew very well the precious gift that was life. Then again, she would not regret the death of her mother's murderer, which must be why she did not mind Leisha killing others—she knew Leisha would only kill murderers. She didn't think it was a

bad thing for Leisha to take the life of someone who would just go out and kill again.

Her thoughts were interrupted when she entered the building next door. This one held the cafeteria where most of the immortals ate. It was incredibly large and could hold five hundred people comfortably. The floor was lined with industrial carpeting, eliminating much of the echo. Still, there was always a little reverberation of everyone's conversations.

Samantha scanned the long rectangular tables and didn't see Tafari or Arthur. She turned to go when Rinwa entered. Samantha was still not sure what to think of her. The woman was nice to Samantha whenever they saw each other—Samantha had even sat with her and some other immortals in the cafeteria. It was pleasant, the atmosphere laidback and easygoing. They were very casual with each other, unlike the vampires who operated with strict formalities.

Rinwa smiled at Samantha, her sunglasses on as usual. Samantha had yet to see her without them. Ian commented that Rinwa liked to use them as part of her "tough girl" image, although Samantha didn't think Rinwa needed them to accomplish that at all.

"Are you here to eat? You can sit by me if you like," Rinwa offered.

Samantha shook her head. "Actually, I was looking for Tafari. Have you seen him?"

Rinwa shrugged, her loose sweater jacket falling off her

right shoulder to reveal a black tank top underneath. "I haven't seen him since this morning. He's been in a lot of meetings with the elders. Poor guy, they're working him so hard."

"Really? Is something going on?"

Arching an eyebrow, she gave a sardonic look. "Something is always going on around here. But I would never be able to divulge the information. No offense, but especially to you."

Samantha was getting used to Rinwa's frankness—the woman didn't give out insults lightly. "Well, if you see him, please let him know I'm looking for him."

Rinwa scrutinized Samantha from behind her sunglasses. "Why? Is there something going on with you?"

Samantha paused. For just a moment, she had the urge to explain the situation to Rinwa, but thought better of it for the obvious reason that Rinwa hated Leisha and all vampires, just like the rest of the immortals.

"Nothing that I can share with you," Samantha responded apologetically.

Rinwa nodded in understanding, curiosity flared in her face. "I'll let Tafari know if I see him."

"Thanks." With that, she left the cafeteria.

Samantha spotted Ian near the entry to the building. She waved for him to wait for her. "We may as well walk together since it's your shift to follow me," she explained when she caught up to him.

Ian had the decency to look sheepish. "I like you,

Samantha," he started, "but . . ."

She shook her head and interrupted, "It's totally fine. I understand why they want to keep track of me." She smiled up at him. "But you and Sean are really bad at sticking to the shadows."

He laughed. "You think we were tryin' to be discreet? Oh lass, if I had not wanted to be seen, you would never have known I was there."

"Then why didn't you just walk with me?" she puzzled.

"The elders wanted you to know that you were being followed so you would behave yourself, is all."

Samantha dismissed it with her hand. "Whatever. So, have you seen Tafari around?"

Nodding, Ian pointed. "I have. I just saw him headin' for his room."

She relaxed a little. "Okay, well let's go get him."

It took no time at all to arrive at the building where Tafari and his men stayed. Tafari answered right away and, after the formalities, he stood, waiting to hear what it was that Samantha had come for.

"It's about Leisha," she began, a little hesitant now that she was actually confronting him. "She's getting . . . um . . . hunger pangs." Before he could ask, she said, "Don't worry. She's not really bad yet. She had the wisdom to tell me instead of trying to deal with it on her own, but it will become a problem if she doesn't feed soon."

Tafari sighed. "I knew it had to come up sooner or later."

"Can't she just go to a dance club or a pub for one night?"

Ian scoffed. "We do not condone murder and will not help her commit it."

Equally disgusted, Tafari nodded.

Before Tafari could say anything, Ian sighed in resignation. "I will donate my blood this time, Tafari. You don't have to burden yourself with it again."

A range of emotions fluttered through Tafari's eyes, but Samantha could not read them. "Thank you for your offer, Ian. But you do not need to make this sacrifice." He motioned for them to come in, heading to the kitchen. "As I stated, I knew it would happen, so the university had a blood drive a week ago that I volunteered to help with." He opened his fridge. The two bottom drawers and the shelf above it were stuffed with plastic pouches of blood.

Samantha would never have thought the sight of blood would make her feel so relieved. She grinned at Tafari, who looked mildly embarrassed, or even guilty, for what he had done. "This is great," she exclaimed. "You are pretty resourceful, aren't you?"

"Would you mind helping Samantha carry these to her apartment?" Tafari turned to Ian. "I am certain Leisha will have need of them presently."

"Of course, Tafari." Ian grabbed a brown grocery sack from under the sink and filled it with the bags of blood. After he had the second one filled, he scooped them up in his arms and waited for Samantha to walk with him.

"Thanks, Tafari," she said as they left his apartment.

When they arrived at her room, Ian plopped the two

bags filled with blood on the floor and closed the door behind him without so much as glancing at Leisha.

Leisha inspected the bags and sighed. "This will do. Tell Tafari thanks for me."

"I already did." Samantha felt a surge of disappointment at Leisha's lack of enthusiasm. "How long will this tide you over?"

"I am not completely sure . . . maybe a week or so."

"But, I thought when you drank blood it would last you for a lot longer than a week!"

Leisha's usual calm and serene mask faltered for an instant, and Samantha could see how weary the vampire truly was. She sat on the floor with her legs crossed and opened a bag to sip out the blood. "Remember how I said we take on the life source of what we drink? Well, this blood has no life source to absorb, so it will only sustain me for so long. Does that make sense?"

Samantha gave a half shrug. "I guess so."

Leisha changed the subject. "We need to get in touch with Ptah somehow," she said. "He'll be getting impatient for my report."

Samantha stayed silent, not wanting to give herself away. She had already emailed each address they had made her memorize together with a detailed report of everything that transpired during their stay with the immortals. She forced herself not to think about how much she was betraying the new friends she was making here, or how much she was betraying Leisha. Samantha had berated herself daily for being such a coward and giving Ptah exactly what he wanted, but every night she dreamed about what Annette had done to her. Even worse were the dreams in which Leisha was bloody and battered, looking at Samantha in disgust as she said, "You could have saved me this torture!" The thought of keeping Leisha safe kept her mouth closed, even if reluctantly.

She barely slept at all with the combination of her nightmares and the guilt that ate away at her. "You can't contact him with the immortals watching every move you make."

"But you can. I will give you his contact information and tell you what to say to him." Leisha gave Samantha a meaningful look. "I am not intending to betray Tafari like Ptah wants me to, and I need you to report to Ptah exactly what I tell you to and no more. Do you think you could handle that for me?"

Samantha felt her stomach sink, the impulse to tell Leisha everything that had happened to her resurfacing. Instead, she stayed silent. She still was not protected from Annette's punishments unless Leisha made her a human servant.

It was then that Samantha realized if she could convince Leisha to make her a human servant, she could tell her everything and she would receive complete protection. But she couldn't bring it up now; it might be too obvious. Leisha would be able to connect the dots. She would bring it up later that night and figure out how to convince Leisha to mark her without giving herself away.

If she were Leisha's human servant, Leisha would also be stronger. Maybe they could go into hiding together so Leisha wouldn't have to face such horrendous torture alone. Samantha felt the need to protect her vampire friend from the terrors she constantly faced in her past.

In the meantime, she would have to continue to report everything to Ptah just as he demanded.

CHAPTER 23

Leisha was pacing in her room again, trying not to give in to her feeling of restlessness. The blood that Samantha delivered the other day had helped quite a bit, but she was still confined to her room. She was only tortured a few times by Esteban and Arthur—they had been discreet so Samantha wouldn't be exposed to it. Leisha hadn't answered any of their questions. Esteban's torturing techniques were a cakewalk compared to Ptah's.

She was imprisoned before in much more unforgiving circumstances. Most of them consisted of Ptah executing his grueling punishments. She knew she should be grateful she had a bed and room where she could even pace back and forth, but her body did not seem to agree with her mind.

She stopped when she heard footsteps approaching her room from down the hall. When Leisha caught Tafari's

scent, she unconsciously reached up to smooth her hair and smacked her lips together to give them more color.

Tafari stood in the doorway, his handsome features unreadable as his piercing gaze studied her.

"Yes?" she asked quietly.

"Samantha told me you will already need another supply of blood in the next week or so. Is this true?"

Leisha nodded her head and explained to him the same thing she told Samantha about absorbing a life source. He nodded grimly; no doubt, Samantha had already told him all of it before he came up to see her. "I am afraid I had not planned for this. The last time your hunger needed to be sated was almost a month ago."

"Yes, I understand."

"I suppose you will have to drink more of my blood when your hunger comes back. At least that will keep it at bay for some time." His tone was dripping with something she couldn't identify. "Hopefully, that will be the last time I will have to donate any to you."

His attitude and the memory of what had almost transpired the last time drove Leisha to protest. "I will not drink from you if it repulses you so much. All you have to do is let me go to a bar or a club. Being in such a largely populated area, I've no doubt I can find a murderer, or at least a serial rapist to knock off."

He snorted. "And you think I would allow you to take a life if I can stop it? Sorry, vampire, it will not happen."

Leisha's exasperation was beginning to show. "Oh

please, Tafari! Like you have any right to judge? At least when I kill someone, I have the knowledge that I'm helping make the world a better place to live in. I never kill the innocent!"

Tafari stalked closer. "Even if I were to believe that, what about the other vampires? Do you tell them which humans are allowed to be killed? Do you turn your back on the innocents as you watch your fellow vamps take them? There are vampires who are more sadistic and insane than the murderers you claim to prey upon. Do you do anything about those vampires?"

He was a foot away from her now, towering over her in his anger. It would have been intimidating if Leisha had allowed it.

She narrowed her eyes and tilted her chin up at him defiantly. "Do you think I want to just sit there and let them take innocent lives? Do you think I enjoy knowing exactly what kind of sadistic rape goes on behind closed doors? I can't do anything to stop them! If I protest in any way, the vampires demand that I be killed. But since Ptah has no desire to be rid of me, he doles out a punishment that is worse than any death imaginable. Because of my 'example' no other vampire has dared to defy Ptah or the way vampires have lived for centuries now!"

Face stone cold, Tafari's eyes flashed more silver than blue, showing the rage he was fighting to contain. "Is that really true?"

Leisha turned away, not wanting to show him the

vulnerability she felt. "I don't lie if I can help it, Tafari. Yes, it's true, and, of course, you won't believe me. I don't even know why I bother trying to explain myself to you."

"I do not understand," he said in a faraway voice. "If you do not condone taking innocent life and do not like the way the vampires live, then why the hell did you agree to become one?" He sounded genuinely perplexed.

Leisha's spine stiffened at the question. She had thought Adanne had already told him everything that had happened on that terrible night. Tired of him continually judging her, and tired of her own self-loathing, she bit out harshly, "To save Adanne from being tortured, you idiot! Why else would I ever agree to become something so completely vile?"

She kept her back to him, trying to get her emotions under control, her usual impassive exterior slipping. Clenching her jaw, she stiffened her fingers so she didn't pull them into fists and give herself away.

Tafari was silent for so long that Leisha was tempted to turn around and see his face. But she still couldn't bear for him to see her heart in her eyes. He moved quickly, grabbing her arm to roughly spin her around, leaning down until their noses were almost touching. She had never seen him look so fierce, and was uncertain of what he might do. "Is this some kind of ploy?" he asked in a dangerously soft voice. "Some trick to make me trust you while you stick a knife in my back?"

Swallowing, Leisha answered in an equally soft voice. "I

speak only the truth to you, Tafari. Maybe if you had given me the chance to explain two thousand years ago, we might have been able to salvage our marriage."

He sucked in a breath as if she had physically struck him. "Adanne told me that you were standing with Ptah on some kind of platform above her while other men *hurt* her. She said all you did was stand there and watch while they brought a whip to her." His tone rang with accusation that stung Leisha to her core.

She could not keep herself from showing the bitterness she felt with that memory. "Ptah forced me to watch and threatened to do worse if I did not agree to join him."

He was shaking his head. "No, it cannot be true. Adanne told me—"

"She was only four years old, and was absolutely terrified! How could you have expected her to remember anything accurately?"

"She also had vivid nightmares of that night for years! Are you telling me that they were simply nightmares and not actual memories?"

Leisha took a deep breath to steady herself, ignoring the bruising force of his hand. "I'm sure that she dreamed of things as she remembered them, but that does not mean that they really did happen in that manner."

"And your father? He said that you almost killed him."

"*Almost* would be the operative word in that sentence." She wrested her arm free of his grasp. "You have seen what I am like when The Hunger takes over, Tafari, and that is

after centuries of working to control it. I had no way of curbing it when it arose. But I did not kill him, and I ran away so that he and Adanne would be safe from me."

It aggrieved her to relive the memories that had apparently made her daughter hate her so. She knew Adanne could not be blamed for perceiving her own mother in that way, but it still hurt to know it. To know that even in her dying breath, she cursed her own mother.

Leisha turned her back to him again, staring at nothing out the window. "I should never have contacted you," she murmured. "It only dredges up painful memories while we talk ourselves around in endless circles."

She heard Tafari swallow. "I am sorry," he whispered.

Pivoting back to him, her eyes widened. "What?"

"I am sorry, Leisha," he said again, his face completely sincere. "I do not know if I can ever believe your story, but you are right. I did not give you a chance to explain before. I should have sought you out and asked you about it. For that, I will apologize."

Leisha swallowed the sob that was trying to escape. She cleared her throat. "Thank you," she said. "You don't know what those simple words mean to me." She paused, and then asked hesitantly, "Did Adanne have a happy life?"

This time, it was Tafari who turned away. "For the most part, she did. Your father took great care of her, and he and I both did everything we could to shower her with love."

For several minutes, the room brimmed with a sorrowed and emotional silence. Eventually, Tafari's shoulders sagged in defeat, shifting back to face her. "If you were to snack, as you put it, on a human, would that sustain you along with bags of donated blood?"

Leisha considered. "It could work for a while, but we would still come to this bridge again in the near future."

"For now, I will allow you to go to a pub when the time comes for you to feed again. I will be going with you, and you will consume little bits of blood from people while under my scrutiny. Do you understand?"

"Yes," she agreed softly. She was too stunned by his willingness to give her this leeway that she said nothing else as he left her room.

Slumping onto her bed, Leisha pondered what this could possibly mean for them. It was a small step Tafari was taking, but the fact that he was taking any steps at all was miraculous. For the first time in two thousand years, Leisha allowed herself to feel a twinge of hope that she and Tafari could actually reconcile their differences. Maybe he could forgive her, after all.

CHAPTER 24

Samantha was trying to enjoy herself, but her anxiety over what Ptah had just told her was making it incredibly difficult. Just after she finished talking to him and was on her way back to the dorms the immortals occupied, she bumped into Willem. He was one of the immortals whom she sat with in the cafeteria on a regular basis. She was not sure if he could read her worried face, or if he was just being friendly, but he invited her to join him and a group of friends to watch a movie.

Samantha was not sure why she said yes. Maybe it was the idea of pretending she was in a normal environment with normal people. After all, only regular human beings got together to watch a movie and eat popcorn, right?

Well, it was almost normal. They ended up watching an action flick, and everyone was commenting on whether those fighting techniques would actually work when fighting with a vampire. It was obvious this was not the first time they had this discussion.

"It's not comparable," Rinwa said. "They used guns throughout the movie, while we fight vampires mostly with blades. We would have to get a movie that uses the same weapons as us in order for the comparison to actually have any bearing."

"Why don't you guys use guns?" Samantha asked.

Willem shrugged as he explained. "The only way to kill a vampire is to decapitate it. Some also like to cut out their heart, just to err on the side of caution. Anyway, the point is that it's impractical to use a gun against a vampire when your ultimate goal is to get close enough to cut off their head. It is the same way the vampires kill us. We sometimes use guns to slow them down, but that is only when we are certain there will be a fight. Generally, it's just too difficult to stay unnoticed by humans when you're carrying around that type of machinery."

"Could you ever develop bullets that can kill a vampire? Like that *Underworld* movie, where they had bullets that gave out ultraviolet rays?" Samantha continued her curious questions.

Rinwa gave a bored expression as she shifted next to Willem on the couch. "Trust me, we have already explored those kinds of ideas. They didn't work. We were able to manufacture bullets that contained ultraviolet rays, but they weren't lethal enough to have the desired effect." She turned and studied the girl through her tinted glasses. "Why

are you so interested, anyway?" The immortal smirked and rested her elbows over her knees. "Thinking of leaving the dark side to join us?"

It was asked lightly, yet Samantha felt a small amount of tension filtering into the room as the rest of the immortals turned their attention on her, awaiting her response. "I haven't joined any side, nor do I plan to. I guess you could just say I'm a neutral party, trying to get an understanding of each side."

Rinwa huffed, "It doesn't work that way, little girl." She took a breath and visibly forced herself to relax. "I like you, Samantha, I really do. All of us have gotten to know you over these past weeks, and we've enjoyed your company. But you are living in a fantasy if you think you can come and go between the immortals and the vampires. That's a very deadly line you're walking, and if you don't join with one of us soon, you will have no protection from the things that go bump in the night when they come for you. Understand?"

With that bit of harsh advice, Rinwa stood and adjusted her black fitted shirt before saying goodbye to everyone and left the room.

Samantha felt the truth of Rinwa's words sinking in. She had chosen a side, but she did not like her decision, especially since it was not much choice at all. Ptah had used fear to make her do exactly what he said. How was she ever going to get out of the mess she was in when Leisha flatly refused to make Samantha her human servant? Samantha and Leisha had two very uncomfortable discussions in which Samantha tried to look like she was not begging, while Leisha kept grilling her on why she would ever want such a thing. The talks went nowhere, leaving both parties incredibly frustrated.

Interrupting her thoughts, Willem said, "I'd like to tell you to disregard what Rinwa said, but I must admit she is right. You can't sit on the fence when we are so close to war with each other. We battled before, and from what I've heard, that was bloody enough." He took a swig of beer from the bottle he was holding. "This time around, though, my gut is telling me it will be far worse." His hazel gaze was intense. "Want my advice? You better go back to where you came from and forget everything you've seen."

When it was time for Samantha to leave, Willem said, "I'll walk you to your building. Rinwa said you got lost on the campus before."

"That was my first night here," she defended, but he still followed her out the door. Once they were outside in the chilled night air, they settled into a comfortable silence as they sauntered over the walkway.

"Your heart seems heavy tonight," Willem said. "Everything all right?"

"I'm a human teenager stuck between vampires and immortals. What do you think?"

He chuckled lightly. "You're fun to be around. I'm sorry that our world is making you grow up faster than you should, but I think you've the potential to handle this situation."

Feeling uncomfortable with the compliment, Samantha changed the subject. "So, do you guys always watch action movies?"

"No, but that's what usually gets Rinwa to go with us. I'm sure you can tell she likes to think she's a 'bad girl.'"

Samantha raised her brows. "She only *thinks* that? I don't know, she seems really tough to me."

"You don't know her like I do." There was so much emotion in that one statement that Samantha sensed wistfulness combined with sorrow.

"You're in love with her?" she asked softly.

He glanced over at Samantha in surprise, then looked in the direction of their destination. "I suppose you could say that." He blew out a breath. "We were lovers for a time. I thought she was happy with me, but it didn't work out. That was when I first joined the immortals, two hundred years ago."

"Does she know how you feel about her now?"

Willem kicked at a loose stone. "It's best that I maintain my distance for now. She's . . . not available at the moment."

"Right." For a while, she forgot that Rinwa and Tafari were together. Her heart went out to Willem. It had to be hard for him; Tafari was practically impossible to compete with.

They arrived at her building and she thanked him for walking with her before returning to her room. As she walked, her mind wandered back to her own predicaments. She thought of all the different options that were available to her, and still decided she really didn't have much of any choice. She had to do Ptah's biddings.

Enforcing her resolve, she did her best to keep an impassive face upon arriving at her room. When she opened the door and saw Leisha dancing to music, she could not help but to smile, temporarily forgetting her troubles.

Leisha might just be releasing her stored up energy from being cooped up for so long, but she looked like any normal college girl dancing around her dorm room. The problem of being around all the "otherworldly" people was that they all just seemed so normal and ordinary. That is, unless they were talking about battles and memories of things they did hundreds of years ago.

Leisha turned off her iPod when Samantha came in. "How was your day today?" she asked casually.

That was always the first question she asked when Samantha entered. Samantha usually told her everything about her day. She figured Leisha was trying to live vicariously through Samantha's interactions with the other immortals. Leisha knew each person whom Samantha named, including their quirks. Samantha even suspected that the vampire was starting to soften her attitude towards the immortals since she was beginning to know them as individuals. But even so, Leisha would never admit to it, so Samantha never voiced those thoughts.

This time, Samantha did not tell Leisha anything about her day except what was most pressing. "I spoke to Ptah on the phone today." When Leisha nodded, she continued. "He

. . . he is planning to fly out here in a few days. He wants to talk with you in person."

Leisha crossed her arms. "Why? I thought you were reporting to him everything I told you to."

"I am!" *And more*, she thought. "But he wants to speak with you directly, in person. We somehow have to make arrangements to get off the campus for one night and just see what he wants."

Leisha's eyes unfocused slightly and she looked at the wall. "I already did, but it's only because Tafari is beginning to trust me again." She sat on her bed and held a pillow in her lap, her usual unreadable expression in place. "If Tafari finds out that I'm using him to meet with Ptah, he will never be able to forgive me."

That made Samantha gasp. "You really think he's open to that idea? Of forgiving you?"

Leisha summarized what their conversation consisted of, and Samantha was grinning by the time she finished.

"Leisha, that's wonderful! You guys are starting to make progress with each other. There's hope!" Her smile faltered a little when Rinwa popped into her thoughts. She was really beginning to like the immortal and would not want to see her get hurt if Leisha and Tafari rekindled their romance, but on the other hand, she knew in her heart that Leisha and Tafari belonged together.

Leisha made a calming gesture with her hand. "We don't know what will happen here, Samantha, so don't get carried away. There may be some hope for us to at least have some neutral ground with each other, but I doubt it could go beyond that."

Samantha chose to ignore that and focus on more pressing matters. "So, do you think it would be possible to meet with Ptah while Tafari takes you out to feed?"

Leisha did a good job of hiding the strained expression, but Samantha had learned to read her little tells. She did not like the idea of betraying what little trust Tafari had for her, and Samantha could not fault her for that.

Swallowing, Leisha responded, "I do think it is possible, and it's probably our best chance to meet with Ptah . . ."

"I get the feeling that you were going to say 'but,' right?"

"I find myself torn on what to do."

Samantha's heart clenched at the hopelessness Leisha was feeling. "You are more torn because of me, aren't you?" Samantha asked.

The vampire met her eyes with a puzzled frown. "What?"

"Are you still worried about my safety, Leisha? Because I'm betting that if you didn't have to worry about me, you would probably not worry about Ptah and would stay loyal to Tafari." Samantha pursed her lips. While Samantha wanted Leisha to not worry about her so much, the girl still had horrid nightmares about what Annette had done to her, and she knew it could have been much worse.

"Samantha, even if you were not involved, there would still be complications," Leisha said.

"Make me your human servant." The words came out

more desperately than she had meant, and Samantha flushed with embarrassment.

Leisha's response was instant. "No. We have already discussed this and you know where I stand. I cannot in good conscience do that to you, and you must not ask for it again."

"But if I were your human servant, you wouldn't have to worry about me so much. I would be protected by your powers, and you would have more freedom. You would be more powerful and we could hide away from the vampires, and I could help you with your feeding. It's clearly the best solution. You are simply being too stubborn to acknowledge that!"

Leisha was losing her patience. "You are wrong, Samantha. I will not make you my human servant, and that is final. But do not worry about my freedom. I can and will tell Ptah that I am unable to meet with him, and he will have to continue getting reports from you." She jutted her chin. "I will not betray Tafari again if I can help it, and I will go out with him to do exactly what we agreed upon and nothing more."

Leisha ended the conversation by putting on her earphones and lying down on her bed with her back to Samantha. Samantha lay on her own bed, anxiety overwhelming her as she contemplated what she would tell Ptah tomorrow.

CHAPTER 25

Tafari opened the car door and muttered, "Does this look sleazy enough for you?" It was obvious he was quickly losing his patience. Leisha had refused the first three pubs he took her to, because they looked "too nice."

Leisha tried to be patient herself when she explained to him that she needed to go to a location that would invite the less reputable kind of people. She could not understand why that bothered him so much, but was finally able to convince him to take her to one of the trashier bars.

"This should work just fine," she said pleasantly, ignoring his irritable tone. It had been almost two weeks since he agreed to take her out to feed and she had hardly seen him before today. She was embarrassed to admit to herself that she was looking forward to going out with Tafari, restraining herself from looking at this arrangement like a

date. It was a foolish inclination, and she had silently berated herself for acting like a silly, giddy teenager.

Once they left, it was easy for Leisha to fall back into her customary manner and forget that she had been thinking giddy thoughts. Tafari was his usual gruff self and did a superb job of making her feel like a burden. She did not allow herself to feel bad over his attitude. Instead, she decided to take comfort in the fact that Tafari would never change.

She pulled her attention back to the reason they came to the bar when they entered. Together, they walked through the smoke-filled room and bad lighting to a table in the back corner away from the lights.

"Remember what we agreed upon?" Tafari reminded.

Leisha nodded. "I remember. I'll be sure to make out in a dark corner where you'll be able to see me *not* kill anyone."

He still seemed unhappy with the arrangement, but sat back in his chair and humphed, "Good." Leisha started to get up when he requested, "While you are at the bar, would you bring me a glass of red wine, please?"

Leisha hid her smile, but was certain her eyes sparkled with amusement. "I think a beer would be the wiser choice in this kind of establishment."

Tafari gave a long suffering sigh as he nodded. Leisha chuckled a little as she sat on a stool and ordered a beer.

It did not take long at all to attract attention from the men around her. She had an easily amused and open expression on her face, and had no trouble flirting with each man who approached her—all of them wanted to take her back to their apartment. No one seemed enthusiastic about lingering in the pub. Feeling exasperated, she decided to try the other end of the bar. She got up and sent a fleeting look towards Tafari as she walked to the opposite side toward the backdoor.

Just as she was about to sit on another stool, Tafari grabbed her arm roughly. "Where do you think you are going?" he hissed.

Leisha allowed her face to show how aggravated she was feeling. "I was just finding a different seat. I wasn't having much success where I was. What's the problem?"

He glanced over to the backdoor meaningfully.

She rolled her eyes. "And you were supposed to start trusting me, remember?"

"It could hardly be referred to as trust, and I am not going to take the chance of you running off and reporting everything you have seen of the immortals to your beloved master."

Leisha jerked her arm from his grip and glared. Just as she was about to retort where he and his own beloved immortals could go, she noticed they were attracting an audience. She smiled at the guy closest to her and giggled. "My ploy worked," she said animatedly in a Cockney accent. "I made my boyfriend jealous. Now we get to go home and make up!" She gave Tafari a quick kiss, ignoring the fiery sensations it created within her body. "Come on, sweetheart. We'll need to stop at the store so I can get something

extra special I'm sure you're going to enjoy."

There were scattered chuckles throughout the bar as they walked out.

"Well, I hope you know of another place to go to now," Leisha said grimly.

Tafari sighed. "This is going to take all night."

"I could have found someone if you hadn't made a scene in there."

Tafari grunted. They were almost at the Audi—Tafari digging the keys out from his pocket—when Leisha heard the heartbeat before anything else. She glanced behind them from the corner of her eye.

The man approaching had his gun out and ready. He was targeting Tafari.

She waited until he was almost on top of them and aiming his gun before she acted. She hit his forearm with a swift karate chop. The man cried out and dropped the weapon. Before he could move, she pulled his reeking body closer to the shadows of the building and held his arms behind his back at a painful angle.

"Who is he?" Tafari asked.

Leisha looked into the man's flat brown eyes and read his thoughts. It took a few seconds to sort through them since he was high on crack, but Leisha was finally able to decipher his motives.

"No one you need to worry about," Leisha said. "He's a bum off the streets and was planning on killing us and taking our valuables." She looked down at the man. "Thank you for seeking us out, Baxter. You just saved us a lot of time."

Baxter flinched. "How did you know my name?" he slurred.

She smiled. "It's not important."

Pulling his neck toward her mouth, Leisha bit into his jugular. His blood had a bit of a sour taste to it, but it would sustain her as well as anyone else's, so she continued to drink. She tried to ignore the memories of his pathetic existence as they washed over her. After he had been drained, Leisha dragged his corpse into the small alley behind the bar and left him to rot.

It was difficult to read Tafari's face when she returned.

"You really do have the ability to read minds," he said slowly.

She could not help but smile a bit smugly. "I did tell you, Tafari. I only lie when it's necessary."

He studied her for a minute, and then folded his arms against his chest. "I thought we had agreed there would be no killing."

Biting back a profanity, Leisha kept her tone reasonable. "Can you honestly call that murder? He would have killed you over your car if you had been human. Come on, Tafari, just chalk it up to self-defense and let's get out of here."

Tafari stayed quiet as they climbed into the Audi, not betraying any emotion one way or the other.

They did not speak much on the way back to the campus, although Leisha felt perfectly comfortable sitting with

Tafari in the silence. It reminded her of the days when they were together, which made her feel a little nostalgic. She could picture all too clearly their small hut made from twigs and mud and the sense of happiness that filled it. She would give anything to have that life back again, to be able to watch Adanne grow, and to be with Tafari.

When they pulled into the parking lot near their building, Leisha saw that Samantha was waiting for them. She looked a little nervous and Leisha became fully alert.

"What is it?" she asked as soon as she stepped out of the car.

Samantha shrugged. "I just want to talk to you about a personal matter." She glanced at Tafari.

"I hope everything is all right." He looked at Leisha. "It was a most . . . unusual evening." With that, he turned and headed toward his own building, calling over his shoulder, "Do not bother trying to escape. You cannot tell how many immortals are watching you right now."

Leisha didn't watch him walk away. Instead, she focused her full attention on Samantha. Something was definitely up. She stood and waited for the girl to say something.

"Let's go someplace a little more private. I know this little spot between some buildings that is pretty concealed."

Leisha followed after Samantha. "I know this has something to do with Ptah. Did you talk to him tonight?" When Samantha didn't respond, Leisha sighed. "You better tell me as soon as we get there."

Nodding, Samantha held her spine stiff while keeping

her hands clasped tightly in front. Leisha recognized the spot at once. Samantha had given her full details about the location of the payphone she used to report to Ptah. She also quickly recognized that they were not alone. Vampires surrounded them. She could feel their penetrating eyes on her as she walked all the way through the trees to the secluded spot with the park bench and phone.

Ptah was sitting on the park bench, patiently waiting for her with a small smile on his face. "My dearest Leisha," he crooned. "I have been looking forward to this moment for some time." He motioned to the empty spot on the bench. "Come, sit with me. There is much to discuss."

Leisha looked over at Samantha and saw her staring at her feet intently. Her face was filled with guilt and anguish. Leisha bit back a groan. She knew there was no one to blame but herself for this situation. Samantha was only sixteen years old, practically helpless with a master manipulator like Ptah. Leisha had been a fool to think a girl would be able to handle reporting to Ptah on her behalf. Now, the vampires were there in the immortals' home.

She kept her face blank as she sat on the bench beside the master vampire. "What do you want, Ptah?"

He looked displeased at her lack of respect, but did not comment on it. "I would like to know why you have been so slow to give me the information I wanted."

"I'm not certain of which information you speak," she answered vaguely. She needed time to think on what her course of action would be. She had to consider Samantha's

safety and try to get the vampires away from the immortals without getting any of them in danger. The situation didn't look positive.

"Do not try to tarry me any longer. I have been patient long enough and I feel that it has not rewarded me sufficiently." He looked hard at Leisha. "You have not been loyal to me."

Leisha kept herself from reacting. She wanted to shout that it was true. That she held absolutely no loyalty for him in her heart, but she was too concerned about Samantha's welfare to speak in such rebellion. She had to get Samantha away. To do that, she would have to placate Ptah.

It took only a few seconds to mentally steel herself for the performance she was about to enact. "Ptah," she purred in a sultry voice, "how could you possibly think that I am not loyal to you? Have I not given you centuries of my services?"

"As I recall, this last century your services have been exiguous," he responded dryly.

"I just needed some time to myself. You know better than anyone how quickly a hundred years can go by." Even as she said the words, she knew the attempt was futile. Ptah was no fool, and Leisha would not be able to convince him that she wasn't trying to manipulate the situation. She could see her future easily enough—at least one year, if not more, of severe beatings and public humiliations. She would be slave to any of the vampires' violent and perverse machinations. It was a bleak future, but that was not forefront in her mind. She did not know what Samantha's future would hold. Would she simply be killed, or would she become another vampire's human servant? Forced to live in a world of darkness and pain. Samantha would not survive such a world.

Ptah stopped her pain-filled thoughts with a tolerant smile. "I do understand that, Leisha. I know you better than anyone, including yourself."

Leisha hesitated in confusion. He could not be buying her act, could he? A trap was being baited for her, and she was unsure if she should continue to go along with her deception. After a moment's deliberation, she decided that the mess she had landed herself in couldn't get much worse, and at best, Ptah might have actually believed her lies.

He leaned forward and lightly caressed her cheek with the back of his hand. "You do need me. Would you deny it, my Leisha?"

She looked into his onyx eyes and shook her head.

"I have spoken with Annette," he said, pleasant smile escaped his face. "She has agreed to share me with you. Was that not thoughtful of her?" His fingers made a light trail to her throat and then to the back of her neck.

Leisha was confused and equally repulsed. She could not fathom why Ptah would say such a thing knowing that the other vampires were clearly within hearing distance.

"How gracious of her," she said absently, trying to figure out what he was doing.

"I knew you would be pleased." With that, he grabbed a fistful of hair at her nape and pulled her in for a kiss before she had time to protest.

As soon as his cold lips touched hers, Leisha felt her body react the way it had all those years ago. She withdrew herself mentally as her body stilled—a survival mode she had used to keep her sanity whenever Ptah treated her as his prized possession—melancholy and despair now reaching out to her. She came to life and pulled away from him, suppressing a shiver of revulsion, and failing.

Ptah appeared to misinterpret her reaction. "Your passion is incredible, Leisha." Resting his hand high on her thigh, he was rubbing it affectionately. "We must always keep our kisses leashed, is that not so? Otherwise we would embarrass those around us with our unquenchable desire."

Leisha was wondering if Ptah had lost his mind. What in the world was he talking about? She had always acted like a lifeless doll when he had touched her. Whatever game he was playing, she did not buy it.

Ptah pulled her closer, wrapping his arm around her waist. "I have a gift for you, my sweet. To celebrate our reunion. I know you missed me as much as I have missed you while you were spying on the immortals for me."

A feeling of foreboding snaked down her spine. Was he going to try and make Samantha a vampire? Leisha immediately discarded the idea. Samantha might have been a little naïve, but she would never succumb to the temptation of immortality so easily.

Ptah nodded to Natsu, his personal guard. Natsu disappeared through the trees and returned with another vampire. Between the two of them was Tafari, his hands chained behind him, his mouth gagged. Tafari's beautiful silver-blue eyes were cold, staring hard at Leisha.

She felt her stomach drop as soon as she saw him. She didn't miss the accusation and bitterness that shimmered through his stare. That was what Ptah's performance was all about—he was undoing the small bit of trust she and Tafari had just started to build with each other.

Ptah had known everything. He knew that Leisha had absolutely no plans of helping the vampires defeat the immortals, and that she had no intentions of betraying Tafari. Ptah had come here to fix what he would consider her blunders, and in a scant few minutes, he had accomplished just that. Tafari would never believe her if she tried to explain it to him.

The hope that had been growing inside of her for the last few weeks was stomped and obliterated.

Samantha gasped when Tafari came through the trees, and he sent her a concerned look.

"Most clever, Ptah," Leisha remarked in a cold voice. "I didn't see it coming at all."

Ptah chuckled. "That is because you were clouding your judgment with your feelings. They only serve to hinder you."

He looked at Tafari. "So, I finally have you within my grasp. I must say that after all these years of us trying to

kill each other, it is unfortunate that we arrive at such an abrupt ending. Quite anticlimactic, wouldn't you say?"

Tafari glared icy daggers at Ptah.

The master vampire only smiled in satisfaction. "Would you like to hear what we will do tonight? Obviously, we have disposed of your supposedly well-trained guards around the campus. I know where the council meets, and I am aware that they are having a meeting early in the morning, before sunrise, which is all too convenient for my plans. It is unfortunate that you will not be able to witness their downfall. I believe that we will be passing the time with torturing you to death."

"No!" Samantha screamed. She moved to run to Tafari, but Victor grabbed her around the waist and held her back easily.

Ptah nodded to Natsu again, and he pulled Tafari out of the clearing to disappear behind the trees once more.

Leisha sat frozen, trying to think of what she could do to prevent Tafari's death. She had to think of something, and quick. Her mind swirled with possibilities, but nothing seemed plausible enough.

Ptah's chilling, thin lips on her neck brought her out of her considerations.

"It is true, you know," he said in a confiding tone. "You truly do need me. You would not have survived without me all these years."

"I seemed to have done just fine on my own for the last hundred years," Leisha replied.

"There is something I have not told you about becoming a vampire," Ptah said conversationally. "I made you feel coerced into agreeing to turn by torturing your daughter, but did you know that there has to be an actual desire to become one? You cannot simply agree to become one of us, but you have to possess the want, the deep yearning." He paused to give Leisha his full eye contact. "If you really had not wanted to become a vampire like you have been telling yourself all this time, then you simply would have died that night two thousand years ago."

Outrage and indignation were Leisha's initial reaction, but the idea of what he said made her ponder. Had she truly wanted to become a vampire? She would have never wanted to leave her family behind, and that would have obviously driven her to deny having the smallest desire. But if she really did hate what she was, why did she not let the immortals kill her? Why did she continue to fight for survival? Why did her body make the transformation if she sincerely detested the idea of becoming a monster? That realization, mixed with what she should do in the present circumstance, only filled her with more confusion and despair.

"Do you not see, my Leisha? You really do belong with us, otherwise you would have died that night," he repeated. "You are a vampire, and we vampires have always amalgamated. It is time for you to stop wallowing in this convenient self-pity and embrace your true fate. Unite with your family of vampires as we have so willingly embraced you."

Ptah turned her face to his. "There is much that I have kept hidden from you, but no longer. When you come back home with me, I will reveal to you everything about the other world I am from and how that may relate to the prophecy child."

Leisha's curiosity about Ptah's demon world deepened since he first mentioned it in his quarters, but that was not enough for her to return to him.

As if reading her thoughts, Ptah whispered, "I know your father."

She shook her head in puzzlement. "Of course, you do."

"No, not your foster father. I speak not of the shaman. I know your true, biological father."

She hadn't considered who her true parents were since before she'd become a vampire. "How could you know him?"

Ptah's smile was full of arrogance. "As I stated, there is much ignorance in you. You have no concept of your true parentage; of how special you are." He stroked the side of her stomach to her ribcage. "You have powers and abilities that I could awaken for you. I could give you so much more, Leisha." His voice grew husky. "I could make us unstoppable; more powerful than anything you could ever imagine!"

The idea of discovering her true identity was enticing. She needed to know what Ptah meant about her special abilities and wondered if she could even become more powerful than the master vampire himself.

"Leisha," Samantha pleaded from a few feet away. She was crying and her expression was filled with torment.

In that moment, Leisha knew what she had to do. The sense of purpose filled her, bringing peace to the storm that was waging within her. It was a shame that she would not be able to please Samantha in her actions, but it was what she had to do. She was a survivor, after all, and the grim situation that they were in did not leave her with many options. Samantha's feelings would have to be sacrificed in this.

Leisha closed herself off from the compassionate side she tried to keep alive all these years, and opened her darker side. She allowed that part of herself that enjoyed the killing to come out in full force. She would need it in order to survive the night.

Looking at Ptah, she swallowed. "You're right. I did have some desire to become a vampire all those years ago, and I do take pleasure in my powers even now." She took a deep breath. "I have judged my own brethren unfairly because I didn't want to admit that I could be like them. Thank you, Ptah. You've helped me this night to see what it is I must do."

Ptah studied her with intense scrutiny, his vacuum eyes swallowing her within their depths. "I do believe you are actually being sincere. I almost cannot believe my eyes." He gave a genuine smile. "What is it that you have decided you must do?"

"Help you defeat the immortals, of course," she said with complete resolve. "Though I do have one request."

"And what is that?"

"I ask that you not torture Tafari, as a personal favor to me. In return, I promise to kill him myself."

"Leisha, no! You can't!" Samantha was hysterical by now. The girl struggled in vain against Victor's grip before finally slumping against him in broken defeat.

Ptah continued to observe Leisha, trying to decide if she was using a ploy to save Tafari.

"I promise to kill him in front of your very eyes, and I will do it tonight," she said.

After an entire minute of contemplation, he finally agreed. "I will allow you to give him a painless death, as a personal favor. In return, I expect you to give me at least one night of unparalleled passion." The thought of actually giving herself to Ptah with enthused passion made her want to peel off her own skin. But regardless, she agreed.

"Most excellent. This night is turning out even better than I had planned." Ptah gestured to the right, and a young man of Eastern descent stepped out. "I do not believe you are acquainted with Annette's human servant, Timur. He happens to be a genius with anything relating to electronics. For instance, he has been able to disable any security system he has ever encountered." Ptah turned to Samantha. "Since you first told me of your location, Timur has been on campus posing as a student. He has been able

to deceive the immortals into thinking that their security hasn't been infiltrated." He looked at Timur with affection. "What a useful asset to us."

The bargain was set and Ptah's plans were in action. Leisha, Ptah, Victor, Natsu, and eight other vampires snuck their way into the room where the immortal council would meet in just a couple of hours. They brought the bound Tafari with them so Leisha would be able to kill him in front of witnesses. Samantha also came along because Ptah wanted to keep an eye on her.

"Besides," he said in a menacing voice, "I would like to see this girl's reaction to the victorious bloodbath that is about to take place."

CHAPTER 26

Samantha felt as if she were about to be smothered by the endless torment of emotions that racked her. She was bewildered that Leisha gave in to Ptah's demands without so much as a protest. She grieved for the horrid change that had come over the vampire within a matter of minutes, and to think that Tafari would be slaughtered in front of her was excruciating. Mostly, she was consumed by guilt. She knew that if she had not given in to Ptah, none of this would be happening right now. If only she had told Leisha or Tafari about that night with Ptah and Annette.

She did it to protect Leisha, but she realized now that she didn't have enough faith in Leisha to protect her. Because of Samantha's fears, everything was ruined. Tafari would die, the immortal council would be slaughtered, and it was all her fault.

Victor had prodded her along the campus as they snuck their way into the building toward the room in which the immortal council met. At that very moment, Samantha was walking toward the damnation of the world. There was no escaping the horrors she would witness this night, but what made her even more terrified were the atrocities she would experience in the near future. She knew Ptah would not let her go, but she had no idea if he meant to simply kill her or make her a human servant. If it was the latter, she feared who she would be servant to.

She was pulled out of her gloomy thoughts when Ptah handed Leisha a sword. Leisha wore absolutely no expression. Samantha couldn't tell what the vampire was thinking.

Leisha took the sword from Ptah and weighed it in her hand. "It will do very nicely against the immortals," she said with no inflection.

Ptah looked at her hard. "My intention in giving you this is that you may be able to fulfill the bargain we had agreed upon just moments ago."

"I'll come get it from you when I'm ready."

"I want him killed *now*," growled Ptah.

Leisha gave him a chilling smile. "Don't worry. I simply plan to drink his blood first. Believe me when I tell you he will take great insult to being weakened in such a manner. Then, I'll finish him."

Cold tendrils of panic seized Samantha as Ptah chuckled in approval. She didn't know this woman who stood

before her. This was not the Leisha that she had felt so close to over the last couple of months. It was as if her decision had closed the door on Leisha's personality and produced this bone-chilling, merciless monster instead.

She could not help but think of the irony. Leisha told her so many times that she was a monster, and Samantha denied it every time. Now Leisha was allowing herself to become the thing she never wanted to be.

Victor spoke up. "The council will be coming in less than an hour."

Ptah nodded in acknowledgment and turned back to Leisha. "It is time."

Leisha slowly walked toward Tafari. He was on his knees with a vampire on each side of him, pointing the tips of their machetes into his back. Even when bound and gagged, he looked fierce.

He didn't whimper or struggle, but kept his back straight with his shoulders back, his chin jutting proudly. He looked Leisha directly in the eyes with disdain. If he had not been gagged, Samantha would have expected him to spit on Leisha when she reached him. But he did nothing.

Leisha knelt beside Tafari. "You knew it would come to something like this," she said softly.

She grabbed his head between her hands and tilted it to the side so she would have better access to his neck. Samantha wanted to turn away when Leisha leaned her bared teeth toward Tafari, but she could not move, paralyzed, unable to do anything for the immortal, unable to close her eyes to his humiliation.

She felt a pang of hope when Leisha paused and whispered something in Tafari's ear, but it instantly died at the fiery look in his eyes. Whatever she said did not inspire any hope in Tafari. Leisha moved her right hand to the back of his head and clutched his short hairs in a fist as she moved her left arm around his waist. Without any more delays, she sunk her teeth deep into his flesh.

Samantha could hear the tearing of skin and thought she might throw up. She kept her gaze on Tafari. He had closed his eyes and clenched his teeth into the gag, his body rigid and proud for as long as he could.

Samantha was not sure how long it took for Tafari to begin slumping forward, but when she saw his face begin to pale, she felt the tears flowing freely. She was witnessing the murder of someone she had come to love and respect, and she could do nothing but stand there and watch.

She barely managed to contain a sob when Leisha pulled back to let Tafari slide to the floor. She stood and looked at Ptah, her eyes feral, deadly.

"He is ready for his demise now," Ptah said casually.

Leisha's smile chilled Samantha's blood. She looked like she was high. There was an energy resonating from her, and her eyes were a deeper green than Samantha had ever seen. When she answered Ptah, her voice seemed to fill the room with small vibrations of power. "Yes. Now I will use your sword."

Looking truly pleased, Ptah held out his hand for Leisha to join him. She moved with even more deadly grace than

she usually did. When she reached Ptah's side, he pulled her in for an urgent kiss. His kiss was long and deep, and Samantha shuddered to see Leisha returning the embrace with enthusiasm.

Tears returned to Samantha's eyes. Her friend was truly gone. She felt as though she were witnessing two deaths instead of one.

She looked down at Tafari on the floor. He was obviously weak, groaning softly. Unadulterated rage tore its way out of her despair, filling her head until she saw red. Samantha didn't think it would be possible to kill Leisha, but if she got the chance, Samantha was going to cut off her head and spit down her throat. With that thought, her weeping trickled to a stop. Bitterness now replaced the despair she had experienced just moments ago.

Leisha was pulling away from Ptah with the most complacent, victorious smile on her face. Samantha could see the blood on her lips, smudged from her kiss. Ptah handed her the sword with deliberate slowness and Leisha took it in kind.

Samantha would never be able to describe what happened in the next instant. She played it over and over in her mind afterward, and her memory could only register so much—that Leisha had been smiling up at Ptah one moment, and in the next, she was standing just a few inches away with a grim, yet triumphant demeanor. Samantha glanced down and saw that her sword had a very thin layer of dark liquid on it. It reminded her of reddish colored motor oil.

Ptah was staring at her, a strange expression on his face. It was a mixture of surprise and confusion. A black, oily tear appeared out of the corner of his left eye, slowly trekking its way down his cheek, leaving a noticeable trail on his bronze skin. He took a step toward Leisha before falling to his knees. The head fell to the floor first, then his body, dropping forward on its stomach. As soon as it hit the ground, dark blood as thick as molasses spurted forth to blacken the floor.

The moment Samantha saw it, she realized with a jolt that the scene before her had been a part of her vision. When she came out of her paralyzed stupor, Leisha was bending over Ptah's body with the intent to cut out his heart.

Samantha immediately looked away and saw Victor. By the expression on his face, Samantha could see that he would not be exacting revenge on Leisha for killing his leader—the girl was still trying to put everything together.

Leisha turned to Victor. "It is done," she said.

Victor nodded once in acknowledgment. "It was truly an amazing sight," he commended. "I could only follow a blur of your image. Did you gain extra powers from drinking the blood of the immortal? That is definitely something to consider."

Leisha didn't answer his question. "About our deal."

"Of course. You will make an excellent mate for me. Together we will take the vampires to the next level." He grinned.

Leisha shook her head. "I just want to be left alone. You take the vampires on your great adventure. My only request is that you leave me out of it."

Victor seemed taken aback by Leisha's request, but recovered quickly, inclining his head. "I do want to respect your wishes. However, I must insist to be able to keep in touch with you. None of us can predict what the future will bring. After all, you are one of us."

"I belong to no one," Leisha said, her personality once again shining through. "But I'll contact you in a month's time. Like you said, who knows what the future will bring."

He gave a fleeting smile and glanced at his watch. "I assume you will be staying to help us fight the immortals."

It was not a question, but Leisha answered just the same. "My first priority at the moment is to leave. If I must fight immortals to accomplish that, then so be it."

There was no time for Victor to respond to that as they heard sounds of people approaching the door. All of the vampires went into fighting stances, holding their weapons at the ready. Samantha ran over to where Tafari was lying on the ground. She had enough time to see that the wound at his neck had closed just before the door opened and light spilled into the room.

As soon as the door burst open, Natsu rushed forward and decapitated the first council member to step into the room. Arthur was behind him and immediately backpedaled while pulling out a dagger from under his sleeve.

Leisha was suddenly crouching next to them, blocking

Samantha's view of what was happening, although she could certainly hear metal against metal, the sound of steel slicing into flesh, followed by grunts of pain.

Leisha pulled on Tafari's limp arm and hoisted him over her shoulder. "Stay close to me," she said, grabbing Samantha's arm. Instead of leading them to the only exit where all the fighting was taking place, she took them to the opposite wall and set Tafari down.

Leisha moved faster than Samantha could see, but she was able to discern that the vampire was repeatedly kicking the wall of the windowless room. In only a few seconds, a cloud of dust settled on piles of brick and drywall. Above that was a gaping hole, inviting them to freedom.

It was only a few feet above the ground and Samantha ran through without any prompting. She turned back to see Leisha right behind her, shouldering Tafari once again. He must have passed out.

"Is he going to be all right?" Samantha asked.

Leisha grabbed her arm again, pulling her through bushes and trees. "He'll be weak for quite a while, but he'll survive. This was the best solution I could come up with at the time."

Samantha wanted to respond, but was panting too hard. She knew Leisha could move much faster than this, but Samantha was having a hard time with the pace regardless. She wanted to know what, if anything, Leisha planned next. She also wanted to know a great many other things,

but decided to save her breath for the running. Her friend was back, and she smiled at the thought.

Samantha could not describe how light her heart felt with the knowledge that her original faith in Leisha had not been misguided. She truly did know Leisha like a sister. It was a comforting thought and she tried to focus on that instead of the people whom she had come to know so recently being slaughtered at that very moment.

CHAPTER 27

Leisha tried to be patient with Samantha, knowing that the girl must be exerting herself as much as she could, but it was still difficult. She knew that Tafari's blood would make her faster and stronger, and it was the only way to kill Ptah without any kind of a fight. Now, she wondered how long this intensity would last. It took all of her concentration to move at a slow pace for Samantha's sake when her body was screaming to roam free with so much power and energy.

She was tempted to hoist Samantha on her other shoulder and run faster than the speed of sound, but that would likely injure the girl. So instead, she was heading toward the car Tafari had driven that night. It was not too far away and she knew how to hotwire most Audis. After they were well away from the immortals and the vampires, they would head to Germany. There, Leisha had secured a safety

deposit box with money and identities she could use. After that, they would just have to see.

Leisha was almost feeling giddy—it was more than just Tafari's blood. She actually felt independent now that Ptah was gone. No longer could he manipulate her or Samantha to bend to his ways.

Her contemplation on inner peace was interrupted when she heard footsteps headed in their direction. She halted and pulled Samantha with her into the shadows at the side of the building. It wasn't much cover, but she hoped the immortals rushing by would be in too much of a hurry to notice them.

Her theory proved true. There were ten of them with their swords and machetes held at the ready, but their focus was on the building she and Samantha had just fled. She waited until they were inside their destination before gently prodding Samantha out of the shadows and toward the parking lot.

Leisha was completely caught off guard when a solid mass crashed into her. She had not noticed any of the stealthy movements of the immortal who was waiting for them to make their move. She immediately dropped Tafari to fight off her opponent. From the corner of her eye, she could see Tafari was coming to, and that Samantha was trying to drag him out of the way. But Leisha's main attention was on the woman before her.

She knew it had to be Rinwa from the way Samantha had described her. Rinwa was wearing sunglasses in the early morning darkness, clad in Goth attire. Her long blond hair was pulled up in a ponytail. Her face was full of disdain as she rushed toward Leisha with her machete raised for a striking blow.

Leisha waited until the last moment and then stepped to the side, using Rinwa's momentum to take her to the ground. She deftly knocked the immortal's hand to the pavement in a blow that released her weapon.

Leisha straddled her and held her sword to the immortal's neck. "You are allowing your emotions to rule your fighting techniques," she said casually. "It makes you very sloppy." She was more than happy to draw out the fight, since her body was humming with energy screaming to be unleashed.

Rinwa spit in her face while simultaneously kicking her feet up and around Leisha's neck, pulling her backwards. Rinwa sprawled on top of Leisha, pinning her down with her body while she tried to pull the weapon out of the vampire's grip.

Leisha was able to maintain her grip as she brought her knee up and pushed against the ground with her foot, causing her to roll over with Rinwa. She sprang to her feet, crouching in a fighting position, waiting for the immortal to come at her again. She was just beginning to enjoy their little sparring and wanted it to last a little longer.

Rinwa was up and ready at once. She looked for her machete but decided it was too far. "I'm going to kill you, and you will not torment us any longer," she vowed in soft voice.

Leisha quirked a brow. "You seem awfully confident considering I am the only one with a weapon at the moment."

"I can twist your head off your neck with my bare hands."

Tafari was sitting up against Samantha and was trying to yell something to Rinwa, but his voice was too weak for either of them to interpret what he was saying.

Rinwa rushed at Leisha again, but this time she managed to surprise the vampire when she dipped down and swung out her leg to trip her. Leisha went flying and Rinwa took no time to knock the sword out of her hand with a swift kick while Leisha was still in the air.

Once again falling on Leisha, Rinwa used both of her hands to squeeze the vampire's windpipe, crushing it with deadly efficiency. Leisha countered by using the heel of her hand as she punched in and then up Rinwa's nose. The sound of bone crunching left her feeling momentarily satisfied. Pushing the immortal off her, Leisha sent another blow to Rinwa's temple.

Rinwa's glasses flew off in a wide arc. The blow to her head dazed her for a minute, giving Leisha plenty of opportunity to retrieve her sword from the ground. When she turned to finish the fight, she felt weak as she looked into Rinwa's silvery blue eyes. Leisha dropped her weapon. Those were Tafari's eyes. They were also her daughter's.

"No," she choked out through her crushed windpipe.

Rinwa gave a grisly smile. Her teeth appeared stark white against the blood that poured down from her nose. "What's the matter, Leisha? Didn't think I was still around?" She stood and walked over to pick up her machete. "I assure you that nothing was ever going to keep me from living out this moment. I have dreamed my revenge every night since I was twelve and I will finally have it."

Leisha crumpled to her knees, tears pooling in her eyes. She tried to speak, but it came out as nonsense against her broken throat.

Rinwa stalked slowly back over toward Leisha. "Now," she growled out. "You will finally pay for what you did to Tafari and me all those years ago. You'll finally meet justice after all this time!"

Leisha made no move to defend herself as Rinwa raised the blade for a killing blow. She could not deny her own daughter what she deserved, wishing she could tell her the truth, but it was no use. Even if she could speak, her daughter would not believe her.

So, instead, she stayed on her knees and watched Rinwa with a convoluted sense of pride. She was so beautiful, and she moved with such lethal grace, reminding Leisha of what a fallen angel might have looked—flawless beauty mixed with unleashed deadliness. She met Rinwa's fierce gaze and tried to convey all the love she felt for her in her eyes. Leisha was going to die, and she didn't care anymore. She only wished she could say, "I love you," before Rinwa executed her.

A low, baritone roar came from her left. Leisha and Rinwa looked in unison as Tafari slowly came forward, leaning on Samantha for support. He was shaking and

terribly weak. Leisha could see that he was using all of his energy to keep himself upright.

"You will leave her be, Rinwa," he whispered hoarsely. "For your own sake as well as hers, drop the machete."

Rinwa sent a frustrated glare to her father. "She deserves to die. She betrayed you just as much as she did me, even more so."

Samantha shook her head vehemently, but it was Tafari who replied. "If not for her, I would have died tonight." He looked at Leisha with intense emotions she could never read. "You will let her go, Rinwa. I will not have your argument on this."

Rinwa glanced back and forth between her parents, uncertain. "Are you sure it wasn't some kind of ploy? That has been her game this whole time, hasn't it? To trick you into trusting her?"

"I am not so certain anymore." He looked back at Rinwa. "You and I can analyze all of the facts later. But now is not the time to be rash."

Opening and closing her mouth a few times, Rinwa's lips thinned when she finally came to her decision. "You're wounded, Tafari. I'll get you out of here."

Rinwa sent a heated glare to Leisha over her shoulder as she walked over to Tafari. Her father gently pushed her hand away. "Go get the car ready. I would like to speak to Leisha for a moment."

Rinwa looked as if to protest, but Samantha grabbed her hand and prodded her toward the cars.

Rushing forward, Leisha supported Tafari's teetering weight.

Her throat was healing nicely, but she was still not at a point where she could speak well, so she just stared at Tafari. The sky was starting to lighten with the coming dawn, and his skin looked like it had a little more color.

He smiled ruefully. "I honestly do not know what to think of you. I have sworn to hunt you down and kill off your kind." He shook his head. "But you did save my life tonight, and you did kill Ptah. That is something we have been trying to do for two thousand years. You accomplished it in fewer than two seconds." He looked deeply into her eyes. "I owe you for saving me."

Leisha shook her head. "We're even now," she croaked painfully. "You saved my life a few minutes ago." She managed to swallow and looked up at Tafari, pleading him with her eyes to tell her the truth. "Rinwa?"

"The immortals were reluctant to turn a woman into an immortal. When Adanne showed that she was worthy of being turned, they started calling her *Baderinwa;* Rinwa is her nickname."

Baderinwa. It meant "worthy of respect." Pride for her daughter swelled up within her. "So, she's why you sought me out and asked me to stay out of the war."

He nodded.

"I didn't see her in the last war."

"I convinced her to stay out of that one," he said. "I could not keep her from staying out of this next one. It is

somewhat complicated and I do not think we have the time to discuss it now."

Leisha continued to support his weight while she looked at him with her hurt showing in her eyes. "Why didn't you tell me she was still alive?"

"You know why," he whispered.

Leisha nodded solemnly. Because he had thought the worst of her. Not only had Tafari believed she had so easily given in to becoming a vampire, he had somehow believed she had participated in tormenting their daughter. He had felt the need to keep Adanne's existence secret to protect her from her own mother. Leisha turned her face away and moved to help Tafari to the car where Rinwa was waiting. She was overwhelmed with emotions, speechless.

Tafari stopped her and hooked his finger under her chin. "I am sorry," he said softly. He bent down and placed a tender kiss on her lips. He pulled back for a moment, hovering for what seemed like an eternity before he was once again meeting her lips, this time more passionately.

Leisha gave in, permitting her own passion and jumbled emotions to rule her response to him. It was just as electrifying and outrageous as it had been between them thousands of years ago. They gave themselves up to the power of their chemistry and explored each other's mouths with mad fury. In that moment, no one else existed. There were no wars to be fought, no politics to play, and no manipulation games. It was just Tafari and Leisha giving their love to each other as if the last two thousand years had never happened.

Leisha was not sure what would have happened if it had not been for Rinwa pulling the car around and honking loudly. The world full of hopes and dreams was jolted from Leisha and she was plunged back into reality.

They reluctantly pulled apart and Leisha helped Tafari into the passenger seat of the car.

Rinwa leaned forward to give Leisha an icy stare. "I don't care if you did save his life tonight. You stay the hell away from Tafari!" With that, she gunned the engine and made Leisha jump out of the way as the car peeled out of the parking lot.

Standing next to her, Samantha squeezed her hand. "Are you okay?" she asked.

"I have no idea." Her voice was scratchy and broken, but she forced the words past the ache in her throat.

"We'll reflect later. We still need to get out of here." They could hear the screams of fighting and fury. It sounded like the small battle was still going strong.

Samantha nodded. "Rinwa gave me the keys to her car since she took Tafari's. It's just over here. Do you want me to drive?"

Not bothering to answer that question, Leisha simply took the keys. They got into the car and bolted out of the parking lot, leaving hot rubber in their tracks.

CHAPTER 28

Samantha was on hold, her stomach churning nervously as she waited for someone to transfer her call to Mason's cell phone. She wondered with some trepidation if it was taking so long because someone was tracing the call. Could they even track her location on a prepaid phone?

She pushed aside her anxieties when she heard her father's voice in her ear. "Samantha? Is it really you?"

"Yes," she answered in a breathless voice. She cleared her throat. "Yes, it's me, Mason. I thought I should check in with you and let you know that I'm fine."

"You're really okay? How did you get away from that bloodsucker? Where are you? I'll come personally to pick you up. I was able to track you as far as England. I just arrived today." He continued to ramble on about where he was and how glad he'd been to learn that she had gotten away from *that vampire.* The relief and exhaustion in his tone was almost Samantha's undoing, but she straightened with resolve and interrupted him mid-sentence.

"I'm going to be on my own for a while." Her tone did not sound too sure, but she plowed on. "I don't want you to worry about me. I have everything I need to take care of myself. I'm safe and I'm learning how to be happy without Mom. That's all you need to know, Mason. I just wanted to tell you so that you wouldn't worry about me anymore. You can now go back to your old life." Her voice raised an octave as she spoke, but it couldn't be helped. She had said what she wanted to say to him, at least for now.

The silence on the other end was thick and almost deafening.

Samantha took a breath. "Do you understand what I'm saying? Did you hear me, Mason?"

"Perfectly," came the frosty reply. "You're still with your little vampire, aren't you?"

She debated briefly on whether to lie, but decided to go with truth. "Yes, I'm going to be staying with Leisha," she said softly.

"You're choosing that monster over your own father?" His anger was as apparent as if she were in the same room with him.

"I'm not choosing any one person over the other, but I trust Leisha and I know I'm safe with her." She paused a beat. "I can't say the same thing about you."

Mason gasped, then proceeded to use every profanity in

the book, all of it lashing out at Leisha, panting by the end of his litany. "Listen to me Samantha," he said with sudden calm. "I know I wasn't in your life while you were growing up, but I am trying to be your father now. Come back home with me and give me the chance that your mother didn't allow me. I can't promise to be wonderful, but I'll be the best dad I can."

Tears sprang to her eyes, but she blinked them away. "No," her voice trembled. "Not right now, okay? I just need some time to think."

"That brainwashing, manipulative, conniving bitch! She has taken away your will! You're not able to think for yourself right now. You need—"

"I'm still me," she said between clenched teeth. "I'll call you on Christmas or something." With that, she pressed the end button and slumped back into her chair.

After a few moments of staring at nothing, she picked up her mug of hot chocolate, her hands still shaking, and took a long sip.

Samantha was exhausted. It had been five days since Ptah came to annihilate the immortals, and they had been on the move ever since. Leisha drove all the way to Germany, doing little odd jobs here and there to earn money for food and gas.

Leisha's throat healed within minutes after leaving Oxford and she had been able to fluently sweet talk her way through all kinds of near disasters. The vampire charmed her way through the borders even though she had no identification, with bloodstain on her clothes. Most of the people they encountered seemed enamored by the woman's beauty and barely noticed the blood.

After two days of driving, they arrived at a bank, where they met with one of Leisha's connections to get an ID for Samantha. When all was done, they stopped at an Internet café.Returning from using a computer, Leisha sighed.

"Well?" Samantha prompted.

"The vampires don't have all the details on who died in the attack at Oxford. At least, they don't know the deceased immortals. I've been chatting with Nikita on I.M. and he said they know at least five people on the immortal council did not survive, but that's all he knows. Victor has taken Annette as his mate and they are talking about moving to a different base, in Paris or Italy."

Samantha sagged her shoulders. "So, nothing really changed, has it?"

"Well, having Victor for a leader will be different, though I doubt it will change for the better."

"And the immortals?"

"They may have lost half of their council, but they will be replaced. They will find another location and life will go on. In the meantime, both sides will still be trying to find the prophecy child." She smiled at Samantha. "Too bad, they don't have you to tell them that he has not been born yet." She paused. "Are you ready to tell me about the conversation with your dad yet?"

Samantha's stomach clenched at the question. "Maybe later."

Leisha pursed her lips to the side. "You can change your mind, Samantha. You're more than welcome to stay with me, and I promise I'll take care of you, but I understand if you want to try and work things out with your father."

Closing her eyes, Samantha remembered her father watching over Leisha's broken body. His eyes held no warmth at all. "I would much rather live with you."

Leisha nodded, smiling. She knew Leisha loved her like a sister and Samantha felt the same. She could not leave the vampire now. Not while Samantha was grieving over all the immortals who had died because she had snuck Ptah in.

She also couldn't leave now when she knew Leisha was going through her own grief. Her daughter was now alive, yet hated the very existence of her. And Leisha would not discuss it at all, nor would she talk to Samantha about the kiss she and Tafari shared. Samantha was feeling optimistic about them rekindling a romance, but Leisha only showed stoicism over it.

"Samantha," Leisha whispered, "After all that you have seen of me, and after all that I have told you about myself, why aren't you scared of me?"

"That's easy. It's because you are just a person, like everyone else sitting here in this cafe."

"No, I'm not. You know what I am."

"Yes, you're right. You're more than just any regular person. After all, you help rid the streets of murderers and still have a healthy respect for human life regardless of your natural tendencies. No one in this room could top that!"

Leisha looked perplexed for a few minutes, then shook her head and laughed. It was the first time she had heard Leisha truly laugh. "Come on." The vampire stood. "Let's get back to the hotel."

They left and climbed into their car. Neither one spoke as Leisha maneuvered through the busy streets. Samantha was reaching to turn on the radio when a new vision assaulted her senses . . .

A WOMAN WAS LYING ON a couch in what looked like a small apartment. She was screaming as though in agony, but no one was touching her. Then Samantha looked around the room and saw them.

Victor was holding a newborn baby who was squirming at the sound of his mother's screams. Standing next to him was Annette, her gaze fixed solely on the woman. Samantha's blood curdled as she realized what was happening.

Victor grabbed Annette's arm. "That's enough," he snapped. Then he walked over to the woman and held out the child. "Do you want him back?"

The mother was weaker than her newborn babe, but still tried to reach for him. Victor pulled the baby out of reach. "You must answer my questions first."

The woman sobbed helplessly. "I swear," she said. "I don't know what you're talking about. His father abandoned me when I was six months pregnant. That's all there is to it. He's nothing special,

he's just my baby." Her voice broke on a sob. "Please give him back to me!"

Victor sighed in clear annoyance. He turned to Annette. "It seems we have followed yet another false lead." He placed the baby in his mother's arms, the woman barely able to hold him.

Victor walked over to Annette. "Which one would you like?"

Annette gave a sweet smile. "I like the fresh innocent blood of a babe."

"I prefer older blood myself," he said casually. "They always hold so much more terror in their aura."

Together, they walked with menace as they approached the mother and child.

SAMANTHA CAME OUT OF HER vision to see Leisha parked on the side of the road, cars speeding past them, honking their irritation.

"Are you all right?" Leisha asked, clearly concerned. "What on earth did you see?"

It was then that Samantha noticed the tears streaming down her face. She was sobbing uncontrollably. It took her several minutes to get her crying under control before she was able to recount her vision to Leisha. "It was so horrible, Leisha!" Samantha was starting to cry again. "The worst part is that I know I can't save them. I don't know where they are and I can't go up against Victor and Annette."

"We need to find the prophecy child before they do."

Samantha bit her lip. "Where are we supposed to start?"

Leisha was silent for some time before turning back

onto the road. "There's only so much we can do. I think we should return to America, get you back into school and let you have some semblance of a normal life. We'll just have to pay strict attention to your visions while I spend my time in libraries and online doing research." She reached over and gently squeezed Samantha's hand. "We'll figure this out together, and we'll make sure the child is protected, from both immortals and vampires."

Samantha wasn't sure if she believed that, but Leisha sounded so sure of herself that the girl relaxed. Maybe they could really save this poor child, whoever he was.

ACKNOWLEDGMENTS

Many thanks to my critique group, who helped me turn my writing weaknesses into strengths. Jessica Bradshaw, Brett Monson, Ruth Craddock, Ashleigh Miller, Roxy Haynie, and Karyn Patterson.

I would also like to mention my first fans, Shantell Ewell and Esther Montgomery. They loved my manuscript and instantly became enthusiastic supporters for this book to get published. Erica Miller was a great help at polishing my work and submissions.

A special thanks to an unknown intern at Jolly Fish Press, who believed in my manuscript so much that she pushed for it like an agent would have.

Of course, I have to mention Christopher Loke, who was willing to take a chance on a nameless author, and has encouraged me to finish the trilogy. My publicist, Kirk Cunningham, has been a lot of fun to work with and loves to try new campaigns with me.

And finally, my husband, Adam, who has supported me through my dream of becoming an author, and has been monumental in building my online platform.

I couldn't have gotten to this point without any of these people, and I'm so grateful for their friendship and support!

ABOUT THE AUTHOR

ADRIENNE MONSON, WINNER OF THE 2009 Oquirrh's Writer's Contest and the Utah RWA's Great Beginnings, has immersed herself in different kinds of fiction since a young age, but she has always found herself to have a voracious appetite for vampire novels. She currently lives in American Fork, Utah, with her husband and two kids.

CPSIA information can be obtained at www.ICGtesting.com
Printed in the USA
BVOW031849200213

313806BV00006B/292/P

9 780984 880195